TUMBLEWEEDS BURNING
A Novel

TUMBLEWEEDS BURNING
A Novel

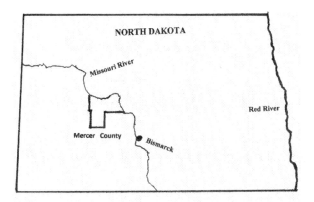

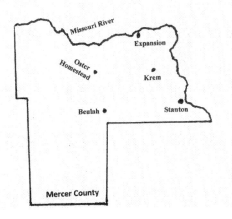

MILT OST

To order additional copies of this book, contact:
Xlibris
1-888-795-4274
www.Xlibris.com
Orders@Xlibris.com
550213

Contents

To Delores, precious soul mate,
and
All our family who own my heart

Foreword

The story of a million German-Russian people is a love story untold. They loved the old country, but they loved their new land more. And more than both, they loved their God.

While they spent a hundred years in Russia, they were determined never to become "Russified" and woe to the son or daughter who brought a Russian to the father's house for anything more than playtime.

This is the story of one of those families, across five generations of time. The story rolls through a significant number of powerful historical events and traces a family's attempts to live meaningful lives in the midst of them. Life portrayed in the czarist court sounds bizarrely surreal at times, but numerous sources verify the descriptions as only too real. Life portrayed on the great American frontier may seem equally surreal to smartphone users but in that harsh frontier lay the roots of much we hold dear today.

When those masses yearning to be free reached American shores, they longed for land. And while some settled in Alberta, Saskatchewan, Texas, and even South America, most took root in the great American heartland.

To be nourished in the bosom of these people, speak their dialect, absorb their idiosyncrasies, but most of all to be steeped in the profound hope and faith that colored every page of their life, was a privilege indeed. It is my hope that every heart that joins them on these pages will experience a touch of that as well.

M. Ost

Glossary

Arbusa—watermelon, sometimes called "wasser melon."

Bessarabia—province in southern Ukraine, west of Odessa and the Black Sea.

Blatchinda—pastry dough rolled out and filled with pumpkin, sugar, cinnamon, folded over, and baked.

Borscht—"poor man's soup," made with cabbage, onions, carrots, potatoes, garlic, salt, and pepper. Some used beets instead of cabbage (made "red soup") and topped it off with a dollop of sour cream. Could upgrade with tomatoes and pork sausage or pork shank.

Czar—Russian equivalent of "Caesar." When writer speaks, it is "czar." When characters in story speak, they always make it "tsar." Czar's family is: wife—tsarina; sons—tsarevitch; daughters—tsarevna (German = Kaiser).

Dah—Russian for "yes." (Nyet for "no.")

Dampf Nudla—yeast dough rolled out, then rolled up like cinnamon roll, put in covered pan with onions, garlic, and water, and cooked.

Dessiatine—Russian land measurement, equals 2¼ acres.

Dorf—German for "small village."

Fleisch Kuechla—dough rolled out and filled with hamburger, onions, salt, and pepper, then folded over and deep-fried in lard.

Gatch—slang for a person who is a "really weird duck."

Gurke—pickles.

Halupsy—cabbage leaves rolled and stuffed with onion, hamburger, rice, spices, covered with tomato sauce, and baked in the oven.

Halvah—sweet confection, served as candy; made from sesame seeds, nut butter, sugar, glucose, and honey. Variations could include sunflower seeds, cocoa powder, vanilla, almonds, orange concentrate, or pistachio nuts for different flavors.

Hectare—German land measurement, equals 2½ acres.

Hootzla—slang for "a big bunch of nothing."

Ja—yes, pronounced "Yah."

Kaladyetz—head cheese, jellied dish similar to Schwarta Maga, scrap parts boiled in broth, poured into pan, layer of boiled eggs, carrots, parsley added, cooled, and sliced as luncheon meat.

Knoepfla—dumplings; flour, eggs, milk mixed and dropped by teaspoon-size into boiling water.

Kase Knoepfla—cheese buttons; noodle dough rolled into sheets, stuffed with cheese mixture, folded over, and boiled in broth. Similar to manicotti or pyrogies.

Kuchen—yeast-raised pastry dough rolled out, put in pie tin, covered with half-inch layer of cooked custard, slices of fresh or canned fruit laid in (peaches, apricots, blueberries, prunes, or rhubarb), sprinkled with cinnamon, and baked in oven.

Kuechle—fry bread, flour dough fried in lard.

Kvass—low-alcohol Russian drink made by fermenting black bread in water, adding yeast, sugar, malt extract, and flavoring with mint, strawberries, apples, or raisins.

Schwarta Maga—made from pig's head, snout, ears, brains, feet, and other scrap parts, all fine ground, broth added, cooked, and poured into cleaned pig's stomach. Thin sliced and served with bread as breakfast meat.

Stirrum—pancake batter stirred until it fries up like scrambled eggs, sometimes mixed with raisins, sprinkled with powdered sugar and cinnamon. Often served with lettuce-and-cream salad as a light supper.

Swabian—or Schwaebisch, German dialect spoken by German-Russians coming from Bavaria and Baden-Wuerttemberg area.

Tanta—used variously for aunt, grandmother, or honorific for older woman.

Verhuddle—a tangled mess (pronounced "fer-WHO-dle").

Verst—Russian measurement roughly equal to kilometer or six-tenths of a mile.

Wurst—sausage; also word for measurement of one foot (Russian "fut").

Chapter 1

Feeling Alive

"What a dance," GP said to himself as he lay down on the straw mattress. "Crazy stuff."

Several young women had just come home from Bismarck and wanted everyone to learn the new Charleston. The girls, hair in tight waves and wearing formless flapper dresses, squealed and giggled at the sheer exuberant delight of the Charleston's motion. One of the boys said, "If I want to jump around that much, I'll go chase calves in the corral."

Crazy, thought GP. *All they want to do is show off their wiggles. What's the use of dancing if you can't hold 'em tight.*

The mantle clock in the next room struck three, and he remembered tomorrow was church so he and his brother Freddie had better get some sleep. But his mind wouldn't settle down.

Their night at the dance was pure fun until that cow-witted Wiedeman came along.

The Osters had immigrated when there was still decent homestead land in the valley. The Wiedemans came just enough later that the remaining homestead land was in the hills of the high country. For that, along with some unfortunate history from the old country, the sons of the Wiedemans hated the sons of the Osters.

This elder Wiedeman brother, Emil, was from his shoulders to his feet a Clydesdale horse of a man. When he saw GP and Fred at the dance, he and his brother stomped over, with Emil ending up just a half step away from GP's petrified face.

Wiedeman had a habit of lifting his Roman nose in the air and from a head taller than GP, looked down that nose and bellowed whiskey breath deep into GP's nostrils, "So, Ostie, let's see what them soft little 'cordian fingers 'r made of!"

Emil, solid Aryan, maybe even Viking warrior stock, was not the swiftest bull in the pasture, and his few bullish words told GP that he had spent a good part of the night dipping deep into the Redeye bottle.

GP's cheek muscles rippled, his stomach tightened, hands clenched. He backed up two steps to where the air had less fumes in it and snapped, "These fingers are good at breakin' teeth."

At that, Emil spat a chaw of Copenhagen at GP's feet. "C'mon, show me," he slurred.

GP balled up his fists and started for Wiedeman, but seeing a number of women in the crowd around them, he backed off.

"Ostie, the little chicken," clucked Wiedeman with a slurred laugh.

GP's eyes narrowed to slits, his insides boiled, but he turned and walked away.

"You wait," he shot over his shoulder.

Now, as he thought of it again in bed, he snapped wide-awake, blood boiling anew.

"That sumbuck'n jackass'll be back in town one of these Saturday nights," he whispered through gritted teeth, "and if he tries that again, I'll take care of him."

After a moment, he added, "Those Wiedemans should both be stomped in a pile of fresh manure."

"Just be careful," Freddie replied sleepily. "That Emil ain't makin' fun, and he's tough."

Still, GP's vision of revenge on Wiedeman made for good sleeping.

****

Though this land was old, the thing they called Dakota was barely out of its teens, named for the natives who lived and loved here through countless flowerings of the chokecherry tree. And while people in other parts, who thought themselves much more sophisticated, dubbed it the untamed wilderness, its newest inhabitants pictured themselves as very much up on the latest things in life. They would take no backseat to Boston's fabled elite.

With fall harvest over, and threshing done, tonight had been the first big dance in the valley. All the young singles were there. Lot of young married couples and kids galore. Portly grandparents whirled the polkas, hardly touching the floor, and flowed together like swift Missouri River waters. Little ones jumped and shouted, twirled and ran, with no pattern but full-throttled delight.

In bed, GP's mind flipped between pictures of Wiedeman and pictures of the accordion player at the dance. GP just recently bought an accordion and was trying to learn to play it by ear. They said he had *the gift*. He could hear any tune once and play it. But for now he had to learn the bloody keys. He did fine pumping the bellows but fingering the keys with his right hand while at the same time managing the 120 little round white buttons with his left hand would indeed be one big challenge. He was hoping that Uncle Pete, an accomplished old-time accordionist, could help him.

The next Saturday, GP and Freddie parked their Model-T and started down the board sidewalk when Freddie looked down and muttered under his breath, "Here they come."

"Who?"

"The Wiedemans."

Emil approached with unsteady gait, nose in the air, and looking down at GP, sneered, "Hey, Ostie, we got some stuff to settle!"

With that, the spitting Wiedeman uncorked a glob of brown snus on the toe of GP's boot.

Before Wiedeman could even wipe the remaining slobber off his chin, GP shot his right fist into Wiedeman's cheek with such lightning force that his head snapped against his shoulder. He crumbled on the sidewalk with a sickening gasp, unconscious; his eyes rolled up in their sockets.

The younger brother started at GP, but when he glanced down and saw blood running out of Emil's mouth, he bent down and lifted his head, shaking him to bring him back from the dead.

Within seconds, a crowd gathered, pushing to see the bleeding body and shouting, "Hey, what happened? What's going on?"

As the buzz continued, Freddie grabbed GP's arm and whispered, "Let's get out of here, right now."

"Go."

"I wonder when we're gonna see the rest of this," GP said, rubbing his hand when they reached their car, "or if that dumb ox got enough."

"We better watch our backs for a while."

"One of these times he'll be sober, and it could be big trouble."

****

It was times like those that made GP even more thankful for his special place. In the changing seasons, he had, quite by happenstance, found a refuge. Three quarters of a mile from their settlers' sod house stood a hill that many claimed was the highest point in Mercer County. At the very top of its peak sat a four-foot-high mound of weathered granite rocks. And because of the secrets this mound held, GP grew to develop a special mystic bond with this place.

The massive glaciers of aeons ago, built up by inches and moved by inches south, had picked up great walls of granite rocks, from who knows where in the far north—maybe the Arctic Circle, maybe Winnipeg—relentlessly crushed them and then with seemingly malevolent vengeance scattered them across these hills and plains. Here these rocks were gathered by the Native Americans and stacked as cairns to bury their dead, while for the white settlers it became a cursing ground as they wrestled the endless rocks to break the stubborn sod.

But no glacier's force pushed this mound together. Human hands did this. And those same hands gathered more rocks, each a foot or more across, from the hillsides around, and made a trail. For every step, a rock was placed in a path a hundred yards down to a lower knoll on which sat another cairn of rocks.

Below the two stone mounds, on a grassy lower plateau down the ridge, some twenty tepee rings dot the high prairies. Each measures fifteen feet across, with one rock missing—where a doorway served entry for a family to come home—to rest, to sleep, to share both stories and love.

This place held a secret, and since the Osters homesteaded here, they only managed to uncover one little part of it.

An elderly Native American matriarch mysteriously appeared at the cairns but only seemed to add to the puzzle.

Freddie was too young to remember, but as they grew, he loved to ask GP, "What about the old woman on the hill?"

GP would tell him, "When we were little, every year, one day in the spring, an old Indian woman walked up to that hill from the reservation down by the river."

"Then what?" asked Freddie.

"Well, she walked around that big mound seven times, real slow. Then she'd follow the stone path down to the lower mound."

"And then?"

"She'd walk three times around that pile, then walk back up and sit on the big mound, real still."

"For long?"

"Sometimes an hour. Sometimes half a day."

"Why doesn't she come anymore?"

"One year she never came back."

"What happened to her?"

"Don't know. Maybe she died."

"Who was she anyway?"

"We never found out."

Now, at a recent dance, GP met August Little Soldier who married a white wife and whose grandfather rode as scout with Custer at the Little Big Horn. As they were talking, GP mentioned the rock cairn and the old woman.

"That was probably my grandmother," Little Soldier replied. "And the grave is Raven Feather, her grandfather. She used to talk about him. I guess he was a big man with our people."

Later, GP again walked up the spring-fed ravine, climbed the long hill, circled several tepee rings, and sat on the same high stone cairn. He closed his eyes and tried to picture what it must have been like, when the Lakota Sioux, Mandan, and other bands lived here during the summers of long ago.

Up here, he could feel how they picked up the cooling breezes and spotted the great buffalo herds many miles in all directions. This high "summer cabin" meant food for the coming winter. From here they saw the Great Spirit lift up the life-giving sun in the distant east and lay it to rest on the hills of the cloud-birthing west. During the day, when they turned to where the shimmering North Star stood silent guard of the night, their gaze swept across miles of mighty water as the Muddy Missouri, great river of life, swept past them to the east.

Early every spring they moved their camp up here, from the river lowlands downstream, and waited. Soon the massive buffalo herds, numbering into the millions, began to appear from the south, grazing the long grasses, smelling the fresh waters of the swift Missouri, creeping on like some endless, swarming ant heap. They moved ever slowly on into the verdant north, snorting, bellowing, mothers lowing for stray calves, bulls wallowing in the warm earth, and rolling on their backs to rub off the long hair of winter. They came in a low steady rumble. A practiced ear to the ground could hear it from miles away.

The men of the tribes anxiously waited for them, sharpening spears, sprinting their horses into shape, shooting arrows at full gallop. For the young men it was another time to prove their manhood, for the mature a time to shine their status. For the women it meant hard days of cutting, skinning, lifting, carrying, drying strips of meat, and tanning hides. For all, it meant great feast and joyous dancing around the fires long into the night.

So when the herds came grazing over a range of distant hills, down through another valley, up the closer hills, it was time for sport, for riding, for food. The mounted warriors charged on their ponies from behind a forward hill, paired together to single out a young bull, raced alongside, shouting high-pitched war whoops into terrified, laid-back buffalo ears. Careful to stay far enough away from the half ton of stabbing horns and flying hooves, they loosed their silent arrows. Slowly the frenzied herd began to panic and run in blind stampede, shaking the ground like a rumbling earthquake that knew no end.

One buffalo shot straight ahead, hooves cutting the soft spring earth, trying to outrun the speedy Indian ponies. Eyes wide, terrified, it took the arrows, and after several hundred yards of desperate running, it stumbled, fell, kicked, and ran no more. Another went down, and another, until a dozen lay still, as the thundering herd roared on. The warriors ended the chase, circled back, and set up victorious ululation.

Listening women, knife in hand, ran to the kills. Children whooped, laughed, stabbed the warm carcasses with sticks, in kills of their own. Dogs barked and jumped, nipped at stilled hooves and hanging tongues, excited for their own glorious feast. As daylight faded, the meat was cut up, hides folded, all loaded on travois, and packed back to the high camp.

When Sister Sun laid down to rest, she tossed a last handful of light to the cooking fires. Now fresh gourmet livers, hearts, and tongues were sliced and put on sticks to roast. Glorious fragrance began to rise from the fires, wafting around every circling deer-hide tepee.

A surge of celebration flared through the camp as their nostrils were bathed in the rich aroma of liver roasting over maple-fired cooking pits. Soft popping of burning firewood yielded to the whispered crackling sound of succulent intestines stripped and cleaned and hung on poles over the living flames, slow roasting for crispy snacking chips.

The heavy, scrumptious taste of brain and tongue sparked new power for mind to soar and voice to call the spirits of the mighty Four Winds. This incense of life curled over every morsel of organ meat crossing their lips, for this was the spirit of Brother Buffalo flowing into their spirits for strength to accomplish great deeds.

Every tongue, whether two-footed or four, was satisfied; none left hungry.

By firelight under the great umbrella of stars, it was time to thank Wakan Tanka and Brother Buffalo for the enduring gift of life. They lighted the peace pipe and passed it around, set up the drums, seven men pounding out the powerful, hypnotic rhythm. Light feet picked up the cadence, drumming the earth in dances of thanksgiving. Songs trilled long into the night, past the time of Sister Cricket and Diving Night Hawk whistling down. The countless stars twinkled safe rest.

The fires slowly died, dogs were sated and still, and horses nibbled grass nearby. Out by the evening star, the buffalo grazed, at rest again. In the tents, stomachs were full, hearts at peace, and life was good. The next sun, even the next snow, would be good as well.

Once more, in the sweet stillness of the night, they thanked the Great Spirit for this high and sacred place, where earlier fathers laid their chief, Raven Feather, to rest with the spirits.

****

Now, with passing years, the great prairies were silent, the once-countless buffalo all gone, the Native Americans still nearby but reduced to hunting deer and prairie dogs on cruel reservations. Mixed into the vast stretches of buffalo grass were hundreds of buffalo bones, mostly just skulls with horns surviving. The new white homesteaders earned money by picking them up, stacking them high on wagons, and hauling them to the village of Expansion. Hired crews there load them on Missouri River barges, to be shipped East and ground up for cheap fertilizer.

In this mystic spot, GP still felt a presence. Turning his gaze north with Raven Feather, two miles away he saw the broad expanse of the great Missouri River, mother of Lewis and Clark, and the very route they traversed on their way West. Looking south, he saw Medicine Butte, a hazy thirty miles away, another sacred site to Native Americans. Letting his eyes wander east or west, his eyes rested on row after row of grassy buttes and bluish distant horizons as far as eye could reach. Inhaling deep into the northern breeze and with the buffalo of old, he smelled the rich waters of the Missouri, carrying Montana's silt to the Gulf of Mexico, from source to end all unknown to GP except for this little spot of prairie home.

As he sat on the stone mound and looked out across this land, he realized that it was terrifying, both in its beauty and in its magnetic attraction. Deep inside, he felt its power to draw his soul to rapture with its endless sunsets and its miles of waving virgin grasses.

The realization was just beginning to dawn on him that if he challenged this land, it could destroy him in an instant with its unrelenting winds and hungry flying things; this land that less than a century ago played host to those endless weaving herds of buffalo so vast that no one could number them, their wallows still denting the sides of the hills all around. This land that mothered a native people who left their tepee rings and laid their dead in sacred mystery to this day under cairns of rock atop the highest hills for spirits to keep watch and guide the way. *This land, this little spot of earth, is life,* he thought. *It shaped my soul. It speaks of what I was. And will be. It is Mother Earth,* he realized, *in ways more subtle and more profound than I can really know. My soul was suckled at its breast. I breathe it, walk, smell, taste it, until I can't lay a hand on just where it ends and I begin. Even as God holds it in the hollow of his mighty hand, so his gentle arms reach out to draw me in with it and dare to let me be husband of it all.*

Ei, yei, yei, where is all this wild stuff coming from? he suddenly reflected, shocked at the thoughts that this place inspired in his cascading mind. *Maybe Raven Feather is breathing in my ear.*

Up here, he thought, *I feel like Moses standing on Mt. Nebo, looking into the Promised Land. Funny, I sure don't see any of Sinai's tablets with Commandments lying around.*

Maybe, his mind continued to churn, *that's why this high place was so special to the Indians, too. Kind of like church, where they worshiped.*

His heart would not let go: *A wise man led his people and gave his last days to this place. And now his body lies here under these heights. Ei, how much he feels like a brother.*

But as his gaze slowly turned once more east and west, north and south, his heart stretched beyond his gaze.

"So beautiful, but I want more than this," he breathed into the north wind.

Chapter 2

A Good Place to Be From

GP was born here, in this North Dakota *erd Haus,* earth house, made of sod.

He had been baptized "Gottfried Peter," but as he grew up, things got too complicated because his uncle who lived on the neighboring farm was also named Gottfried so they took to calling him "GP."

For GP, this was home. But his homesteading parents, John and Fredericka Oster, could not yet think of this hard new land as home. Their home was Russia and before that Poland and Germany before that. Their people were peasants, serfs to Germanic kings, people who lived on the land but only at the whims of the nobility who would bless or execute as they saw fit. Their people lived to serve the king.

GP remembered his father, John, and Uncle Gottfried talking one cold winter's evening about the long journey to this new world.

"It was two hundred years ago," John had mentioned, "that Tsarina Catherine passed a law in Russia, inviting our people in Germany to move to her land."

Just then the mothers sounded a call to make homemade ice cream. The boys dressed and ran to the shed for an axe and then to the barn for pails to go chop ice on the stock pond.

"Be careful," John shouted after them. "You know that axe works real good for chopping toes too. Don't fool around out there."

In the house, the mothers got the girls organized to dip milk out of the cream can in the entryway and get cocoa powder, vanilla extract, fresh cream, chopped walnuts, sugar, and salt all set out.

"Now, girls, you run out to the chicken coop and gather a dozen eggs," Mother sang out while she snaked the big, gallon ice cream freezer out of the cupboard from behind the cooking pots.

Several minutes later, the girls were back in the house, laughing, with little Martha bitterly crying, "Mamma, Mamma, that mean old speckled biddy hen pecked my hand really hard when I reached under her for an egg. I think it's bleeding, Mamma."

"Here, let me look at it," Mother replied. Then, kissing it, she rubbed it firmly and chanted the age-old grandmother's incantation, *"Heile, heile, Katza drek, bis morge frueh isch's alles weg,* Heal, oh heal, like kittie poop. By tomorrow morning it'll be all gone." Its very ridiculousness made little Martha and all the rest roar with laughter, and the pain was magically gone.

Soon, the ingredients were all mixed and poured into the canister, the crank locked into place, the chopped ice poured in and around the wooden freezer barrel, and the boys started the half hour job of cranking the mix. As it began to harden, GP knelt on the freezer to hold it steady while he cranked. Fred and Wilhelm added more ice and salt to the barrel and helped to hold the freezer from sliding around while they took turns cranking some more.

Finally came the long awaited announcement, "It's so stiff, I can't crank it anymore."

One of the boys unlatched the crank and another lifted the freezing canister out of the slushy, icy, salt-water brine. Mother wiggled the cover off, and staring at them all as they crowded around was a stiff, chocolaty, mouth-watering dessert that turned winter into paradise.

Mother tugged the beater out of the canister, and in a moment, all the little ones grabbed spoons and reached in to help scrape the beater clean and get an early spoonful of one of the heavenly pleasures that brought joy to the prairies.

When the nutty chocolate delight was all dished out and passed around, Uncle Gottfried couldn't help but pick up the history lesson they had begun earlier.

"Well, actually, it was more like a hundred and fifty years ago, in 1763, that our great-grandparents got the invitation from Tsarina Catherine the Great for German people to come and settle in Russia."

The word had spread quickly in Germany and surrounding countries, and thousands upon thousands of industrious Germans, along with several other nationalities, were quick to accept the offer of kind cousin Czarina Catherine's Manifesto.

Little did they know that, should the Tatars invade, they were in the buffer zone and would be the sacrificial lambs for Mother Russia.

Then in 1804, Czar Alexander I reissued Catherine's invitation, and more thousands came.

They were hoping for a new paradise, but silently wondered if instead it might turn out to be a life tortured and dangerous.

Chapter 3

Attack of the Wolves

Heinrich Oster and his wife, Anna Marie Schmidt, living in Ostrow, Poland, heard about the czar's invitation, and it sounded like an offer they couldn't refuse. German peasants like them, living in Poland, did not have a bright future. The young couple packed their few clothes, blankets, a black kettle, and cooking pots into a trunk, hitched their two horses to the wagon, and joined a caravan heading east into a mysterious land called Russia.

"My head is just spinning with all this stuff," Heinrich whispered as they set out.

"Ja, and my stomach is kinda jumpy about the whole thing too," replied Anna Marie.

Reaching the Russian border, however, quickly brought them out of the clouds. Russian government bureaucrats detained them, day after miserable day.

"What are those nuts holding us up about?" Heinrich wondered to a caravan neighbor.

"I could maybe take it, if this lousy rain would quit, and the cold and wind."

During those endless days, however, one of the border guards, who in his younger days served in the czar's elite Imperial Horse Guards, was drawn to watching Heinrich's single younger brother, Gustav. On the journey, he turned into the unofficial horse consultant and part-time veterinarian for the party's horses.

The guard was impressed with Gustav's gentle care of the horses, his quiet confidence among both the immigrant people and the horses as well, and his almost regal bearing.

"Young man," he told Gustav, "I've been watching you, and I like the way you care for these horses."

Gustav was taken aback, stammering one of his few Russian words, "S-*spaciba*, thanks."

"Listen," the guard went on, "I used to serve in the czar's Imperial Horse Brigade, and I'd like to take you to St. Petersburg and get you into the czar's service. You're the kind of man they're looking for. Think about it and let me know tomorrow."

The family was stunned by this unexpected offer that came out of nowhere. All during their supper beside an open fire, they mulled it over and on into the night.

"Don't jump like a dog on a bone here," Heinrich cautioned. "I've really got to wonder about this." His eyes narrowed as he added, "Why would they let a foreigner guard the tsar? Somehow something smells like spoiled meat here."

"But just think," Gustav raved, "this's the chance of a lifetime!"

"Sure is," others chimed in. "The kind of chance you can only dream about," added another as visions of shining sabers and gold-braided uniforms atop charging horses circled their minds.

"Ja, but you could get killed too," Heinrich added slowly, pronouncing each word, furrows wrinkling up his brow as he tried to slow the stampede.

"Hey, but what a way to finish," Gustav laughed, "next to the tsar of Russia!"

"But stop and think a little," Anna Marie said softly, afraid they would think her a sissy; "the whole thing could be a trap. What if they're trying to spy on us and use Gustav to get us all into trouble?"

Gustav's throat tightened as he felt the tide shifting. Suddenly, both his hands shot into the air. "Ei, we're not talking about selling a horse here. We're talkin' my life," he blurted out much louder than he intended.

At long last, with the moon at its zenith, they agreed that Gustav should try it, and two days later, he and the guard were finally ready to leave. Anna Marie embraced Gustav for a long moment, then looked up and held his face in both hands. She couldn't hold back the tears as she whispered, "Dear Gustav, I'm so afraid I'll never see you again."

"Oh, Anna, I'll see you before you know it."

Heinrich reached out to Gustav one last time, and they locked hands with a grip of hot iron that bespoke both the bond of brothers and a sudden gut full of deep uncertainty. They both fought it, but tears rolled down before they could stop and left them too choked up to say anything in farewell beyond a nod and a final deep look into each other's eyes.

Both men wiped their noses with their sleeves, and Gustav turned to join the guard. As they got ready to ride out of the border checkpoint, Gustav turned in the saddle and sang out, "I'll come riding to your *dorf* on a big white stallion," waved once more and kicked his heels into his horse's flanks.

Finally, after two more miserable weeks of waiting, the border guards checked off their names and duly assigned each head-of-family 40 *dessiatines* (110 acres) of free land in what was to become the village of Klostitz, in the Odessa region of the fabled *Schwarzes Meer*, the Black Sea. After being granted passage at the border, it took Heinrich and Anna and the rest of the caravan another miserable month of travel to reach their assigned area.

When they arrived, they found a land thinly populated, in an area where the earth had wrinkled into a series of long north–south ridges and valleys. Their new home was on the lazy Tschaga River, and soon they would be surrounded by hundreds of *dorfs*, villages, springing up in this entire south Ukrainian area of the vast Russian steppes. They would shortly be populated by many thousands of immigrating Germans, with a few other European nationalities mixed in.

Before long, the Klostitz they settled in 1811 would become a "Mother Colony," with a ring of other small German villages around it.

By the time they arrived in their new home, winter was near, cold setting in, and food scarce. This Russian outback had few trees, so lumber for houses was almost nonexistent. Fortunately, there were limestone outcroppings on some ridgetops in the area, and the men set to work mining and chiseling stone for their houses.

Late on a Saturday afternoon, all the other men had ended their work, and only Heinrich and a neighbor remained at the quarry, engrossed in their stonecutting, when Heinrich suddenly felt the hair on the back of his neck stand up.

"Something funny going on," he called to his neighbor. "I feel goose bumpy."

Just then, their tethered horses snorted in alarm. Wheeling around, the men were stunned to see a pack of several dozen huge black wolves racing toward the horses from all sides. They were coming off a long season of hunger, and they didn't seem to be discriminating about whether this meal would be horse meat or man meat.

In one blurred motion, without time to think about the danger, Heinrich dropped mallet and chisel and grabbed his long-handled shovel, the other man his pointed pickaxe, and both sprinted toward the sharp-fanged attackers.

The lead wolf sprang into the air with a snarling leap, landing on the nearest horse's rump. Bucking for dear life, the horse kicked both hind legs in perfect synch to catch a second leaping wolf in midair. Blood splattered as the wolf's head crumpled with the sickening sound of bones exploding, like kindling sticks under a heavy roller.

Heinrich flew into the fray with a fury, swinging his shovel with sudden otherworldly strength, and struck the first wolf still atop the horse's rump. His shovel blade cut deep and knocked the clawing attacker off the horse. Both men screamed at the top of their voices, like demented spirits of the netherworld, and lunged wildly at the snarling wolves.

More wolves closed in, fangs out, hazel eyes ablaze, and locked on target. Vicious jaws snapped with the cadence of blacksmith hammers, saliva slapped in streams from ravenous, snarling mouths. Heinrich screamed so loud that his teeth rattled, and he swung like some berserk madman at anything that came close to him.

The wide-eyed horses reared and whinnied, bucking wildly, while the two men turned into a shrieking army. Wolves snarled and barked, ripping flesh in a furious blur of tumbling motion, as the air turned thick with swirling limestone dust and the feral smell of blood, reeking with hormones of fright—Dante's *Inferno* sprung to life. Soon the meal looked too high a price for the attacking wolves. They lost their nerve, and as a body, suddenly raced away.

Without a pause, the terrified men took handfuls of dirt and plastered it on the gashes in the nervous horses' hides to stop the bleeding and begin healing. Moving as quickly as they could, they harnessed the equally terrified horses to the wagon, all of them shaking, trembling, and the men fumbling at every clasp and buckle. Heinrich shouted, "Giddy-up" at the team and snapped the reins, but the horses needed no encouragement and raced with the worn wagon at speeds neither man nor horse had traveled before.

Their ferocious run raised a cloud of dust, quickly alerting the entire village who ran out to meet them and join in the wild, disjointed story that poured out in nervous stuttering pieces from the frightened men.

"You're all bloody," a shocked Anna cried out. "Are you hurt?"

"I'm all right. The blood is from the horses."

Long into the night they discussed and retold, feeling again those awful snapping jaws, only inches from their arms.

"We need to get out in the morning," shouted several voices, "and hunt 'em down before they attack the women and children."

As darkness settled over the *dorf*, the storied numbers of wolves grew by the hour until hundreds were racing through the grassy steppes around Klostitz.

The wolf attack left the entire *dorf* unnerved. While some wanted to organize a mighty wolf hunt, wiser heads decided that to survive the winter, getting their houses built was more urgent at the moment so stone quarrying and building continued with more energy than ever.

In the meantime, other men of the company took wagons to Russian towns some kilometers away and used their meager settler's government allowance to buy roof timbers and food supplies. The women and older children organized into groups and followed the river up and down, cutting reeds to thatch the roofs.

They finished only a dozen houses before the winter became too cold, so two and three families had to share each of the dingy one-room houses that had dirt floor, with fireplace in the corner for cooking and heat.

Some deep friendships developed that winter. And some became bitter enemies, never quite able to forgive or forget the slights and snubs suffered in those crowded quarters.

In early spring, they began building more houses along two streets, one on each side of the Tschaga River. The stone houses now were larger and divided into two, with a wall separating the two halves. The front half was for the family, and was further divided into two rooms: one for sleeping, one for cooking and eating. The back half was the barn for the horses, a few cows, and several pigs. A little shed housed a couple of geese and a few chickens. Each yard was enclosed with a four-foot high limestone masonry fence. This would be their castle, their good home in this brave new world.

As soon as the ground warmed enough, the men headed to the long, gently sloping land east of the *dorf* and broke up the waving grasslands to plant crops. Life was no picnic, but they owned their own home and a piece of productive land to farm. It was a dream come true.

When a strange rider appeared at the house and rattled the door with his loud knocking, Heinrich quickly motioned the family into the back room and with his heart pounding, opened the door a crack and stuttered, "Yes?"

"I have a letter for Heinrich Oster."

Heinrich was shocked to see the czar's double eagle insignia on the letter in his hand.

Chapter 4

Letter from the Czar's Palace

Lieber Bruder und Familie, Dear Brother and Family,
I was finally able to track down what dorf you were settled in,
and hope this letter finds you in good health.

The border patrol man brought me to St. Petersburg and got
me into the Tzar's special horse brigade. They call it the Tsar's
Imperial Hussars. There are 100 of us, but only 48 go on parade at
one time. I started out as a groom, and really liked it, but I guess
they saw I knew a few things about horses and about riding, so
they moved me up to the horse cavalry, and then up into the Tzar's
own palace unit. We are Company A, 4th Imperial Horse Guard
Regiment, 2nd Cavalry. There are two other German men in the
company, and they really helped me learn Russian and how to live
in this different world.

The Hussars are quite a deal. We live in special barracks right
behind the Tsar's great big Winter Palace. The horses are stabled
on the first floor, and our men live on the second and third floors.
The horse barn is so clean you could eat off the floor. Special
mint sprigs are hung around the walls to keep it smelling good.
Sometimes the Tsar comes to walk through, and it better look good
and smell nice, or we all get extra duty. Or the whip, if it's bad.

We have really good food, our own tailors, and doctors for us
and the horses. We have two horses each. My favorite is Zvizdah,
Star, and he's big, 18 hands high, and shiny black with a white star
on his forehead. We have to do hours of shining and polishing all
our gear, currying our horses and braiding their manes, and we
get lots of lectures on the history of Russia and how to handle all
kind of things that might happen in a parade, especially on how to
protect the Tzar in case of an attack. We do hours of drills on the
big main street, Nevsky Prospekt, and in the big parade ground
square, Dvorcovaya Ploshchat, on the back side of the palace, away
from the Neva River. There is talk of the Tsar putting up a really

big pillar in the middle of the square, maybe 47 meters high [152 feet], to remember Tsar Alexander's big defeat of Napoleon. That should be interesting.

Anna, I thought you might want to know what we wear. Girls seem to like that. For every day we wear gray uniforms with black stripes on the sleeve and leg, with a small, red double-headed eagle embossed over our left breast. For parades it is a really big deal, and we do lot of them. We have to keep our horses in perfect formation, four abreast, heads high, legs prancing. And we have to dress perfect. That means perfectly pressed black pants with red stripes, fire red jackets with double-headed eagles sewn on back, and decorated with all kinds of gold braid. They have two kinds of helmets for us. One is white with long black plumes, the other is gold with a double-headed eagle crest on top. It's all finished off with black knee-high boots with brass spurs, and white leather gloves with fringed gauntlets. Not a wrinkle or spot on our uniform, boots spit shined to see your face in, sit your horse like a statue with no jiggling around, inlaid sabers shining like the sun, saddle, bridle and breast plate shined like gold. One mistake, and we get six lashes across our bare back with the Captain's riding crop. That's only happened to me once so far, and it was bad. I hope never again.

The most surprising thing is how much vodka my comrades can hold. I have to be careful, because I sure can't keep up with them. Some of them get pretty heavy into gambling too when we are paid. I try to stay away from that too, because there have been several fights and a stabbing that got one of the men whipped and kicked out. I have a mustache now. It's dark and thick, and makes me look kind of rough. Sometimes painters paint our picture. If I get enough money together, I'll try to have one painted and send it to you.

Two weeks ago I got to carry the colors of our company with the double-eagle standard, riding right behind the Captain. It was quite an honor. Once in a while Tsar Nicholas 1st mounts up and rides with us. He's terribly fussy, and everything has to be perfect when he's there, and we are told never to talk to him. He sits a horse real good, and sure looks like a king with all his medals on.

But he only rides with us in drills. In a parade he and the tsarina always ride in their gold carriage and six.

Last week we had to lead a parade for the Tzar to go over to Peter and Paul Fortress, across the Neva River, which has a beautiful church with a very high, thin gold spire. There are no pews. Everyone stands for the whole mass as they call it, and it lasts for a couple hours. After everything was over and the Tzar left, they let us sneak a quick look inside. Everything is gold, with many statues and carvings, and marble of every color. Even Peter the Great's marble casket is in there close to the altar, and it is really big. Part of the fortress is also a prison, where they say some pretty terrible things happen, and we didn't get to see any of that. One of our men even said that Tzar Peter had his own son tortured here so bad that he finally died.

I am learning a lot about this country and palace life, and I will write you more when I hear that you got my letter. God keep you.

Your brother,
Gustav

Chapter 5

Clouds over Eden

These German immigrants soon discovered, to their great dismay, that their move left them living still dreadfully far to the east of Eden. Dreams of paradise evaporated in the swirling Russian mists. Life was incredibly hard and harsh.

Marauding bands from the East struck the villages time and again. Lutheran pastor, Ludwig Wernborner, was murdered when he tried to get the Catholic priest of Mariental liberated after he was abducted by the Kirgisians. The Cossack chief, Pugatchev, who had been one of Czarina Catherine's lovers, arrived with a group of soldiers and tried to extract bribes from the settlers. When they refused, he burned a number of villages and, with a smile on his face, returned to St. Petersburg.

"The tsar is boss, and all who serve him must be obeyed!" he yelled over his shoulder as he rode out of town.

"These German intruders in our homeland are scum," he proclaimed to his officers, "and we can wipe them out any time we want to."

Later another group of soldiers drifted through and saw Anna Weiss working in her garden. They grabbed her, forced her to a nearby haystack, and gang-raped her. "If you make a sound, we'll kill you," they told her. She made no sound. Her tears were silent. The entire village was ready to take up pitchforks, but what would it accomplish against armed soldiers?

Then, during the long nights of winter, bands of Russian youths rode through the villages, breaking windows, throwing stones at anyone outside their house, turning cattle and horses loose to run away, setting haystacks on fire. A complaint to the police only brought more trouble so the settlers licked their wounds, cleaned the mess, and said no more.

Every instance of ill-treatment grew more odious and more hateful to the immigrants.

"I wonder," Heinrich told Anna one day, "if we couldn't somehow get my brother, Gustav, in St. Petersburg to tell the tsar about how we are being treated."

"Well, he said he's not supposed to talk to the tsar but maybe he could get his captain to find a way," Anna replied.

Heinrich wrote Gustav a long letter and described some of the miserable ways in which they were being treated, but he expected little to come of it.

Yet, despite all the clouds over their Eden, there was peace. The sun shone. Crops grew. They planted apples and peaches, plums and pears. Long live the Tzar!

Meanwhile, Heinrich and Anna Marie Oster began to raise a family. A son, Christian, was born and then another son, Heinrich Jr.

They made the best of the situation with the local Russians, though language, customs, farming methods, religion, all remained thoroughly German. Their village, Klostitz, was all Lutheran. The next village was all Roman Catholic, and so the villages were clustered by religion and by area of origin in Germany and surrounding lands. Pastors, priests, and schoolteachers followed, small village churches and schools were built, and Germany dwelt in Russia. Tradesmen practiced, midwives labored, farmers worked the good earth, the young learned, and the old died. "Ugly stuff going on around here," they said, "but we just have to make the best of it."

When their cows and pigs, wheat and produce were ready for market, they loaded the wagons, hitched the horses, and drove to the bigger Russian towns. In order to sell and buy, trade and live, they had to learn some Russian language. And staying overnight in town before the long trip home, they learned new Russian foods as well. New spices were sprinkled, new tastes acquired, new Russian dishes tried out in German kitchens by the new immigrant mothers. Flour dishes like *knoepfla,* soups like *borscht,* sweets like *kuchen* and *halvah,* meats like *halupsy,* and pickled everything, all gradually became familiar to German palates. Though most of them were rebaptized with German names, a few like *halupsy, kaladyetz, and borscht* were to keep their Russian identity intact. To this folk, the czar was "Da Tsar," which they spoke with hard rolling "rrr's," like their Russian neighbors.

Though life was hard, Heinrich and his neighbors determined that this was their home, and they were here for the long haul. Still German in their soul, in their language, in their customs, and in their ways of making a living, they would make a "little Germany" in the midst of this Russian wilderness and show these spiteful Russians what real life was all about. They would not be cowed into running away like frightened rabbits.

Chapter 6

Letter #2 from the Czar's Palace

The czar's ministers were finally forced to face the feelings of anger and discontent coming from all directions. Their solution was to urge the czar to increase the education of the court and all the royal attendants. Surely, if they knew the inspiring history of the country and the honored royal family, they would be all the more loyally supportive and dedicated to their tasks.

Since the Imperial Hussars were the czar's closest guards, they were among the first to receive special instructors. To their dismay, the instructors soon discovered that Gustav, as well as a number of native Russian guardsmen, could not read Russian. Thus, they had to begin with the very basics of education. The Hussar students turned into apt learners and soon progressed to further study, with special emphasis on the storied past of the country and the glorious history of the honored Imperial Romanov family.

Gustav was particularly taken with the Romanov family history and most especially with Catherine the Great, since she was born a German princess and shared his German blood. He bubbled with enthusiasm during their supper meal when he and several other Hussar mates got to discussing her. His eyes grew large as he recounted the instructor's words, "They said she was as pretty as a rose in the morning dew."

One of his tablemates rolled his eyes, but Gustav was not deterred. "Remember, she was only fifteen when Tsarina Elizabeth picked her out and brought her here to Russia to be the bride of Peter Feodorovich," he reminded them. They had just learned in their class that Czarina Elizabeth, the daughter of Peter the Great some hundred years earlier, was never married, and thus with no children as heirs, she was worried about the future of Russia. Their class book had said, "She cast her net into foreign waters, and there found Peter Feodorovich, her only nephew, son of her sister Anna, who had been married off to a German duke, Karl Friederich."

Gustav was fascinated to learn that Peter, this half-German, half-Russian princeling, was, at the tender age of sixteen, given an offer to become the next Russian czar, Peter III. And young Catherine seemed the perfect match for him. *Smart move, Tzarina,* he thought to himself. *They were both raised Lutheran,* he mused on, *but I suppose they got that knocked out of them pretty quick around here.*

The instructor regaled them with stories of how Czarina Elizabeth "adopted" the two young royals to live with her in the huge, 1,050-room Winter Palace in St. Petersburg and quite literally became their mother, teaching, coaching, and coddling them as her own. This, despite the mischief these young crown-wearers-in-waiting were able to generate in the cavernous palace complex hard by the River Neva. The Hussars reveled in it and grew to love the newly humanized Romanovs. Particularly enjoyable to the men was the instructor's quote from Elizabeth, "Reading, my dears, is harmful to your health."

"Hey," whispered a bearded horseman in the back row, "love that woman!"

But the Hussar's new education had another consequence. A second set of writings circulated secretly among the men. Supposedly as factual as the official histories, these writings portrayed a darker side of the court, tracing greed and selfishness, along with a cavalier disregard for all their subjects outside the palace walls.

Here Gustav saw Peter and Catherine when they were married—he just seventeen and she sixteen—painted as privileged and spoiled teenagers. One of their wedding presents from Czarina Elizabeth was a toilet seat embedded with emeralds for him and one embedded with sapphires for her. To ensure proper decorum, Elizabeth also added an Orthodox prayer book with large Cyrillic print for Catherine, "to save your eyes, my dear Katherina," she wrote. Gustav shook his head: *Guess that was supposed to make the sapphires holy when she sat on 'em.*

Then another little booklet made the rounds. The authorities deemed this one salaciously inflammatory and anyone in possession of it could expect lashes. It was seductively innocent but still spiked the testosterone level in the barracks and bore the simple title "Wedding Night." It described the wedding night of the young royals, adding that Elizabeth, leaving nothing to chance, ordered powdered rhinoceros horn to be placed into Peter's hot cocoa and Catherine's filmy chemise to be steamed in lavender perfume from the Caliph of Egypt. And as only a czarina would be privileged to do, she personally tucked them into their wedding bed which was artfully strewn with fresh rose pedals.

"Boy," Gustav snickered, "we ought to find us some of that powdered stuff."

It went on with a portrait of the young newlyweds spending their wedding night—playing with toy soldiers. Gustav called over two of his guardmates, and they sat beside him on the bunk. "Shh," he whispered, "listen to this: 'Peter's hands were busy forming and reforming his brigades as the three-inch blue-uniformed Third Dragoons battled valiantly for the tsarina by candlelight against the infidel Turk, across the red-flowered silk expanse of the royal four-poster, fighting from Peter's pencil-chest all the way across to the safe high ground of Katherina's supple thighs. Thus was royal virginity preserved for another night, a portent of things to come. Succeeding nights saw the surge of the dragoons grow ever more intense and intimacy more rare.'"

"Guy's crazy," Gustav quietly chuckled, "doesn't sound like much of a German to me."

"Or Russian. No red-blooded Russian man would pass that up," his friend added and then shouted across the barracks, "Unless he was one of 'those'!" Two other men shot glances at each other, then quickly looked down, saying nothing.

Peter, they learned in these revelations, loved all things soldierly, with uniforms, drills, and dominating shouts of command. But, ironically, he hated most things Russian and was often snappishly critical of the people around him. And womanhood seemed a mystery beyond him. This was to be the czar!

Gustav's mind was torn. This was his home now. These were his people, his leaders, and his life. All this was also becoming his story as well. *What am I supposed to believe?* he silently asked the dark as he tossed in bed. *What's really the truth anyway?* He wasn't sure how much of this struggle he could safely share with his Hussar comrades, and it left him suddenly feeling intensely alone.

The next day at mail call his name was called. His letter was from Heinrich, and the news tore his heart. *How can those beasts treat my people like that?* his mind cried out. All day he stewed in the anguished pain, but he knew this was a pain he could not share. At least not yet.

When he couldn't sleep again, he finally tossed the covers back and walked to the little table at the end of the barracks. His friend was awakened by his tossing in bed, and now, propped up on his elbow, he could just make out Gustav strangely sitting alone in the dark. He got up and silently padded over to the table.

"You sick?" he whispered.

"No, just sick of stuff."

"Like what?"

"Like they're feeding us a pile of crap around here."

"Hey, careful with that," his friend replied, looking around to see if the rest were asleep.

"No, really. Know what? All the damn gold and fancy carriages around here just pull our eyes away from all the ugly stuff happening to the people out there."

"You're talkin' crazy, man."

At that, Gustav slammed his hand down on the table, and the loud "thwack" reverberated around the room, causing heads to pop up in shock all along the dark barracks.

"Hey," someone shouted, "get to bed or we're all in trouble!"

"Just talkin'," the friend shot back. "Go back to sleep."

"You don't know anything," Gustav replied way too loud for the moment, glaring at his friend and not ready to share the disturbing news from Heinrich. "I'm going to bed," he added, and with that, he walked away and slammed himself into the hard bed.

"You be careful," his shocked friend whispered. "These walls got ears, you know," and silently patted Gustav's shoulder as he passed his bed, puzzled and suddenly afraid of the man who was his dear friend.

Gustav felt a lump in the pit of his stomach. *Tomorrow I gotta write Heinrich.*

****

Lieber Bruder und Familie, Dear Brother and Family,

I was happy to hear from you and glad you are well. But your news really bothered me. I've been trying everything to find a way

I could help you, but I just can't find anything. There is no way I can talk to the Tsar, and anyone else will probably get me kicked out or whipped. Or worse. I'll keep working on it.

I'm learning so much history here. Trouble is, there are so many sides to some stories that I just don't know for sure what to believe. It's hard, because the more I find out, the more disturbed and angry I'm getting about the whole thing. But I still like the stories about Tsarina Katherina, about fifty years ago. I'm sure you've heard of her. She was a German girl, you know, born a princess there and brought over here by Tsarina Elizabeth.

Here we have been busy. Last week we had to lead the Tzar and his big party out to Lake Ladoga, some kilometers from here. It was frozen, so they went out on the ice, with a really big sled that's bigger than a lot of houses and needed twenty horses to pull it.

His mind went back to that huge sled, ten meters long by five meters wide, with runners that looked like pine tree trunks. It had a full kitchen with a cookstove in the front and an oversized center table. The back end contained a cluster of couches for people to relax and a heating stove to keep them warm.

There was lots of music inside with fiddles, accordions, and balalaikas, and a lot of people running around on the ice were pretty wobbly from vodka, but it sounded like they had a real good time. We nearly froze to death riding our horses, and I think I froze several toes, but I hope they heal up again.

By the way, Anna, our instructor said Tsarina Elizabeth had her closets full of 15,000 gowns that she loved to wear. How long do you think it would take to try each one on just once?

And, yes, I have been careful with those Russian beauties that you warned me about, but I have to tell you some of them are awfully pretty and looking better all the time.

Well, enough for now. Things are getting kind of edgy around here, with the secret police nosing around and watching everybody. Give those two young nephews a big hug for me, and take care of each other, with God's blessing always.

Oh, I almost forgot. A while back we had to guard the procession of the Tsar out to Tsarskoe Selo, which was Catherine's 180-room palace at Pushkin, a little ways south of St. Petersburg. The Tsar was visited by the English king, so it was a big deal with lots of people. The royals went by train, but our Imperial Horse Guards had to ride out and guard them from the train to the palace. After the royals were done looking and having tea, we were allowed to look at the Amber Room in the Palace. It's absolutely the most beautiful thing I've ever seen, enough to jingle your spurs.

The memory of it stopped his pencil. He recalled the guide saying it was the Eighth Wonder of the World, with all the walls totally covered in precious amber of many colors. Closing his eyes, he saw the treasured white-shaded gems, the oranges, golds, soft browns, all in hues too beautiful for words to describe. *Ei,* he thought again, *a hundred thousand little jewels shaped into faces and animals and plants is almost too much for my little brain to hold.*

Standing in the middle of all that bright golden light, I felt like I was taken to heaven. All in all, it is a good life and I am still glad you let me do it.
Your brother,
Gustav

Chapter 7

Mouchoir for the Masses

Russian czars were absolutely certain about one thing: they were placed on the Russian throne by Almighty God himself. In this enthronement, they stood on the Holy Bible itself. Its word was perfectly clear: "The authorities that exist have been established by God." That meant everything they decided came from the mouth of God right to the czar's heart.

This holy right coming directly from God, they were convinced, gave them absolute power over all things and all people. The biblical word in Romans 13 was also clear: "He who rebels against the authority is rebelling against God."

That basic conviction led to horrendous consequences as lower level functionaries dealt with the people of the land. Added to those actions, some disaffected courtiers who were released or passed over by the court found the courage to speak about what they had witnessed behind the insulated walls of the palaces. And they found ready ears among the intelligentsia and a new host of writers and university thinkers.

At the same time, "seditious" presses sprang up across the land, hawking the word that the czar and all the court were only living for themselves. Labor unions and masses of workers felt they were being cheated and were more than ready to listen to speakers detail the corruption and greed in high places.

One of the biggest lightning rods was Czarina Elizabeth. She befriended the guards during her illustrious reign, and now the instructors returned the favor with effusive praise during the Hussar classes, and Gustav began to appreciate her. But the underground writings about her were also the juiciest and quickest to inflame the crowds and contained a spittoon full of messy stuff that the higher ups did not want anyone to know.

Then one day, on the way out from supper, a comrade slipped a small book into Gustav's pants pocket and whispered, "Be careful with this."

Sitting on his bunk by candlelight in the barracks that night, Gustav looked around to see that he wasn't attracting unwanted attention. Then pulling out the thin volume, he came to a section on Tsarina Elizabeth. It spoke of how, growing up in palaces, she despised all things ordinary and that contact with the masses made her ill. Taking her carriage into the streets, she carried "scented mouchoirs to hide the dreadful smell arising from the unwashed throngs," as the writing said.

"What's a 'mu-choir'?" Gustav asked their instructor at the next session.

"It's pronounced 'mo-shwar,' and it's French for 'hanky,'" replied the instructor. "Where did you come up with that anyway?"

"I don't know. Something I read one day."

The instructor squinted his eyes, and Gustav cringed because it seemed like the man was looking into his soul for secrets, but fortunately, he let the matter drop.

After several of the little tomes had surreptitiously circulated around the barracks, warily guarded against discovery, Gustav and two Hussar comrades carefully smelled each other out over where each stood on the writings. Satisfied that each felt open to this illicit learning, they walked to a nearby inn at night and spent a bottle of vodka sharing their thoughts.

"Some of that stuff really gets your goat," Gustav weighed in.

"How much you think is true?" asked another.

"Wish I knew, but some of it has to be, don't you think?"

A week later, when the men gathered again and the vodka flowed like a river, Gustav pulled out his current little volume and flipped several pages to share a word on Tsarina Elizabeth. Just then one of the officers walked over and pulled up a chair. "You men sure look like you're in deep about something."

Then catching a glance of Gustav's book before he got it into his pocket, "Whatchu got, a good girly book?" he roared with a laugh.

Three hearts pounded in terror at being discovered, one man coughed, and Gustav piped up with a sudden high-pitched laugh, "Wish it were, but it's about horses."

"Yeah, we've been trying to learn," another quickly shot out.

The third nervously asked, "Sir, can we buy you a throat-wetter?"

"Why not."

"Sir, what kinda horse you like best?" one of the men quickly put in.

And with that the officer was off, sharing favorite horse stories, the book forgotten.

After he left, the men looked long at each other, slowly shook their heads, and breathed full again.

"Too close," Gustav whispered. "I'll never bring another cockeyed book!"

While official lessons continued to extol Elizabeth's great accomplishments in international affairs, enlarging the borders of Russia, building the great Smolny Cathedral, and adding splendor to the magnificent Winter Palace and other structures, Gustav still couldn't get away from the indulgent excesses that marked her reign.

The underground writings talked of Elizabeth enlarging the Imperial Vaults to hold her immense collection of royal jewelry, the most valuable in the world, bigger even than the Shah of Iran's or the Crown Jewels of Britain. "Her eyes danced," they wrote. "Her hands grew animated. Words rolled like rain from her lips when she pulled out black velvet-lined trays of diamond pieces, emeralds and pearls, sapphire, opal and spinel, amber and healing amethysts, all set in richest gold. The peerless diamond crowns, sapphire necklaces, and ruby brooches laid on her skin brought her to near ecstasy." Gustav's mind was jumbled between excitement and dismay.

For all his disappointment at such wild excessiveness in the face of grinding poverty all around, he told one of the men, "Ach, what I still wouldn't give for a quick look at all that stuff."

"Don't even talk about it," the friend warned, "or we'll all be in trouble."

Later, Gustav shook his head as he read, "When nights turned dull at the Winter Palace in St. Petersburg, Czarina Elizabeth had a moment of inspiration and ordered all her entourage and nobility transported 650 kilometers to Moscow for a royal gala in the sumptuous grandeur of the Kremlin's five-story Terem Palace. Some twenty-four thousand courtiers, family entourage, and foreign diplomats required thousands of horses with carriages to get all of them to Moscow."

"That probably was nothing special for Tsarina Elizabeth," Gustav told his friend, "because she kept a stable of a thousand horses ready all the time anyway, for any big thing she wanted to do."

Further on, the piece pointed out Elizabeth's prodigality in ordering a full set of Lomonosov Porcelain dishes with matching crystal and silver for 150 guests to eat at one time. It went on to her elaborate, scandalous party when she ordered all attendees, male and female, Russian and foreign, to dress as the opposite sex to get in, a venture that caused great consternation and bitter criticism from both high- and low-level people. Several foreign governments sent sharp protests at their diplomats being treated in such derogatory fashion. Gustav's Hussar mates just shook their heads as well. "Let it go," one said, "it's no business of ours." They were surprised by how eagerly he was learning and becoming a soul mate to them and didn't want to see him get into trouble.

Gustav's astonishment grew deeper when he learned that one of Elizabeth's biggest expenses came early, when she took the throne. Her predecessor, Czarina Anna, loved to hunt, and when the winters turned harsh, she commanded her servants to bring cages of birds into the Winter Palace and turn them loose. Then she shouldered her prized shotgun and blasted away, in any of the thousand-plus rooms, wherever the birds flew. *Ei, she left lotta expensive holes for Elizabeth to fix,* was all Gustav could think of.

Somehow, through it all, Tsarina Elizabeth was the face of Mother Russia for twenty-one years. And what a face it was. That long a reign must have meant she did something right, and the Hussars felt a certain fondness toward her, quirks and snobbishness and all.

To Gustav and many of his Hussar comrades, coming out of a muzhik, peasant background, the indulgent opulence behind the palace walls seemed like nothing short of sinful. But as they guardedly talked about it, one of the men reminded them, "You know what? I'll bet it's no different here than in any court around the world." "Dah," replied another, "they're all like this, don't care snort about all the rest of us."

Still, Gustav was troubled as he continued learning from their instructor and from official sources. He liked the tsar and those before him and was thankful for the opportunities he was given, but all the clandestine documents disturbed him. He and his closest comrades in the Hussar service still weren't sure how much of the material was true, but so much was coming at them that they believed some of it had to be.

And it was dangerous. They did not know which of their comrades might betray them or who might be a secret police informer, so carelessness this close to the czar could get them summarily executed.

Gustav continued to soak up the heavy dose of historical Elizabeth they were given, along with the czars who followed her, but when lessons returned to "Cousin Catherine" and her half-German mate, Peter, he felt that it was also in part his history.

He felt a new warmth for her when he discovered how Catherine endeared herself to the people by becoming fluent in Russian, how she adopted the customs of the land, and how she was approachable and personable to people of every rank. She was skilled and gifted, bright and immensely curious about all of life. She learned the full ritual and converted to the Russian Orthodox faith. His eyes grew large when he read, further, that on her conversion day, Tsarina Elizabeth presented her with a sapphire-and-diamond necklace worth one hundred and fifty thousand rubles. *For that,* he thought to himself, *I might think about converting, too.*

Catherine and her husband, Peter, had nearly twenty years to learn from a good teacher in Elizabeth. But Gustav was further disappointed to learn that most of Peter's royal education flew right over his head. "When he ascended to the throne as Tsar Peter III upon Elizabeth's death, he was perhaps as flaky a ruler as ever sat upon the Russian throne," the writing said. Later, it called him "as discreet as a cannonball," describing him as sarcastic, hot tempered, given to playing cruel practical jokes on those around him.

So it was no surprise when he learned that while Peter never outgrew his love of all things military, it was the military who joined the nobles and sidled up to his ambitious wife in a coup and overthrew thirty-four-year-old Tsar Peter after only a six-month reign. They immediately proclaimed Catherine as the new sovereign, Catherine II. A short while later, under mysterious and hastily investigated circumstances, Peter turned up dead.

As the piece continued, Gustav smiled when he read, "Soon the Russians learned to love their new Mother, and she loved them back."

Then Gustav read another line that truly disturbed him: "Catherine had great curiosity, but perhaps the only thing that outstripped her curiosity was her sexual appetite. She never remarried, but her bed remained hot for all seasons."

All this left a taste of bitter gall in Gustav's mouth. He had been so proud of dear "Cousin Catherine," his shining star, for all the truly great things she accomplished, indeed earning her the sobriquet, "the Great." But now she felt to him little more than a rich, horny peasant.

Ei, yei, yei, he breathed as he tossed over and over in bed, *my whole heart just hurts. I guess tomorrow I've got to write Heinrich and Anna again.*

He felt good to have someone to write, but his heart was still troubled.

****

Lieber Bruder und Familie,

It was so good to get news from you.

I have some good news, too. I just earned a stripe, so I'm Sergeant Oster, and in charge of a squad of men. Recently we were also issued pistols, and have regular target practice. And my Russian is getting better all the time too. I think I talk better Russian than some of the men in our company. I have to, really, because the Tsar hates foreigners, and I don't want to get thrown out now. I'm kind of getting to like this life. Never thought I'd say that, even though I get so angry at the way the royals seem to think they are above all law and even kill anybody they want to any time. So much isn't fair, but what can one person do?

You know what I miss the most around here? The wonderful hymn singing in our old church back home. There is a big Lutheran Church here, kind of around the corner that we ride by on Nevsky Prospekt. It's called Saints Peter and Paul Lutheran and they said it was actually started by Peter the Great. But I really don't dare go there, because I'm afraid I'd get in big trouble if the Tsar found out. They have one of the Tsar's Orthodox priests do mass for us here, but it's in Slavonic and I don't understand it and get nothing out of it. So I read my Bible and pray alone. Guess that will have to do.

Oh, Anna, you asked about the Tsarina. I have to tell you, last week we led them to a ball in their big carriage. And when the Tsarina was helped out, she had on a monster dress that the Captain said they later told him weighed 34 kilos [75 pounds]. How would you like to dance all night in that?

He laid his pencil down on the little table where he was writing and looked around to see that no one was paying attention to him. And in an instant, he felt all alone inside as well.

The joy he felt in thinking of Heinrich and his family suddenly turned dark as he thought of the danger they could all be in.

What's happening to me? he thought. *I have such a good life here, but so many things seem so gosh-awful messed up.* He glanced around the room nervously and thought, *People in high places just care about themselves and treat everybody else like dirt.* The thought wouldn't let go: *Ei, how power can twist people's hearts, and little by little, they get to believing that sin is fun and evil is actually good.*

His hand slid down to his belt, and he realized he had a lump in his stomach and that his stomach hurt. He rested his arms over his letter on the rickety table and laid his head down on his arms. *Oh God, what is this country coming to?* he pleaded in painful prayer. *And what am I coming to? Like it or not, I'm part of it. It's got me in its teeth and won't let go. Oh God, dear God, reach down and help us.*

Just then a hand gripped his left shoulder. Instantly, an animal howl burst from his lungs, and in one motion, he jumped up and swung his left arm backward in shock. It was the captain who had quietly walked in during his deep reverie and nearly got himself coldcocked.

"Whoa, Sergeant, what the devil's going on?"

"Sorry, Sir, I didn't hear you coming. Guess you startled me."

"What are you doing anyway?"

"Writing my brother."

Gustav's heart nearly exploded when the captain leaned over for a look at his letter. *Oh dear God, I'm dead,* flashed across his mind and his hands trembled. But then he caught himself: the letter was in German, and the captain was Russian.

"Good, Sergeant, glad to hear that. Keep in touch with family. Carry on."

When he left, Gustav dropped down on the chair, hardly able to breathe: *Precious Lord, Jesus, what could have just happened to me here?* In that fleeting moment of sheer terror, tears welled up in his eyes, and his very soul cringed, *Oh dear God, thank you.* In seconds, he was drenched in sweat, his arms trembling with unbelievable fear. For long moments, his fingers drummed on the table, his left heel bounced on the floor, and once more he rested his hurting head on his arms.

He wanted to continue writing, but his hand shook too badly to hold the pencil. Finally, when one of the men on the other end of the barracks began singing a mournful love song in that lowest of rumbling Russian bass voices, he slowly picked up his pencil, drew in a deep, deep breath, and tried to settle down his pounding heart enough to continue writing.

I've learned so much about this place and our new country. I have been going to classes and reading their stuff, and then reading some more in books going around between the men, under the table as they say. Sad to say, the more I get into it, the more mixed up I'm getting about what is really true, and the more it bothers me. I almost get sick about it once in a while.

Anyway, these stories have me so wound up right now.

His pulse went up, and he stopped writing as he thought of an article he recently read that made his blood boil. Dear Tsarina Catherine had seen danger from the Tatar hordes threatening to invade from the east and hit upon an ingenious solution. She issued a broad manifesto inviting her German cousins to come to Russia where she settled them in a buffer band along the Volga River and in the Black Sea area. Her offer guaranteed them free land, freedom of religion, no taxes for thirty years, and "freedom in perpetuity from military service." All this she further sweetened with travel allowances and interest-free loans for those wishing to start a business. *And that rotten business is what brought us here,* he mumbled to the table.

This was Gustav's people, betrayed by one of their own flesh and blood, and he suddenly balled up his fists and felt like punching something, anything. After several minutes, he realized he had to calm down and tell Heinrich the truth and warn him of the danger they could be facing.

Heinrich, I have to tell you something terribly important, and dangerous to talk about. We have been tricked and it has me almost angry enough to quit.

Do you know, dear brother, why we are in this land? Not because our cousin, Tsarina Catherine, liked us so much, but because we are the first line of defense if the blood-thirsty Tatars invade. Our people would be like Isaiah's "lambs led to the slaughter," sacrificed first, to give the big shots time to flee. That was a big shock to me. Hope it never comes to that. I don't know but maybe you should even think about leaving this land.

We've had some secret police types nosing around here, asking a lot of questions. There are a lot of suspicions in high places right now. It is getting risky to say things, and we have to be careful. So from now on, I will sign my name as Silnyj, which is Russian for Strong, Nikolai Silnyj. Hope I can be. When you write, still use my regular name, so the letters get to me.

Yours, Nikolai Silnyj

Chapter 8

Promises Broken

Heinrich and Anna's family gradually grew to a dozen, all full of life.

"Those kids are gonna eat us into the poor house," Anna complained with a smile, glad they were healthy, but hardly able to fill all those hungry mouths.

They went to a few years of school, enough to learn the basics, and then, one by one, the older ones were loaned out to neighbors to help in the fields or in the kitchens when extra hands were needed.

The younger boys joined Heinrich in the spring, walking to the fields a half mile east of the *dorf* and hand-scattering the precious kernels of wheat that would grow to feed the family next winter. In the fall, they helped to drive the team of horses out to pick up the sheaves of wheat that had been cut down with long-bladed scythes and tied into bundles. In between, they led the few family cows out to join the herd of village cows in the commune pasture, and once a week, they took their turn as shepherd-for-the-day in charge of the whole herd. Every noon, they brought the herd back to the lazy Tschaga River, to walk in the water, fill up, and then back out again.

The younger girls joined Anna in full days of cooking, boiling, baking, canning garden vegetables, hand-washing clothes with scrub board and tub, learning to crochet, patching endless torn clothes, and by candlelight at night, darning sock after holey sock. When they laid down their needles, it didn't take long to fall asleep in the welcome dark.

Still, life wasn't all work. They had time for play as well, joining neighborhood children, teasing favorite girlfriends and boyfriends, and throwing snowballs in the long, cold winters when icy Siberian fingers clawed at their skin.

The whole village joined in building an impressive, high-spired limestone church, a hundred yards up the gentle slope from the west bank of the Tschaga River, to practice their three-hundred-year-old

Lutheran faith. And up the hill from there, in ground too steep to plant crops, they platted their cemetery, where their dead could await the Lord in glory.

They learned the catechism and the Lutheran faith at the hands of village pastors, who steeped them in the rich history of the Bible and every Sunday led them in singing hymns which, after enough times sung, they knew by heart.

Heinrich, now forty-nine, and Anna had been quietly reviewing the short list of eligible young women among the thirty German families of *dorf* Klostitz. Son, Christian, was twenty, and it was time to find a wife for him. During the sermons and hymns in church, they casually glanced around and did some mental measuring. *Which young woman is strong enough to carry on the hard work and bear the children to ensure our family's fortunes? Which one comes from the best family that could be joined to make ours a bit more prosperous?*

They settled on Karolina, of the Wolt family, and met with them to negotiate and arrange a marriage. After several meetings, it was done, and there would be great festivities on that June day to come. To get ready, a pig had to be butchered and sausage made. Crocks of sauerkraut readied, potatoes cleaned and boiled, carrots washed, kuchen by the dozens baked and set on high shelves to keep them away from cats and little kids, vodka and beer laid in from Russian Odessa, yard raked, and the dirt floor in the house wetted and swept clean.

The four-foot high limestone fence around their yard needed to be whitewashed for the occasion. Neighbors Miller and Boeshans and Kleinschmidt agreed to get out their accordions, fiddle, and mouth organ to play snappy songs for happy dancing and carefree singing. Hair needed to be cut, beards trimmed, long tresses curled, the best dresses ironed, shirts starched, shoes cleaned and polished.

By three in the afternoon of the joyous 23rd, that June Saturday of 1860, the entire *dorf* began walking to church. Out of every humble house, down every dusty artery they came, family meeting family, men joining men, women arm in arm. Smiles and laughter grew louder, children skipping, teasing, shouting but without being so loud they'd get shushed. Several buggies arrived, carrying relatives from neighboring villages. They unhitched their horses and waited.

On the front steps of *St. Johannes Luterische Kirche,* St. John's Lutheran Church, the excited buzz grew quiet as Reverend Gerhardt Kussler met them, opened the door, and led them inside, taking Christian, Karolina, and their two witnesses to the railing that surrounded the altar.

Behind them, women sat on the left, men on the right, young girls in Sunday best sitting on backless benches in front of the women, boys in front of the men.

Christian, fresh shaven, hair oiled, sported a new black wool suit, starched white shirt and black tie. Karolina's veil and sash and collar were delicate white lace handwork; her floor-length dress was black so she could wear it for funerals in coming years. Her face glowed with the inner radiance of knowing she would be safe, cared for, hopefully even loved. No smiles now. This was not a time for levity, especially in the house of God.

With soft Bessarabian sunlight filtering into the dusky sanctuary, Reverend Kussler, in black gown with white collar tabs, intoned, *"Im Namen des Vaters und des Sonnes und des Heiligen Geistes,* In the Name of the Father and of the Son and of the Holy Ghost." After hymns and Scripture lessons and prayers, he preached a mighty hour, reminding Christian and Karolina, and, of course, the whole assembled *dorf,* of all the duties and responsibilities of the married estate, sternly instructing, counseling, admonishing, encouraging, building bridges to the future, and talking with great surety of children that would come. *Yes,* the grandmothers nodded, fanning against the clinging heat. *Surely, surely.*

The young bride felt a joy in her heart that she had never known before. So many glorious visions danced through her mind during that worship time: being enfolded in her beloved's strong arms for hours on end, baking him rich chocolate cakes and watching as he hungrily devoured them, sitting on chairs outside their new little house and listening to the crickets at sunset, twisting and tumbling together for hours with all the passion that only new lovers can bring to their wedding bed.

And Christian? Well, Christian had heard enough and just wanted to get it over with and out of there. All this talk was getting old, and his collar was choking him. Flies buzzed, sweat flowed, horses snorted outside the open windows, but who cared? A new house was being put together, a new family aborning in this holy hour. Amen.

Then back home. Drink to slack the terrible thirst of forced sitting. Piles of food to still the pangs of empty stomachs. More drink, *kvass* and things stronger. Sweet, rich *kuchen.* More talk and laughter, romping children of every age. Soon dishes were stashed, and all headed for the granary, where the accordion was unlimbered. Long into the Black Sea night, feet flew and hearts rejoiced together in the miracle of a fresh virgin union, life being continued across a new rainbow of hope arching across nature's way.

Before they knew it, the dimness of the fabled Russian White Night gave way to eager sun searching them out from the eastern horizon, and Christian and Karolina took leave, trudging the dusty path to the tiny new house the relatives had built for them. There would be no wedding night. Night was already gone. But the wedding bed was fresh and asked them in. The circle would continue.

Yet these vast steppes where hungry bands of wolves ranged and witches were said to hover over deadly cauldrons, where even mighty czars could disappear overnight in a stealthy coup, these steppes could turn on peasants, too—not all at once in a mighty cataclysm of sudden change, but slowly, incident by troubling incident.

One morning, there was a knock on the door. Two grim-faced Russian policemen stood there and asked Karolina, "Where is your husband?"

"Out in the fields," she replied. "Why?"

"Because someone told us he stole their horse."

It was a total fabrication, but there was little they could do to defend themselves. It was up to them to prove they hadn't done it. The police didn't come back. There was no further charge of any kind. None was needed. The knock on the door had done its job, and Christian and Karolina were frightened out of their wits. So were the neighbors. When would one of them be charged with another crime? When would one of them be hauled away to be seen no more?

Another day, neighbor Nikolaus Unruh drove to a neighboring Russian town, unhitched his horses, and tied them to the wagon. A young Russian child pestered one of the horses, and it kicked him. Although there was no serious injury, the family sued Nikolaus, and the judge awarded them a sum that Nikolaus labored two years to pay.

With numerous incidents like this, the Germans grew to severely dislike Russian lawyers, judges, and the entire court system. To go up against them meant to lose, simple as that.

Then government officials rode through the villages announcing, "All farmers will be required to pay land taxes beginning next year." That meant the end of the Homestead Decree guaranteeing, "No taxes." Another promise broken.

Two policemen accosted Constantin Keller. "What have I done?" he asked. "Why are you doing this?"

"Because we don't like you. That's enough."

They hauled him to jail and left him there four days. His family was terrified, not knowing if they would ever see him again. When he came home, all of Klostitz was afraid.

In village after village, similar scenes played out. Word spread. The settlers were powerless to fight back. Protesting only brought more trouble. The authorities were deaf, nor did they care. Incident melted into incident, and as word spread, the settlers slowly realized that it was flowing together into a river of persecution. They were no longer wanted; they were being welcomed out. Every passing month made it more clear.

Yet, through all this, life went on. Crops were raised and so were children. Three times, a frightened Christian would rush over, knock on the midwife's door, and shout in the dark, "Come, quick." Thus three children were born, and all safe. Ten more times in coming years he would knock, but more calmly. Each time Tanta (Grandma) Rueb grabbed her ready-bag and fast-pedaled her stubby legs to Karolina's side. And after Tanta Rueb's mustache grew thicker and darker, her daughter, Rosina, scrubbed her hands and guided the borning. Eight of the children lived; five more were early laid into the Russian ground, including a set of twins, too soon born. And with each death, a little piece of Karolina's heart broke off and fell into that tiny grave, making her old before her time. Life was precious. Life was hard. "Dear God this, too, Thou hast ordained," she whispered into her pillow through silent tears, but she wasn't ever completely sure she really meant it.

St. Johannes's scrabbly cemetery had two rows of little graves with lambs carved atop simple headstones bearing heartbreaking messages: *"Friedrich, sonnes Gustav und Matilda Pfenning, geboren* (born) *3 Juni, 1865, gestorben* (died) *4 Juni, 1865."* One day of life!

Still, somehow, Karolina felt blessed of God: in all these pain-filled times, she had not been called to join the many young mothers who ended their childbirth in the ground of St. Johannes as well. Several times before she was done weaning the child at her breast, another was already growing inside her. During these weary stretches when she had no strength left, there were nights she cried herself to sleep, but the tears were silent, and Christian must not know. She believed this was the role God chose for her, and yet her tired back curled in soulful prayer: *"Dear Lord, why did you give Eve such a hard and heavy load, and why must I carry it all over again? Does it really have to be this way? Will this be my lot until the way of women ends for me? Yet, Lord, not my will, but thine be done. Amen."* In the morning, none would know her anguish. The children were her love, her life. They needed to be fed.

****

Through all these seasons of anguish and blessing, Christian and Karolina had never spent a night apart. Though they never talked about it, they realized more and more how much they meant to each other and how close their hearts had grown together.

One day, Christian was out in the fields, walking up and down the rows behind the team and singing a hymn. Suddenly, his mind turned to Karolina, and he found himself smiling. *Such a gift, dear Lord, you gave me in that woman.* His mind flashed through so many of the things she did for him and for the children and the good conversations they shared. *Holy God, she makes me sing, just like you do.* He felt so good that he almost told her.

These stolid Aryan men were not given to displays of emotion nor to great romantic actions, either in public or in the privacy of their own homes. Yes, you loved your wife, but *if you give the woman a new washboard for her birthday, that shows your love aplenty,* was more than just idle talk.

Where the women found the freest bonding was with their children and with neighbor wives.

Where men bonded more freely was with their horses. Twelve hours in a furrow together, through cold and drizzle and stormy heat, and a closeness developed. Horse and man learned to depend on each other, and they did. Twelve-hour days in the field and man and horse knew each other's language, both voice and body. Even Fido, walking in the furrow, knew the feel.

Thus, their married love was deep, but not a thing ever discussed. "Love" was used in God-talk, in singing and praying and worship, and never for human beings or any other thing. Karolina cared for John more deeply than anything else in life, but speaking about love would have unnerved both of them. Slowly stirring a kettle of soup over the fireplace, she found herself for some unknown reason thinking of the Virgin Mary's great prayer of praise in the Bible, and her own heart turned to prayer: *Merciful God, as you blessed Mary with a holy Son, so you gave her a good husband, too. Thank you for my children and for giving me such a good man. Amen.* Holding her ladle still for a moment, her mind went on: *And thank you for the joy of being faithful to each other and caring for each other more than life itself. How rich we are, how rich. Yes.*

Such caring was for a lifetime, but yet what really got a man's blood pressure up was anything to do with his prized horses. When a good horse cost him hundreds of rubles, he cared for it like a chestful of gold. Their Russian neighbors had a proverb for this: *"His wife dying won't crush the farmer, but his horse dying fills him with terror."* These men wouldn't say so, or even necessarily agree, but they understood.

So when Marya was about to throw her first foal, it was a nervous time around the house. During the night, Christian got up and lit the lantern to go check on her. When he opened the barn door, Marya was lying down, groaning, snorting, whinnying with fear in her throat. One look and he realized she was in trouble.

One quick look and he ran to get the two oldest boys, Gottfried and John. Shaking both awake, he tried to sound unruffled, but his loud whisper betrayed him, "Quick, get up, Marya is having her colt."

Running back, they saw Marya's eyes rolling in fear, short breaths coming through her snapping mouth, belly heaving. Christian spat out machine-gun orders: "Gottfried, lay easy on her neck. Stroke her cheeks and her nose. Do it easy, e-easy. Talk soft to her. Let her know you'll help her."

"John, get the rope down. Throw a loop over each of her back legs. Hurry up. Then string it over to the post. Snug it tight. Come on, don't fiddle. Move! Loop it three times around the post so it holds. Don't let her kick me with her back legs.

"Gottfried, be careful if she starts thrashing with her front legs. She might try to get up. Don't let her. Hang on to her. Stay awake here, don't get careless, or we'll have a dead colt," he continued, barking orders.

"John, hang on to that rope. Don't let it slip. Watch out!"

His normal low voice had gone up half a dozen notes. He was trying to show calm, but the boys knew calm was long gone. This was serious, and they'd better not slip up.

The colt was coming out back end first, and it was stuck. Christ would have to reach inside and turn it around. He stroked Marya's flanks for several minutes, to keep her from panicking when he began to reach inside. Slowly, ever so slowly, he started gently pushing the colt back and off to one side. Just then it kicked and jerked and flipped around, head first. Christ reached in and grabbed the front legs, slowly guiding them out, then pulling, an inch at a time. Marya heaved and shuttered and birthed the little one. In one big, wet sack, it whooshed out.

Christ cut the cord and snapped, "OK, John, quick get the rope off so she can get up. Gottfried, get off, let her stand."

In one kick and roll, Marya was up, wheeled around, and began licking the colt clean. Suddenly, she paused, looked at Christian and the boys, as if to say, "Thanks. You were a big help."

"How about," said Gottfried, "how about, if we name the colt, 'Peter'?"

"Sounds good," Christ replied. "Peter it'll be, just like the old tsar."

They got back to the house just as the big rooster sounded reveille. Karolina had the coffeepot on. This morning, the boys would be drinking coffee too. Their boyish days were at an end. This night marked the beginning of manhood. Coffee this time was terribly serious. The boys were in their cups. No words were spoken. Karolina looked over and met her husband's eyes. Both broke ever so small a smile. Both knew that new days were dawning.

Chapter 9

Let 'em Eat Steel

Czar Alexander II, in 1861, freed the serfs in Russia, two years before Abraham Lincoln signed his fateful Emancipation Proclamation to free the slaves in America. Both shook their worlds. And at the end of the day, both would be assassinated, each in part for his role in bringing freedom to the littlest of the least among their people. The royals and rich nobles, losing free help on the land, sought revenge any way they could get it. They "would not go gentle into that dark night" of financial loss.

In the Black Sea area of southern Russia, to the grassy rolling steppes to the west, through the oak stands of the northwest, and on to the rich black soils of the north and east along the Volga River shores, strong winds were blowing change. The Russian peasants, freed from the bonds of serfdom, now demanded land of their own. And they were violently angered that a group of émigrés from foreign places, speaking foreign tongues and worshiping in foreign ways, were given land—free land, no less—by the crown.

"Where's *my* free land?" went the cry as they hammered their tankards in smoke-filled saloons.

Bitterness was born full-bitch and grew faster than the robust dandelions of spring in conditions such as this.

The disgruntled headed for the big cities, filled with rumors of work abounding from the industrialization that was slowly building factories. But wages were low, unions were formed in protest, and anger was flowing as dirty as the Volga.

Dostoyevsky, Tolstoy, Pushkin, all thundered strong imprecations across six thousand miles of fractured Russian landscape, exposed corruption, revealed the moral chaos that was rotting out palace halls and offering government for sale to the brightest bribes.

A new czar felt no compassion for the people fomenting unrest. They were disobeying God's chosen sovereign and must be brought into line. "They got plenty to eat," he said, looking out the palace windows. "They want fruit? Fill their bellies with the taste of steel." That became the dictum of the palace, and the military stood ready to indulge the troublemakers in a savory feast.

In all this shuffle, the new Germans suddenly found themselves labeled "New Enemy" by their neighbors, the long oppressed native Russian peasants.

****

Karolina and the girls continued to find joy in the big, waddling white geese they were raising. The geese laid eggs and were hunkered down over nests of a dozen eggs each. Then one morning, daughter Katherina walked out into the grass behind the barn and noticed a little yellow fluff-ball peeking out from underneath one of the geese.

She raced back to the house, "Mamma, Mamma, the eggs are hatching!"

Mother grabbed Katherina's hand, picked up baby Anna Maria, and dashed outside. Picking up a stick, she gently pushed the goose off her nest. The hen, not pleased, hissed and bit the stick in angry protest but finally yielded, moving off to the side, but only a step. If need be, she would fly at the intruders and flap them hard with her strong wings. She didn't like leaving her precious children exposed.

Karolina and the little ones squatted down and watched as another egg mysteriously shook and softly rolled from side to side. Mamma goose stood across from them, neck arched, eyes blazing, tongue out, ready to fly at these calloused intruders. A crack appeared in the trembling egg, then another, until it split open. Out popped a tiny yellow beak and a wobbly wet, straggly head that bobbled on rubbery neck. Exhausted, its head dropped and stayed down.

"Did it die?" Katherina wanted to know.

"Sh-h," said Karolina softly, "just watch."

After a minute of nothing, the lifeless little neck swung up, beak pointed to the sky, and the little gosling kicked its legs. It bravely tried to stand, tumbled over, and kicked at air. Now it was free of the egg, and in another moment, it feebly stood up, rocking around like one of the over-vodkad Russian neighbors.

With practiced hands, Karolina picked up the first hatchling that by now was dry and fluffy and walking wobbly steps and gently placed it into Katherina's hands. The gosling nibbled her fingers, ever so softly searching every pore for a morsel of goose food, finding none, but searching all the more. Katherina giggled at the tickling, nearly dropping the fluff-ball but totally immersed in the pure joy of holding this new little sister-creature, both of them so young, with so much to learn, so much to cram into the time ahead. She slowly bent down and set the little one back into the nest. As she backed away, mamma goose, in a huff, annoyed at being shushed aside stepped in, poking the broken eggshells out of the nest with her beak, and spread her long wings back over the downy nest. Ruffling her feathers, she settled down, free after all the stress, to be the goose mamma she was intended to be. Watching all her careful fussing, Karolina couldn't help but smile and told the girls, "Ach ja, I know, a mother's work is never done."

Every family in the *dorf* had their own gaggle of white geese, and every morning one of the village boys was assigned as "goose-herd" to walk through the village and gather all the geese into one big "herd," taking them out to graze on grass at the edge of the village. In the afternoon, he brought the entire gaggle back into the *dorf*, and at each door, the geese from that house peeled off and waddled into their own yard without a word being spoken. They knew where they belonged.

But it seemed like a lot of people around the country didn't. Unsettling events were swirling around every corner of the land. Yet, in the German *dorfs*, life remained quiet and peaceable, for the most part, and stories of harsh happenings elsewhere seemed a long way off. Still, to the men of the village, they were a frightening portent of what they might face in the time to come.

Chapter 10

Package from the Czar's House

Heinrich and Anna finished a light supper and were sitting on chairs in front of their house when a military courier arrived.

"I'm looking for Heinrich Oster."

"Ja, I am Heinrich Oster," he replied, frightened by this uniformed stranger.

"Package for you."

Heinrich soon recognized the czar's familiar seal on it, but when he noticed its black color, his heart fell.

A group of neighbors quickly gathered, eager to see what magic had struck the Oster house. Heinrich got his jackknife out of his pocket and slowly opened the blade. He tried to appear calm, but his hands were shaking so badly that he nearly dropped the knife, though his practiced hand made short work of the paper wrapping.

Inside, laid an eight-inch long, highly polished maplewood box and a large envelope.

Heinrich started to undo the delicate silver clasp, but his hands began to tremble uncontrollably. Unsure and afraid, he glanced at Anna, his eyebrows raised and eyes imploring help. His chin trembled as he finally handed the box to Anna. Her arthritic hands could do no better with the clasp, and finally, one of the neighbor women reached over her shoulder and gently unlatched the clasp. As Anna opened the box, all crowded in, with necks craned to get a closer look inside.

"Oohs" and "Ei, yei, yeis" burst from every throat. Never had eyes in that little gathered clan beheld anything so magnificent.

Pinned to the black velvet lining of the polished box was a radiant, three-inch princely gold cross on a scarlet ribbon. The arms of the Greek cross were inlaid red gemstones, and between each of the four arms of the cross was an intricately wrought, golden, double-headed eagle, wearing the crown of the Romanov House. On each eagle, one talon bore the Royal Scepter and the other, a small cross atop the orb of Mother Russia. The white enameled center of the cross showed a gallant warrior on a rearing white steed. In the bright sunshine, it glistened like a fallen piece of heaven.

"Gustav must have done something really great," Heinrich stammered, suddenly hoping the medal might still be good news, "but why would he send it to us?"

Just then, Christian came in from the field, and after glancing at the radiant medal, he opened the large envelope and took out a letter.

The little party laid their eyes expectantly on Christian, hoping to hear about heroic deeds.

"*Jetzt was*, now what?" Christian exclaimed. "This thing is all in Russian."

Its full page of formal Cyrillic script was obviously done by a highly trained hand, but no one could read the Russian words. Finally, Christian looked back into the envelope, and there was another piece of paper folded up. Some thoughtful soul, knowing Gustav's background, had translated the entire letter into German and quietly included it in the envelope:

> *Dear Master Heinrich Oster,*
>
> *It is my sad duty, and with a heavy heart, that I must inform you of your brother Gustav Christian Oster's recent death.*
>
> *He was killed in the line of duty, heroically defending our Most Illustrious Czar Alexander. While the Czar and Czarina were riding in their carriage, a small rabble horde suddenly surged forward and attacked the carriage. When your brother witnessed what was happening, he raced his horse back from his patrol position and placed himself beside the Czar's window. He killed several of the anarchists before two bullets intended for the Czar struck your brother in the chest.*
>
> *If it be the least fragment of comfort to you, know that your brave brother's soul left this world instantly. He gallantly sacrificed his life for our beloved Czar and all of Mother Russia. His murderers were caught and his death avenged.*

For Gustav's extreme bravery, His Royal Majesty, Czar Alexander, hereby posthumously awards him the Imperial Order of St. Alexander Nevsky.

Your brother was buried with full military honors in the Palace Cemetery. Should you find occasion to visit his grave, present this letter to the Royal Guard at the main entrance of the Winter Palace, and you will be escorted to the tomb.

May Blessed Mary, Holy Mother of our Lord, together with St. Alexander Nevsky and all the Saints, Bless and Comfort you.

Your Eternal Servant,

General Dmitry Prokhorov

Special Military Aide to Czar Alexander

At the bottom of the translation was added: "The Order of St. Alexander Nevsky Medal is the highest award for military bravery, in honor of the great hero, Alexander Nevsky, the mighty Russian warrior and leader in the 1200s Anno Domini."

"*Lieber Gott,* dear God," muttered Heinrich, "*Ach, Lieber Gott.*"

His shoulders sagged; then tears streamed down his face as he stared at the dusty ground. One by one, the neighbors quietly walked by and gripped his hand or clasped his shoulder. In that silence no word was spoken, as grief was shared, concern poured out, and the bond of neighborly love pulled tighter. Their eyes never met.

Anna quietly closed the polished medal case and carried it, with the letters, into the house, where she carefully packed them into the bottom of her travel trunk.

For Grandfather Heinrich, the tragic news made hard days even harder. When they first came into Russia, he had agreed to let his brother experience the "good life" in the palace, and this death was all his fault. His heart was broken; he couldn't talk to Anna or to anyone else. He drew into a lonesome shell and yearned for home. And in this new Russian place, his heart sadly never quite felt at home. He never learned the language, beyond a few words and numbers to do trading in the larger towns. Now his eyes were clouded over with cataracts, vision became fuzzy, hearing almost gone, and people had to shout so he'd hear. His knees bothered him, and even walking to the outhouse became a huge burden. Food no longer had any taste. Life offered no joy. He slept alone on a rope bed in the corner, snoring—Anna said—louder every year. Then one morning, when Anna called him for breakfast, he didn't answer.

For Heinrich, one more bath by loving family, a short funeral with Reverend Kussler reading biblical promises over the quick-nailed wooden casket the relatives had made, and the Russian soil was his next bed and the longest.

Within a year's time, Anna Marie joined him on that barren, windswept hill above their town, the spot marked by a fragile, white-painted cross with only her name to remember the whole lifetime of a tender helpmeet and faithful child of God.

Chapter 11

Tsaritsa Katrigold

In the bigger towns and faraway cities, unrest continued to grow. Unionists fomented anger; fiery speeches agitated crowds that grew larger with every passing year.

Where popular Czar Alexander II had loosened the reins, his son, Alexander III, succeeding him, got nervous and tightened them hard and fierce. He would show the upstarts what the face of power looked like.

Russian air carried the smoke of rebellion, and when Alexander III's son, Nicholas II, in turn became czar in 1894, the smoke coalesced into deadly clouds. Riots broke out, and people were killed. Japan was sounding war in the East.

Nicholas needed soldiers, and his ministers told him the quickest way to enlarge his military was to draft the "outlanders," the Germans who had begun to feel too smugly settled in, too much like they belonged in the land, and too quickly prosperous next to their Russian neighbors.

True, Catherine and Alexander I had solemnly covenanted with the Germans that they would not be subject to Russian military service "in perpetuity."

"But that was a hundred years ago," argued Nicholas's ministers, "and the world was different then."

For Christian and Karolina and the older generation of settlers, that all seemed far away, and they felt a deep loyalty to the new czar, Nicholas II. With their rural Russian neighbors, they still thought of the czar as the true father of the land. What he commanded must be done. When they spoke of him, it was "The Tsar." Unlike their city cousins, they did not feel the heavy hand of the government or the dreaded bureaucracies that seemed to squeeze too tightly the air they breathed. Their horses were healthy, crops grew, school and church ran on as the seasons came and went. They butchered a hog, made sausage, canned chicken, packed sauerkraut, visited his eleven and her ten brothers and sisters and their families, and paid their taxes. Yes, there were scattered incidents, but they were bearable.

But for the younger ones, things were different. With the irreverence of youth, Nicholas was no longer the tsar, but "Nicki." Palace intrigues in faraway St. Petersburg were, unfortunately for the royals, not as private as they thought. Their royal cocoons were being split open; the masses chattered their affairs.

Other news from outside was filtering through as well. The unrest spreading across the land was endlessly fascinating, intriguing, and exciting. On occasion, Gottfried and John rode their horses an hour north from their village of Klostitz to the nearby Russian town of Frumuschika. Ordering a plate of smoked, dried eel and a glass of vodka, they were soon encircled by the stories going around. Riding home, their heads were reeling with spicy details.

"Did you hear that?" asked Gottfried. "The tsarina sounds like she's really good-looking."

"Yeah, but it sounds like she's a witch. Can't get along with anybody."

"Well, but they say she's kinda bashful, and those high-hat types around the palace can be some nasty, you know?"

"Can that really be her name, Alice Victoria Eleanor Louisa Beatrice? So why do they call her Alexandra Feodorovna?"

"I sure don't know."

"And she was Lutheran too, came from Germany, they said, but now she switched over to Orthodox? Too bad."

"I suppose Nicki made her do it."

"And her father-in-law, old Tsar Alexander."

"You can bet on that. Otherwise, Nicki couldn't marry her. Maybe that's where the 'Alexandra' part comes from too, to keep the papa happy."

Riding on, their thoughts turned back to more exciting things: the three alluring Russian girls they met on the way into the village. They had tipped their caps and said, *"Dobryj dyen,"* good afternoon. The girls tossed their long black hair, giggled, and waved a small wave, interested but trying not to be too obvious in case they were being watched by a nosy grandmother behind her crocheted curtains. John's eyes especially noticed the girl on the right—his mind named her his *Maria,* after the sainted mother of Jesus. Riding by in the narrow dirt streets, they were only two cow-lengths away from touching the girls, close enough that John was struck by *Maria's* twinkling dark brown eyes and silky black hair reaching down to the middle of her back. Vivacious smile danced across her face, slammed into his heart. Her long, gathered blue skirt effectively did not hide well-rounded hips that swayed, oh, so wondrously as she walked. A white ruffled blouse was filled out amply enough to set John's mind reeling. Juices shot through his brain, and other parts, and in high fantasy, saintly *Maria* suddenly became the other Maria, the Magdalene. His loins tingled against the saddle leather. Breaths came short. His heart pounded in his ears.

"*Lieber Gott,*" he whispered to himself. "*Lieber Gott,* dear God, what a beauty."

A few of the blonde Aryan girls of his village were attractive in their own right, but *Maria* set his mind on a different track completely, enough to bring color to his cheeks and rattle his whole body with thundering emotions.

Trying not to show his Vesuvian excitement, John asked secretively, "What do you suppose would happen if we brought two of them home?"

"That'd be the last time we went to town," replied Gottfried.

From as far back as they could remember, they, and all German boys in the villages, were commanded, "Don't you *ever* bring home a Russian girlfriend!" Girls were told the same thing. Only more often and louder! There would be the devil to pay and exile around the corner for any who so much as bent that rule. Any of the young who married a Russian crossed the line and brought on the wrath of the Almighty and the father!

One of the Meidinger girls rebelled and brought home a Tschaikovsky. The distraught family tried to persuade her to drop him, but they ran off and married. Father Meidinger announced to his family and to the entire village in church the next Sunday, "We no longer have a daughter Kristina. Her name will never be brought up again. To us she is dead." The mother's heart ached, and long she grieved for her precious child, but Kristina was never mentioned again.

Several months after their trip to Frumuschika, curiosity along with increasing doses of testosterone got the better of Gottfried and

John, and they asked Father for permission to ride there again. When he agreed, they were soon on the road, up and over the high ridge, riding fast. As they approached the outskirts of town, they slowed the horses to an easy walk. Though they hadn't talked about the girls, their minds had pictured many a delicious scene with them.

"Do you suppose we'll see the girls again?" John wondered out loud.

"Hope so. They're sure nice."

This time the three special girls were not all out. *Maria*, however, was walking with her mother! They rode by as slowly as they dared, trying to get off a subtle wave to her, but the mother's eyes were glued to them every step, and the girl had to pretend she didn't see, nor care. The boys respectfully doffed their caps—to the mother, of course— hoping the girl would notice their special interest. Drums boomed in John's brain, his heart pounded, his legs grew limp with ecstasy. His mouth grew dry. In a flash, he pictured kicking his horse and at full gallop leaning far down like a fiery Cossack of old, sweeping her up in his arms, swinging her up behind his saddle, and riding off hell-bent through the tall prairies to Tsar Peter's magnificent secret hideaway and there consorting with his voluptuous *Tsarina Maria* until life was ended and all breath hushed. He couldn't live without her.

In the moment this lightning exploded in his head, two mangy dogs came running up, barking at their horses. What awful pain it was to come crashing from that height. But his vision could not come to pass. *No,* his mind whimpered, *no more of this. Keep moving. Look calm. Ride on.*

Hearts thumping, the boys rode on to the tavern, ordered up their plate of smoked eel and glass of vodka, nodded at the locals already in their bottles, and listened to the conversations. In the run-down tavern, clouds of smoke rose from every table, fighting to kill the dim light poured out by the flickering kerosene lamps hung on the walls. Some moments the burning wicks won, but more often great sheets of smoke won the battle in the reeking, stale saloon.

John nudged Gottfried as nearby conversations inevitably turned to the czar. The tables seemed to be a veritable encyclopedia of czarisms.

"Where do they get all this goofy stuff?" Gottfried asked as one Russian voice sounded off: "You know all the Romanovs have been big, strong men. Tsar Peter stood two meters three *(about six feet, nine inches)*. And all the tsars since then have been big."

"For sure," yelled another voice.

"And here's our little rooster, Nicki, barely half as big."

"What a castrated skunk," shouted another, over stomping boots and pounding glasses, as raucous laughter swept the room.

A few timid voices defended the czar and lifted up his strengths, but before long, more ribald descriptions grew louder, words more slurred, the atmosphere profane and bawdy. Gottfried kicked his brother's foot, under the table, and nodded toward the door. Time to go before trouble found them, and the locals counted them in as enemies along with Nicki and his gang.

On the ride home, they reflected on the image of Czar Nicki that was developing for them. They wanted to like the great czar, but the stories in the tavern painted a sordid picture of contradictions. Living in their little country *dorf,* they couldn't begin to imagine the czar's thousand-room palace in "Peterburg" or his three-hundred-room summer palace with its gold fountains by the sea, all so vilified by the czar's own subjects in the smoke-filled tavern.

Through all the wild shouting, they came to see a handsome, dapper man, smart and educated yet one who could not make decisions, a loving family man yet one who played hide-and-seek in the palace gardens with his courtiers and foreign diplomats, and a deeply religious man yet who prayed to a room full of icons. It all left them confused and troubled.

"I can't see where those pictures of saints can ever do you any good," Gottfried suddenly blurted out from his saddle, "no matter how much gold and rubies they got around their faces."

"That's for sure."

In the dark, with a million brilliant stars shining overhead to accompany the quiet creaking of saddle leather and the steady cadence of the horses, it was easy to get reflective, to let the mind drift to bigger things. "But maybe that's why he can keep his head and stay calm when all the rest seem to losing theirs over dumb stuff," said Gottfried.

"Well, if I had four different palaces to run to, and my own train to get there, I'd probably be pretty relaxed too," chuckled John.

"Poor guy. They sure don't like him around here."

"Wonder what'll happen yet?"

"I sure wouldn't want to be in his shoes, that's all I know."

"I just hope they don't end up shooting him like they did his grandfather."

Long after they got home, undressed, and into bed, their minds were still replaying the trip, the gossip, the pictures of strange Nicki and his pretty Alexandra Feodorovna. Even the three dolls couldn't match all that for excitement.

****

While they were gone, Karolina had put the youngest, Anna Maria, to bed. But she wasn't quiet for long.

"Mamma," cried little Anna Maria, "I can't get to sleep."

When Karolina came back, the little one begged, "Tell me a story, Mamma."

Karolina was tired from a day already too long and snapped, "Go to sleep!"

"But, Mamma, I can't, I can't. Please, Mamma, please."

"Oh, all right. I'll tell you a story our teacher told us about the tsar."

"Is he a nice man, Mamma?"

"Well, this is about a tsar a long time ago. His name was Tsar Igor. And he was very rich. He had many palaces, and in his main palace, he had a big room where he kept all his gold, piles and piles of gold. Nearly every day he would go into his special room, lock the door, and count his gold. He loved nothing better than to feel it run through his fingers and hear the clink of the coins falling back into the chests of gold. Now one day, as he was bent over a pile of gold, he glanced up and suddenly there beside him stood a tall man dressed in a long shimmering white robe."

"Who was he, Mamma, who was he?"

"I don't know, child, and neither did Tsar Igor. But the man said to him, 'Tsar Igor, you have more gold than you can ever use. Why don't you give some of it to people who are hungry and cold?'

"'Oh, someday I will,' said Tsar Igor, 'but first I need to get more so I never run out. I wish, I just wish I could get more.'

"The man replied, 'Do you wish that more than anything else in the whole world?'

"'I do,' said Tsar Igor. 'I do, I do!'

"'Then go to sleep,' said the man in white, 'and see what happens.'

"Tsar Igor went to sleep, and all night he dreamed of gold, piles and piles of bright, shining gold. In the morning, he woke up and looked around. But nothing had happened. There were no piles of gold anywhere.

"Then Tsar Igor threw back his bedcovers, and immediately, they turned to gold. He jumped out of bed and reached for the glass of fresh juice his servants had put on the table beside his bed. But immediately the glass and the juice turned to gold. He picked up the fresh flower in the vase beside the juice. It turned to gold. He grew hungry and picked up the bread and cheese in the plate. More instant gold. He reached for his shoes and at his touch they turned to gold. He walked outside and leaned against a tree. Its trunk, every branch, every leaf became instant gold. He shouted and screamed. Never had he been so happy. Everything was gold. He had more gold than he knew what to do with. Now he would never run out.

"Just then, his precious daughter, the Tsaritsa Katrigold, came running to him as fast as she could go, shouting, 'Papa, look at the beautiful tree glistening like gold in the sun!' She threw herself into Tsar Igor's arms."

"What happened, Mamma? What happened to Tsaritsa Katrigold?" Anna piped up.

"Well, child, like the man in white had promised, things would happen. And the minute the tsaritsa touched Tsar Igor, she turned into a gold statue.

"When the tsar saw what his greed had done, destroying his own precious child, he fell to the ground and cried, great sobbing, heartbreaking cries. Suddenly, he felt someone beside him, and looking up through his tears, he saw the same man in white. 'Oh, what have I done,' said Tsar Igor, 'what have I done!'

"The man answered him, 'But now you have all the gold in the world. You are the richest man alive, and if you want more, just touch anything and you'll have still more.'

"'But it doesn't mean anything at all if my daughter is dead. My life is over. I am the poorest man alive.'

"'So which do you want more,' asked the man, 'your daughter or the gold?'

"'Oh, if only I could have my daughter back, I'd give up all the gold I own.'

"Just then, the gold statue cracked and out stepped his beautiful daughter, her long hair curling around her shoulders in the pleasant breeze.

"'Now I know what's important,' said Tsar Igor, 'now I know.'"

"So do you see, child," Mother went on, "your family is more important than all the gold in the world."

"Yes, Mamma, thank you. And I'm glad you're my mamma."

"Now you can go to sleep," said Mother. "Goodnight, child. Sleep tight."

All that night, Anna Maria saw laughing children running through beautiful green trees, on softest grass, dodging slender golden statues that looked like little girls. When she woke, a smile formed on her lips as she thought, *The tsar must sure be happy to have his little girl back.*

****

Soon it was time for harvest. Christian went out to the shed and took down the long, bent-handled scythe and sharpened its three-foot iron blade until it could cut fingernails. Then he unhooked the long wooden grain cradle. It also had a scythe blade, but in addition, it had four wooden tines that matched the curve of the iron blade. With it, the harvester could cut the grain and in the same motion drop it into little piles, which the younger ones would gather, heads pointing up, and tie into bundles. Christian set both the cutters outside the door of the house and looked out over the fields stretching from the edge of the village all the way up the gently climbing ridge toward the rising sun.

The heads of wheat in the fields had turned gold and now stood tall, beckoning the farmers. Yesterday, Christ walked out, plucked several stalks, rubbed the grains out of their stiff jackets, blew the chaff out of his hands, and decided, "Ja, they're ready. Tomorrow we harvest."

In the morning, before the sun could wrestle its way up the east horizon, Christ shouted to all in the house, "Let's get moving. The sun won't wait for us."

Karolina, already up, lit a fire in the kitchen stove, put in more thin logs, and got the coffee and sausages going. Eggs would follow in a minute. *You can't swing a scythe and bend a thousand times, pick up clumps of wheat and tie them in bundles, all on an empty stomach.*

After breakfast, Christ and the boys walked the several *versts,* kilometers, from the village out to the fields. The neighbor men and their boys were all on the dusty paths to their own plots as well. The women and girls would finish the dishes and follow them, bringing lunch and helping them tie the cut grain into bundles.

After their five-hectare fields were harvested and stacked, the boys were "farmed out" to neighbors who needed an extra hand. The girls, too, were loaned out to help in neighbors' kitchens. For all, in field or kitchen, work started at sunrise and ended long after dusk.

When the grain was all cut and stacked, it was time to gather at the village "threshing floor," a flat area of smooth, hard-packed soil, thirty feet across, at the edge of the *dorf.* One by one, the farmers loaded their bundles on racks and hauled them to the threshing floor. They pitched the bundles into a loose pile and drove horses around and around on the pile, crushing the heads to pop the wheat kernels out of their husks. Fifteen minutes of this "grinding," the horses were pulled off, and Christ and the men gathered around the pile with long-tined wooden hayforks.

"*Druf,* get on it," shouted Uncle Phillip, and the young men leaped on the pile and pitched the straw high. Around the edges, the older men pitched the straw, all working to further disgorge the wheat kernels from the husks and straw. As the golden kernels fell to the bottom of the pile, they pitched the straw aside and hauled it off to a separate pile, later to be fed to the livestock and used as bedding for both cows and sows. Now only a pile of kernels was left, mixed in with a lot of fine-ground chaff. Again, they threw the pile into the air, this time with shovels, to let the chaff blow away in the wind and the kernels drop back into a much smaller pile. Finally, they shoveled the wheat into sacks and loaded them on wagons to be hauled home to the barn.

Then another farmer hauled his bundles to the threshing floor, unloaded, and the whole process started over for his grain. And another. Women and girls carried jugs of water, bread, meat, and cheeses to fuel the process.

Twelve days, fourteen, first light to dark, with Sunday off to worship, and harvest was finished, the grain all stored for winter's grinding and ready for spring seeding.

A few weeks later, when three of the men hauled loads of wheat to sell in Frumuschika, they came home with disturbing rumors.

"There was talk about a new weed spreading up north of here."

"They say it grows fast after the wheat is cut."

"Ja, grows round, bigger'n a pumpkin, and later in the fall breaks off its stem and the wind tumbles it across the ground like a great big ball."

"Each ball has a thousand seeds and drops them all in a row when it rolls."

"Sure hope," Christ chimed in, "the darn thing doesn't get here."

But tumbleweeds were not the biggest worry for Christ's brother Jacob and his wife, Natalia.

Chapter 12

Tragedy for Aunt Natalia

Aunt Natalia birthed three fair-skinned daughters with hair the color of little lambs and raised them into beautiful growing children. But then she had two miscarriages: one early in a pregnancy and another just before the baby was due. She was devastated for months. Then, after another anxious pregnancy, she delivered a son. David, they named him. "That means, 'Beloved,'" said Jacob to his family, "and so he is."

A busy, vivacious lad, he soon became the toddling pride of Father Jacob's life. Then, one day, the little one took sick with a fever, nothing especially serious at first. The second night he started coughing, crying in pain. As the fever grew worse, Natalia got out some old, well-washed diapers and wetted them down to make cold packs. Jacob sat on the bed and held his hurting child. During the long dark hours, little David became more fevered, weaker, and grew more pale in the glow of the smoky oil lamp flickering on the wall.

At first light, Jacob hurried to get Tanta Schmidt, the village healer. In minutes, she was there. With one series of whirling motions, she tossed back the blankets, pulled little David up, raised his nightshirt to his chin, laid him back down, and began rubbing down his whole body with a mixture of goose fat and special healing herbs that smelled of mint. Bent over the bed, with gentle master-healing-grandmother's hands she continued rubbing him down, soothed his anxious little heart, turned him over, and rubbed some more. Ten minutes she massaged him, fifteen, then set a kettle boiling to make steam, and said a prayer for the Lord to hear and heal, "*Lieber Gott, Himmlischer Herr Jesu,* Dear God, Heavenly Lord Jesus, hear our prayer for this dear little lamb and heal him with your mighty hands, that he may bless you with a long life of serving you. Amen."

For an hour he was better, calm in blessed sleep. Then suddenly, his tiny body jerked and twitched, and he let out a hoarse, piercing, guttural scream. "*Gichter,* convulsions," said Tanta Schmidt, anxiously shaking her head. She didn't like the looks of it. Mother Natalia picked him up and held him tight against her breast to stop the awful trembling. His hands shook; arms, shoulders, and legs twitched beyond control for several terrifying minutes.

By now several other women had gathered in the little house, along with younger cousins who were not out on the threshing ground. Jacob didn't want to insult Grandma Schmidt, but she had done all she could. Now, suddenly louder than he wanted to be, he ordered one of the young ones, "Get Doctor Schultz! Run!" He lived some houses down on the dirt streets of the village, and in minutes, he was there. Walking in with his meager medical bag, he asked Natalia to lay the little one on the bed. He bent over, felt the infant's head, opened his mouth to look down his throat, pushed on his abdomen and his side, and straightened back up. A deep breath, a long pause looking steadily at the little patient, and he thought to himself, *How do I tell this beloved family . . .* A long moment more, he drew another deep breath of resignation and blew it out across his graying goatee. Without realizing it, he let his proud-doctor shoulders fall and slowly shook his head.

"Convulsions. There isn't anything I can do. God watch over him, and you."

Nothing more needed to be said. The family, Grandma Schmidt, and all there knew. With no other word spoken, Dr. Schultz, eyes brimful, shook Jacob's hand and silently left the house.

Tears streamed down Natalia's cheeks.

How can God do this again? she wailed silently. *What have I done so wrong that he is punishing me so bitterly? How many times can I take such terrible suffering?* A long pause.

Why put my little baby through this?

Tumbling over one another, anguished thoughts streamed across her mind like the tears across her cheeks and threatened to overwhelm her. She yearned to put her baby to her breast and let her milk pour rich new life back into him. But even that could not be.

Jacob saw her tortured face and blurted, "Go get Reverend Mueller." More women had gathered, taking turns standing beside Natalia's chair and patting her shoulders. Now one of them hurried out to the reverend's parsonage.

Their beloved young pastor, Rev. Michael Mueller, had just arrived from seminary studies in Germany, brimming with *Seelsorgen,* care of souls. He was eager to be a meaningful shepherd of his new flock, and in just minutes, he, too, was there. As he entered, all stepped back away from the pale little body, now seemingly shrinking by the moment. Reverend Mueller stopped to shake Jacob's hand, quietly proclaimed *"Guten Morgen,* good morning" to those gathered and then softly stepped to the bed. Natalia moved to sit on the bed, her hand brushing her baby's hair and cheeks. Little David's eyes were filmy and staring, his breathing shallow and rapid, brows raised in silent fear from everyone watching him. Tiny lips trembling, he started to whimper. Leaning over, Reverend Mueller gently laid one hand on Natalia's shoulder, the other softly stroking the frightened infant's head. *"Liebe Mutter, lasst uns Beten,* dear mother, let us pray." From memory, he spoke Jesus' word, "Let the little children come to me and do not forbid them, for of such is the kingdom of God." He prayed for God's healing on the little lamb and strength for the flock, recited the twenty-third Psalm, and started into *"Vater unser,* Our Father who art in heaven." All joined in prayer, many fighting tears, throats choked to a whisper.

"Now," he announced, "we must leave it in God's hands."

Somehow Jacob's frazzled soul could not settle for that. "Get my brother, Frederick, from threshing. Tell him to ride to Frumuschika and bring the Russian doctor. Be quick."

Reverend Mueller frowned, but kept quiet.

After some moments of silence, the young pastor walked over, laid one hand on the baby's head, and gently taking Natalia's hand in the other, looked long into her eyes, and softly said, "The Lord be with you and watch over this little soul." He turned and took Jacob's hand, "The Lord give you strength." Then as he raised his arms, every head bent to receive the powerful benediction that had been spoken over God's people for more than three thousand years:

"'The Lord bless you and keep you.
The Lord make his face to shine upon you
   And be gracious to you.
The Lord lift his countenance upon you
   And give you his peace. Amen.'
Now I go back to church to continue praying."

With that he bowed, bade *"Guten Tag, Liebe Seelen,* Good day, my dear souls," and took his leave.

Word had spread from man to man around the threshing floor about Jacob's little son, *"Gichter,* convulsions." Now when the runner came, Frederick dropped his pitchfork, ran home, saddled his neighbor's fastest mare, kicked her flanks, and flew the dusty rutted road up across the high ridge and down to the nearest large Russian town. While the German villagers had a deep visceral mistrust of Russian doctors and wanted no part of them anywhere near, Jacob was desperate. In this terrifying moment, he would sell his very soul to the devil if only it would save his precious child.

Little David by turns slept and wailed weak cries and suffered more convulsions. Natalia picked him up, rocked him, and held him tight.

At the threshing floor, work came to an abrupt halt when Frederick was called to ride, and a number of the men slowly drifted to Jacob's house. They stood around, leaning against walls, sitting on the fence, unsure. Some pulled out pipes and lit up, some rolled cigarettes from the little tobacco pouches they carried. They talked about most everything except the sick little lad in the house. Women with dish towel-covered bowls glided silently into the house, whispered their concern, set the food on cupboards and table, took some outside for the men, and held each other's arms.

Tanta Louisa brought a cup of milk and a spoon, and Natalia touched it to the little one's cracked and fevered lips. After two spoonfuls he turned his head away. No more.

The heat in the humble house became oppressive, heavy. The silence even more. Finally, Tanta Louisa quietly started singing a hymn. Others soon joined until all were singing the hymns they sang together every Sunday, every holiday the year around.

The Russian doctor preferred not to treat these outlanders, and rarely did, nor would he learn their language. Now as he neared the village in mid-afternoon, his shoulders shuddered as he pictured the scene that would likely unfold in just a few moments, *They'll be packed all around me, chattering in their mongrel tongue and expecting miracles. I hate this stuff.*

As he drove up in his carriage, following Frederick on horseback, the older boys ran to take his horse.

In top hat and long coat, with rather pompous formality the doctor stepped down, carried his bag into the house, nodded politely, and without a word walked over to the failing child. When Natalia turned her son to face the doctor, the baby, now weak and limp, again went into convulsions. The doctor looked into his mouth, felt his neck and abdomen, opened his eyelids, and listened to his flailing chest. With many words and more gestures he tried to explain something, but with their limited Russian, they couldn't quite connect. Then slowly he held out both hands, shrugged his shoulders, shook his head, and said, *"Nyet pomashch, nyet pomashch!"*

That they understood: "No help!"

Jacob, beaten down, with his last hope destroyed, stepped up to him and asked, *"Skolka,* how much?"

"Adin roobl, mozhna," he solemnly answered, "one ruble, may I?"

Jacob turned and lowering his head, glanced sideways at the women, set his lips and slowly walked to the cupboard, got out the silver Russian coin, and handed it to him.

"Spasiba. Dobryjdyen, Thank You, Good afternoon," and with what they took to mean *"I hope the child recovers and gets well,"* the doctor climbed into his carriage, the boys let go of the horse, and he drove away. The clopping of the high-spirited horse's hoofs soon faded in the distance. The dust from his wheels spun into the sky and slowly filtered back down into the nearby grass, as hope fell with it.

One of the Tantas muttered the old proverb they had learned from the Russians, *"Only a fool makes the doctor his heir."* The Russian doctor was gracious to come this far and indeed had tried his best, but it was all for nothing.

As the sun stretched to reach the western hills, the baby gasped and suddenly stopped breathing. His eyes rolled upward, one more gasp, his tiny arms shot up and then relaxed. It was over. Natalia shook him, patted his back to make him breathe, and screamed a wailing cry, "No, dear God, no, no, *no-o-o!"*

Three little sisters each held on to Mother and joined her bitter crying. The women rushed to hold them and tried to comfort hearts so cruelly broken.

Jacob sighed, eyes full, and walked outside. *Dear God, how can this be?* But it was over.

One by one, the mournful neighbors slowly drifted away. Jacob and Natalia sat at the table, stunned, unable to feel, to think, to talk. Finally, exhausted, they laid on the bed, minds whirling through long tortured hours until the early roosters cheerfully called forth another day.

By early morning light, across the village, cows were quickly milked, pigs and chickens fed, and after fast breakfast, black suits and dresses taken off the hooks. Uncle Phillip and Tanta Louisa, the new boy-angel's godparents, took charge of getting the best white cloth, along with pine boards, to build a mini casket. Tiny David, now at such seemingly peaceful sleep, was bathed, white hair combed, dressed in white high-button nightshirt, infant hands folded in prayer, and reverently laid in the dreaded box.

Godfather Phillip hoisted the weightless casket on his shoulder and led the way to St. Johannes Church. Jacob and Natalia followed, leading the stunned little sisters by the hand. Natalia could see no path beneath her feet, no little blonde heads at her side, no somber family and neighbors behind her. This grief was heavier than her back could bear, an anguish that shut down her mind and almost her heart. Her shining baby should be walking here and she should be in the silent box! The torture grabbed her soul with such a choking that no sobbing could break its grip.

In hushed stillness, the solemn procession, with many joining from every direction, continued toward the church. Brave sun could not beat down this autumn day's cold wind, but few noticed. Their suffering hearts were joined to the suffering parents. When they reached the church, Reverend Mueller, in black gown, led them slowly down the center aisle. With the organ playing, Uncle Phillip solemnly set the casket on a small round table in front of the circular altar rail, opened it, and laid the cover aside, and all were seated.

Over the quiet sobs and tears, Reverend Mueller intoned, *"Im Names des Vaters,* In the Name of the Father, and of the Son, and of the Holy Ghost."

In their tongue he was the *"Pfarrar,"* the pastor, now their comforter. His heart, too, was hurting with the grieving parents, but he must not show it. In seminary, he had been taught, *"Hold up the Word. Let your voice be strong in the certain hope of eternal life!"* He led them in prayers, turned with them to the comfort of God's word and then with strong voice backed by strong pedal-organ led them in singing hymns they all knew by heart from many singings before.

Totally untrained musicians though they were, these humble folk stood heir to Johann Sebastian Bach and Martin Luther, and now they broke into stirring four-part harmony and poured their hearts into surrounding Jacob and Natalia with majestic chorales of life. Hearts so full make music just as full. Voices blended and lifted the great words to the rafters, reverberated back down, and swelled to turn the presence of death into at least a glint of living hope.

Words came hard for these people, but in song, they joined the angels. While most sang the familiar melodies, two high sopranos soared, several expansive altos joined, a few tenor voices added body, basses rumbled as they heard their Russian brethren do in the raucous, smoke filled saloons where the only female present was the *saftig,* ample, barmaid. But here they lifted voices to the glory of God who even in death was still Lord of all life.

In no one's mind was this moment even close to celebration, but in their abiding faith, they stared death down and with moist eyes joined St. Paul in daring to proclaim, "O, death, where is thy sting? O, grave, where is thy victory?"

And they sang some more. "*Jesu, geh voran, Auf der Lebensbahn,*
Jesus, still lead on, till our rest be won; and, although the way be cheerless,
We will follow, calm and fearless; guide us by your hand, to our father's land."

Generations of their young had been trained in the Lutheran faith of their fathers, and all of them had learned this song by heart as part of their confirmation passage into adulthood.

The melody of more song swept that sacred space and steeped into the pain-filled pores of brokenness to offer the eternal hope of life beyond that tragic little box in front of them.

Reverend Mueller mounted the rear stairs of the decoratively carved ten-foot high pulpit and under its octagonal, acoustic canopy spent the next hour in a forceful sermon, trying to bring comfort and hope, talking about the power of a mighty resurrection which God had brought about after another particularly tragic death. Amidst the searing pain, the Pfaffar pointed down from the towering pulpit to the open casket before them and spoke with tenderest appeal, "I tell you, death does not have the final word."

Then pointing up, with gentle tone he added, "Jesus does. *Sein Kreutz,* his cross, fixed that. And on Easter, the father finished it!"

After the last "Amen" they lifted another hymn and processed out to the windswept, barren cemetery a short distance uphill from the church. The stubby grave, two *wuerst* by three, had been dug beforehand, and now Godfather Phillip stepped into the shallow hole and placed the casket. All the men joined in quietly shoveling ground back into earth's breach. The hollow sound of soil striking box decreased to a whisper as the hole filled. The Lord's Prayer, the ancient Benediction, and it was done.

Usually relatives would then gather in the deceased one's home for lunch and sharing hearts, but today was too painful for Jake and Natalia, and everyone shuffled home.

To these people, death was no stranger. They laid many a child into Russian soil and many a mother too young. But all that did not make this death any easier.

For Jacob, it was the hardest blow he had ever taken.

For Natalia, the world caved in. There was nothing left inside her mind, her heart rubbed raw, and the blood too cold to flow. Numbness strangled her soul. Nothing looked good; nothing tasted good; nothing felt good. People touching her in love made her want to vomit. Arching over the ugly black emptiness in her soul was an animal rage that made her feel like tearing at her precious daughters, tearing at her Jacob, and tearing chunks out of her own flesh.

She grew afraid of going to sleep. Then afraid of waking up. Talking hurt; listening hurt even more. The children playing enraged her. Bird song made her cry. Almost everything now made her cry. She felt paralyzed and took to her bed. No bath. No cleaning of self or house. When comforters came to sit by her bed, she turned to the wall, her heart a jagged stone.

Jacob was lost. The three little daughters felt abandoned by a mother who now frightened them. No one in the family knew what to do.

When Jacob called Reverend Mueller to come and comfort her, she locked her eyes shut in bed and froze him out.

What good, her mind screamed, *were all his pious prayers? Where is his hateful God?*

When neighbors brought foods that were her favorites, with rich smells that before had made her smile, she nibbled a bite, two, rare times three, and pushed the rest away until their puzzled hearts could bring no more.

One who brought food tried to bring comfort, telling her, "Don't worry, you're young yet. You can have more children."

Another added, "Don't be discouraged. Remember, you still have three other children." Words meant to comfort only deepened the rage.

During these days, even having Jacob around seemed to lead her more to anger than to comfort. She brooked no touch from him. Having him anywhere near her made her sick.

As autumn days grew short and winter snows shrank that cruel world yet more, their little house turned into a silent cave—no, a prison made for five. Neighbors began to wonder if the frozen cemetery had room beside baby David's grave for another. Surely it would not be long.

"Yes, you *can* die from a broken heart," they said. "Keep the black dress clean and ready."

Jacob gathered the kitchen knives and put them in the barn, in case she got ideas. Days and nights ran together like a muddy slough full of every terrible creeping thing on earth. Would it never end? What was the use of going on? *How long, O Lord, how long?* he silently cried.

Occasionally, one of Natalia's sisters came by to straighten the rumpled house, cleaning the dust and clutter that Jacob didn't see and the little ones had learned to live with. She washed the few scummy dishes setting around, scrubbed the dirty dish towels and bedclothes that had taken on the smell of rotting fruit, and swept the fouled-up floor. In between, she cooked up a company-sized kettle of soup to keep the family going for a few more days.

Before leaving, she sat for a long while by Natalia's bed, by turns silent or singing a hymn or the fun songs of youth on which they had both too soon grown into womanhood. Natalia said nothing, looked briefly into her caring sister's eyes, and turned away. Then it was time for Sister to return to her own family, hurting, heavy of heart. *I don't even know if I have a sister anymore,* she silently cried, *or for how long.*

Evening time, when Jacob was finished with all the work of being both father and mother, he put the three little ones to bed. Most nights he knelt by their bed and in his pleasant bass, softly sang to them the prayer his mother had sung with him:

"Muede bin ich, geh zu ruh,	-	I'm tired, Lord, time to rest,
Schlieze meine Augen zu	-	Close my eyes in sleep.
Vater lass die Augen Dein	-	Let your eyes watch over me
Ueber meinem bette sein.	-	And may my bed be blessed.
Amen."		Amen.

Jacob prayed, talked to his brother, several neighbor women, and Reverend Mueller. They all tried to lift her wounded soul, and all had failed as well. Only they didn't have to live with it day after day, month after month as he did.

Where are you, God? he silently begged in bitter despair. *Why won't you answer? If you are there, why won't you help us?*

In the dark night hours when sleep escaped, he began to turn over thoughts that maybe leaving would be best. Take the girls and go. What happened after that would happen. It was hopeless. He could do no more. Maybe when the weather got nicer . . .

And then, something strange. Early one morning when the fragile snowdrop flowers just began poking their heads through the last piles of snow, little Maria crawled into Mamma's bed and curled up quiet beside her. No response. Long she lay until her aching hands would stay still no more and she had to reach up and rub Mamma's face, trace her cheeks, and softly stroke her fluttering eyes. Ever so slowly, Natalia forced open those locked eyes. *Who was this little person beside her that suddenly felt so warm?* "Is it you, Maria, or are you an angel?"

The little girl tingled to her toes, beamed an angel's smile, and said simply, "Mamma, Mamma, it's me, Mamma." Mother caressed her face, then wrapped her up in her arms and almost crushed her in a wordless embrace. It was to her as if some sort of thick, invisible, hazy cloud had suddenly evaporated from inside her and a great breath had mystically blown it away.

In an instant, Mamma smelled Maria's hair and her whole familiar little girl smell and burst into a torrent of tears. "Oh, Maria, my precious baby, Maria, Maria, my child, how good it feels to hold you!"

Words like "I love you" did not much cross the lips of these families, nor did they now. But tears and tight hugs shared the temperature of the heart quite as well. Long they held and kissed and rested in each other's warmth made even warmer by Mother's newly bright, magnetic eyes and focused words.

Then Natalia's eyes swept the darkened house, and she whispered, "Where are the rest? Where's Papa?" Before Maria could get any words out, Mother half-sat her up and announced, "Let's get up. I'm so hungry, aren't you?"

Long-suffering Jacob and the other two little sisters came tearing in from the next room, in shock at hearing conversation. *Could it be? Mother actually talking, stirring, making to get up? Had she lost her mind completely and was getting up to run away?* Their hearts thundered, full of questions. Shock continued as they saw the two locked in tight embrace, laughing, crying, full of Christmas joy. Then all five were on the bed in delirious pandemonium. Such commotion happens only in eagle's nests. But here it was: talking, shouting, laughing, torrents of relieved tears, touching, fingers intertwining, and caressing faces and arms and shoulders. It was like five noisy baby wolves released from the den after a long summer storm.

They hugged and bounced for what seemed like hours until Mother tenderly parted the pack and swung her feet over the edge of the bed to get up. When she feebly wobbled, the girls, like the little pack of wolf cubs, were at her side steadying, leading her to the kitchen table. She asked for sausage, bread, cheese, and a glass of fresh milk. When the girls put a loaf on the table, Mother reached to the cupboard for a knife. There wasn't one.

"What happened to all my knives?"

Jacob, caught off-guard by this sudden turn, felt he could only lie, "I took them out to the shed to sharpen," and rushed out to return the knives, hopefully to a newly safe kitchen.

Mother ate like one homeless for long months. The children, Jacob, all ate with appetite they hadn't known for an eternity. They had forgotten what food tastes like when it was covered with a layer of life. The fruit of Eden could not touch this taste. Then suddenly, a circus broke out with laughter and all talking at once, the girls bouncing up and down around the table, all wanting to sit on Mamma's lap at the same time. Jacob sat in stunned amazement, never taking his eyes off his beloved. His mind whirled, *Can this be? Is it real? Am I dreaming?*

They threw open the door, and in minutes, all the neighbors knew and came running to celebrate. Somewhere, a heavenly nightingale had flown in and the endless nightmare was over, the anguish at an end. Healing would come in the noonday.

Chapter 13

Stick the Pig

For the rest of the village, life returned to full the day after the funeral. Threshing continued until all the bundles of wheat were hauled in and pounded out. Oats to feed the livestock, barley, and flax all brought in. Hay, stacked in the fields, was hauled into the stone-fenced yards and restacked beside the barns. Sacks of wheat hauled to the millers to be ground into winter's flour. Cracks in the buildings sealed up against winter's coming cold.

Gardens were picked and vines cleared. Potatoes and carrots were dug and carried into the earthen cellars under the trapdoors of kitchen floors. Cantaloupe and sweet *arbooza,* watermelons, savored, and some pickled. Beans, beets, and cucumbers all pickled; apples and berries, chicken, beef, and rabbits canned, all in jars. Solid heads of cabbage were picked, sliced, shredded on sharp, tin shredding boards, and packed into ten-gallon wooden barrels. After salt and vinegar were added, it was stomped down hard by barefoot little Anna Maria—after Mother inspected her feet to make sure she had washed them well enough. Sister Barbara chuckled as she called out an old proverb, *"Rather a louse in the kraut than no meat at all,"* adding, "Isn't that funny?" They placed the wooden lid down tightly, with a heavy rock on top, and set the barrel aside to let nature's own fermentation turn it into mouth-watering sauerkraut. Summer was good, and all its hard work would make the winter good as well.

Then it was time for another type of celebration: fall butchering. Neighbors grouped together in each other's yards, and a special huge butcher-kettle of water was set to boiling over the wood fire outside, heavy knives sharpened, meat-saw ready, and the horse harnessed.

In Christ's yard, Uncle Heinrich, the neighborhood "designated sticker," arrived, with his slender sticking knife, which resembled a long, vicious two-edged bayonet, ready to go. In festive gait, the men, with single-shot rifle in hand, walked to the pigpen, where the pigs raised eager heads, snouts a'twitch for morning food.

One unsuspecting pig was singled out and shot.

"Quick, stick it," Christ shouted.

As it rolled to its side, Uncle Heinrich drove the long knife into the bottom of its throat, sticking it so the blood would drain out to make the butchering easier. As blood gushed out and spurted up Heinrich's arm, John bent over and slid a pan under the cut to catch a quantity of the red liquid for making blood sausage later in the day.

The smell of blood drove the remaining pigs into a frenzy, wildly running over each other with deafening squeals that suddenly had a different tone, a high-pitched, shrieking voice that was urgent, disturbed, and filled with fear.

"I wonder what's going through their brains right now," John shouted over the squealing.

"Me too," Uncle Heinrich shouted back.

"You think they understand anything about what just happened?"

"Sure wonder."

Then they led the horse into the pen to drag the carcass out into the yard.

They set three poles in tepee shape and, with ropes and pulley, hoisted the critter up over the heated kettle. Slowly, they lowered it into the boiling water to scald the hard bristle hair and make it easier to scrape off. After a few minutes of softening, they raised the carcass and used wide-bladed knives on edge, like the straight-edge razors on their own beards, to scrape all the bristles down to smooth skin. One more dip and the carcass was lowered to a stoneboat and slid to the barn. Here, they hoisted it to the rafters, its back legs spread wide for cutting, bobble head down, another careful washing of hands with soap and critter with scalding water to rid any impurities. Then narrow-bladed knives would go to work cutting open the belly and emptying all the organs from the steaming body.

Dogs hung close by, wild from smell, while little boys ran around wide-eyed with magnetic fascination.

Practiced hands soon had the hog-insides cut loose and dropped to the hard-packed ground, which they earlier layered with fresh sawdust.

Gottfried cut the organs out of the jumbled mass and plopped them into a separate pan.

Next, Heinrich wielded the fine-toothed meat-saw to separate the head and section the carcass. Each man worked on a different cut of meat, slicing, trimming fat, and cutting all into proper pieces. Hind hams were left with hide on and laid aside, later to be rubbed down with salt to cure and hung up to smoke.

The large scalding kettle was now emptied of water and hung back over the open fire. Boys were busy with buckets, gathering everyone's little piles of trimmed fat and dumping them into the big scalding kettle, where the women began melting down the fat, to be rendered into lard or oils for cooking, baking, and medicines.

Next, it was time to clamp the hand-turned meat grinder onto the table, where John began turning the handle to grind up various cuts for hamburger and half a dozen different types of sausage. Each was mixed with different time-tested spices and turned into one of the palate-pleasing meats.

Uncle Phillip, meanwhile, separated the rope-length intestines, squeezed them out, ran water through them, and turned them inside out. Then he scraped them clean and thin, ready to strip onto the snout of the sausage stuffer as casings for aromatic sausage that would be cooked on many a winter night's pleasured fine dining.

A neighbor wielded an expert axe and split the stary-eyed head into quarters, which were then trimmed clean of every last speck of meat. This was hand-mixed with chopped pieces from the cleaned tongue, snout, kidneys, heart, and lungs, together with back-fat and lard. After they ran it all through John's grinder, Christ mixed it in a large pan with healthy measures of onion, garlic, salt and pepper, and all the rich spices that would turn it into their special *kaladyetz*, headcheese, the next best thing to dessert.

Feet were sawed off from the hooves, cleaned, and set aside for pickling or smoking.

The saved panful of blood was carefully stirred, mixed with ground meat, trimmed fat, cubed bread, barley kernels, and abundant spices, and was now ready to be cooked and ran through the sausage stuffer for the appetizing "black sausage," awaiting a cold days' hunger.

Katherina dropped the brain into a pan to be washed and later fried for supper, while Louisa squeezed the liver and readied it to be ground up, with other fatty meat and a rich variety of spices, into scrumptious liverwurst.

In preparing all these meats, little bags of exotic spices were added to the taste, but finally good old salt and pepper, onions and garlic carried the day.

They carefully rolled up the hide and assigned Gottfried to carry it on his shoulder to the village tanner, who would tan it and in turn sell it to the village cobbler to make shoes. Other strips would go to the leather shop, to be combined with cowhides and turned into harnesses, bridles, and saddles.

Finally, it was time for all to join in major cleanup: disassemble the grinders and stuffers, soak all the pieces, along with saws and dozens of razored knives, in boiling soap-water to melt off the lard film that by now seemed welded on. Scrub the pile of kettles and pans. Dry each piece by hand with a dish towel and carry them inside. Scrub tabletops and carry them to the house. Shovel all the bones and piles of scraps into the cart to be hauled out to the edge of the village.

As John drove the loaded one-horse cart out to the edge of the *dorf,* several dozen village dogs ran alongside, jumping, yelping, and salivating for the feast to come in just mere minutes. Before sunup, they and assorted creatures of the wild would have every last speck cleaned up, and all would be sated and at rest.

When cooling sun let go of azure sky and kissed Ukrainian earth in the bloodred west, it was time again for men to do feeding and milking outside and women to get ready for feeding hungry stomachs inside.

Chores finished, Karolina panfried the fresh-cut rolling mass of the morning's brains.

As the five sisters and three brothers gathered with Mother and Father around the big wooden plank table in the crowded kitchen, some could not handle brain. The aromatic side dish of fried, sliced potatoes, carrots and onions was wonderful, but not enough to make the brain go down.

For them, Mother fried up a pan of fresh pork chops.

"Even the tsar and his nice German tsarina," said Christ after his second forkful, "don't have a feast half this good tonight."

Karolina's eyes narrowed, lips widened, and heart warmed. She knew a high compliment when she got one. She replied softly, "All the rich diamonds and fancy gowns in the world can't buy this. *Lieber Gott,* thank you."

"That's for sure," Gottfried mumbled with his mouth full.

Anna Maria beamed a full-blown smile. It felt so good to belong in a house where love lived without apologies. And the food was good too.

By now they could hardly see across the table, so John struck a match on the bottom of his chair to light the oil lamp. Father reached to the small shelf on the wall and took down the family Bible to read their daily chapter of the holy word. A generation of pastors had passed on to him Martin Luther's biblical insistence that the father of each house is God's priest for that family, and he meant to be faithful to that sacred task. Karolina handed him his eyeglasses, and in the dim light, he opened to the bookmark and began with those special words, *"Im Anfang war das Wort, und das Wort war bei Gott,* In the beginning was the Word, and the Word was with God . . ." from John's Gospel. *Yes, the Word was with God,* he thought to himself. *And so are we. So are we.*

"Dear God," he prayed as all heads around the table bowed, "thank you for being with us through all this day and every day. Keep watch over us this night and over all your people. Amen."

The girls washed and dried the dishes. Shortly, lamp blown out, all lay in bed thinking over the day, thankful for life this good. Silent "Amens" rang in each bed, and blessed sleep soon followed.

Over the next days, neighborhood crews butchered beef, then lamb, a clutch of chickens, waddling geese, and a cage of rabbits. Cuts of meat were salted, dried, or canned, all to preserve them for the harsh weather to come. Some of it was set aside for smoking. The long season of short days and long, bitter cold nights was just around the corner, and it was not for the faint of heart. "If we want to live through the winter," Christ told a neighbor, "we better be prepared real good."

With a timid knock, Uncle Jacob was standing at the door, holding a jar of plum jelly.

"Natalia wants you to have this," he said, holding out the bright red homemade delight.

"How is she doing?" Karolina asked.

"So much better," Jacob responded, "and if we ever have another son, I want to name him 'Gotthilf,' God helps, because he sure has."

Chapter 14

Her Hair Smells So Nice

With butchering done, it was time to fire up the smokehouses. And in the following days, the village was swaddled in the rich, pungent smell of wood smoke.

Christ built a smokehouse in the backyard, between the barn and the two-hole outhouse. It measured eight *wuerst,* eight feet by eight, with racks on three sides, floor to ceiling, and a small cast-iron burner in the middle. Then he and the boys spread a bedsheet in the bottom of the cart, loaded all the sausages, hams, and rinds, and hung them over the racks. After the fire was lit, they laid on apple-wood chips and slightly wet branches to make heavy smoke. Every two hours they restoked the fire to keep the pungent smoke working. Three days and three nights, and they had smoked meat enough for months to come. Let days be dark and snows be deep, they would not go hungry.

On the second Monday of the month, it was time for Avram. Avram Lieberwicz was the traveling Jewish merchant from Odessa who made rounds through all the *dorfs.* His tall, tarp-covered wagon, drawn by two weary horses, had a brace of tinkling bells on the back, announcing his coming.

He had a special singsong call that he chanted as he slowly drove down the street:

"Garn und Knoepfe.	-	Thread and buttons.
Schuesseln and Toepfe.	-	Dishes and pans.
Seife zum waschen.	-	Soap for washing.
Huete und Taschen.	-	Bonnets and pouches.
Ich schleife Scheren und Messer.	-	I sharpen scissors and knives
Das macht Eure Arbeit besser.	-	To make your work better.

Alles was Euer Herz -	Anything your heart	
erfreut	desires	
Kommt Leute und kauft -	Come, people, and buy	
es heut."	it today.	

When Avram came by their house, Karolina and the younger children dashed outside, eager to see what treasures he brought this time.

"*Liebes Muetterle,* dear little mother," Avram sang out, "I have cast-iron cooking pans I brought just for you."

"What would I want with those?"

"With your nice family, you need good tools to keep them fed and healthy."

Nodding at the children and smiling, she laughed, "Do they look sick to you?"

"They look wonderful, Mother."

"So, pots I don't need. But do you have your threads along?"

Reaching up into the wagon, Avram pulled out two drawers of thread that flashed an Eden of eye-pleasing colors.

Feasting on the broad palate of hues, Karolina finally picked two spools of ivory crocheting thread off their thin spindles, along with one black and one gray spool of darning thread, adding, "My bunch always wears holes in their socks."

While she was fingering the spools, Avram pulled out another drawer and with a wink and a smile, handed each of the youngsters two peppermint candies. "*Suesses fuer die Suesse,* sweets for the sweet," he cooed.

Karolina wasn't used to such sweet talk, but it felt nice to her, even if it was only a sales pitch. The warm glow moved her to pick up three more skeins of yarn for knitting mittens, scarves, and caps. She paid her kopecks and thanked Avram again for the candy.

"You should have seen the *meshuggener,* crazy man, in the last village. He wouldn't buy a thing, but he still wanted free candy for his kids. *Oi vey,* isn't going to happen."

In his wagon, Avram had wonders. Under his hat, a silver tongue. With the women he had to be careful, but at night when he made camp at the edge of the villages, oftentimes a few men would drift by, and after a few minutes of smoking, or vodka passed around,

Avram was known to get up and lift a special little wooden chest out of the bowels of his wagon. With a wink at one of the men, he would whisper, "*Jetzt*, now, I have something special for your *Liebschen*, the love of your life." And he unfolded soft mysterious clothing items that the men normally didn't get to handle. Exciting moments, these, when men were allowed to roam in fantasy worlds forbidden by the times—and by their women. Just handling such things was as intoxicating as the fruit of the vine. In those secretive moments, money often flowed freely, if not always wisely.

****

Soon, at home, it was time again to take out all the mattresses, open the ends, shake out all the year-old straw, and give them a good hand scrubbing with hot water and potent lye soap made from the lard of the butchered pig. The boys hauled in a wagonload of fresh-cut oats straw and pitched it into a pile in front of the house. Karolina and the girls then restuffed each mattress with soft nature valley's own fresh bedding. While they had the mattresses off, Christ went from bed to bed, tightened the ropes, and retied the knots, making the rope "springs" more firm to hold the mattress up.

Ah, Tsar Nicki, Karolina mused, *you won't have it any better than this tonight in your fancy gold-inlaid bed. And we will probably sleep better than you!*

****

In the village school, the head master was Herr Peter Goethe. He claimed lineage from Johann Wolfgang Goethe, the great Teutonic philosopher-poet of the homeland, and dabbled in poetry himself, but all that was lost in the dust of the *dorf.*

Goethe ruled the scholars with an iron hand, sitting at his massive desk on the elevated platform in front of the room, befitting the head master. Below him, on their long wooden benches, with writing tops attached, seven boys to a bench on the right side of the room, seven girls on the left, youngest closest to the master's desk, oldest in back. They memorized and recited what he commanded or the stick he carried would find finger-flesh in one swift whirl. They learned to read, to write, to do figures, all in German. And they were introduced to German heroes, German lands, German proverbs to guide their ways in life:

> *"As you cook the porridge, so you must eat it."*
> *"Better to fall on your face than to trip over your tongue."*
> *"A fly won't get into a closed mouth."*

Of course, a little compulsory Russian had to be taught as well, but only enough not to get stuck buying a blind horse. The three "heavy" textbooks were the ABC Primer, the Bible History Book, and the Catechism. Eight years of schooling was enough. Many didn't make it that far. Either way, it was no big deal. When boys were needed in the fields or girls in the kitchen, no excuses were required. Time enough for school when work was done.

Summer heat and winter snow slowly played tag in nature's solemn regimen. Gottfried and John spent more and more time working for neighbors, on fields here, building barns there. In winter, they sometimes worked at the steam flour-grinding mill in a nearby *dorf*, riding horse to get there each morning and home at dark. They were busy saving rubles to start homes of their own. They were not tall men, but hard workers they were, and people were glad to hire them.

While visions of the three Russian maidens still occasionally danced in their heads, their biggest joy was finding new girlfriends among their own people. They found an interest in two daughters of the Boeshans family, with the formidable names of Fredericka and Wilhelmina. For several weeks, the young men managed to find reasons to walk past the Boeshans' house, and more often than not, the girls seemed to find reasons to be outside at the right time, quietly smiling and engaging them in casual conversation.

As children, the two-fisted sisters beat the snot out of the boys on the school yard in the evenings and had a reputation in their earlier years. But as nature sculpted their bodies round and soft, they became living lavender perfume in the nostrils of the young *dorf* lovers they once pummeled. Now the brothers found them alluring and soon spent Sunday afternoons at the Boeshans' home. They came to play cards, but there was much more than cards going on. Father

Boeshans enjoyed teasing the brothers, as well as the serious talks that blossomed so easily with these two developing suitors, while Mother Boeshans made sure to stuff them with sour cream *kuchen* and chocolate everything. The parents found themselves growing fond of the young swains, as did the brothers and sisters.

It was certainly not accepted among their people that young couples would be out alone at night, but each set of parents felt comfortable with the other and with the couples alone as a foursome so the brothers were welcome also at night when work was done and darkness ruled. After visiting indoors with the rest of the family, the four spent precious interludes sitting on the bench outside the front door. There they chatted a while, but soon words fell off and they were comfortable chewing sunflower seeds and just being quiet together. A few wakeful grasshoppers clicked, frogs croaked hopefully, and above them a nighthawk plunged steep in his whistling dive.

Somewhere across the *dorf*, a lonesome dog howled. Suddenly, so far away they could barely hear it, a wolf howled a mournful, spooky answer. The hair on eight arms shot up like arrows, and hearts jumped into racing gear. They hadn't heard that sound for a long time, but all knew exactly what it was. All four instinctively huddled closer together, looked at each other, and nervously laughed. But, oh, it all felt so good, kind of scary, but so good.

In that jittery moment, Fredericka looked up into the starry splendor, and her eyes settled on the Big Dipper. As she pointed up, the rest followed her gaze.

"I'm glad," she said, "that the Big Bear never howls like that."

John teased, "It doesn't howl, but every time I see it, I think of you."

"You mean I'm a bear?"

"No, no, not at all. I just meant in my mind you're always there, just like him in the sky."

"Oh, Johnny, you're so nice."

She leaned her head on his shoulder, and it was quiet heaven. Too soon, it was time to get home. A long, engaging hug, a quick polite kiss, and they had to go.

Coming home a bit later than their own parents liked, Gottfried and John softly stole to their beds, but their minds were still in high gear, whirling with girlfriends, wolves, Big Bears, visions of what might yet be.

Finally, John whispered, "Those girls are something else, aren't they?"

"What do you mean?"

"Well, Fredericka is so soft when she curls up close to me like that."

"Ja."

"And her hair smells so nice. I can still smell it now."

"Ja." Gottfried had his own thoughts. Not of hair.

"And they're so easy to talk to."

"Sure are."

"They seem so much older than some a' the other girls that just giggle all the time."

"But the way Wilhelmina wiggles her tush drives me crazy."

"And they both dance so good."

"Ja, Wilhelmina moves like she's a part of me."

"And they've always got themselves fixed up so nice."

"Ja, oh ja."

In the silence that followed, both brothers rode to fantasyland, their thoughts far less philosophical, picturing wild scenes of pure delight.

Finally, John whispered, "*Gehen wir schlafen*, let's get to sleep."

"Ja, ja."

In the weeks that followed, they turned into regular couples, enjoying walks around town and especially *dorf* dances. When the *blosbalgale*, little accordions, came out, feet were light, and life was good. The future had a smile on its face.

In the Oster home, several years ago, firstborn daughter, Frieda, had married Konstentin Stohler, and they began a home of their own, trying to make something of a living from the little farmland Konstentin was able to rent.

Now, second-born sister, Katherina, reached marriageable age, and Father and Mother got together with the Baisch family to weld a union. Shortly, she would be Frau Baisch.

But before any little Baisches came into the world, the young couple one day quietly announced, "*Wir gehen nach Amerika,* we're going to America."

They were not the first of the villagers to go, but it was deep disappointment to all, especially to Mother Karolina. It would be a death to part of her heart.

In two months, the young couple's papers were in order, things sold, and they were gone.

They were not alone; moving away was in the air. With the unrest around them, and spreading across the land, too many things were becoming uncertain. Leaving seemed the wisest choice, at least for those young enough to dare.

Nearby Jewish villages were being attacked, German people accosted in ugly incidents that left a bad taste in everyone's mouth. Even their Russian neighbors were getting nervous. What were they to do?

Chapter 15

Trouble Brewing

Gottfried talked to a young Russian who said, "The police can't keep order anymore. The tsar is looking for more soldiers to help out."

Another told John, "Remember in the Crimea, a few years back Tsar Alexander the Second got a quarter million of our young soldiers killed."

"Ja," John replied, "but didn't our men kill just as many Turks in that one?"

"Sure, but who cares? *'Russian soil drinks Russian blood pretty fast,'*" he shot back.

The boys saw the worry on their young Russian friends—they could be next.

The tsar was Russia. There was little room for personal aspirations. In this land, people existed to serve the tsar.

Older Russians read the newspapers, now filled with more and more stories about the Japanese threatening Mother Russia in the East. Rumors were going around that a million men might get called to defend the homeland. Others told of two million needed to teach the mongrel tribes of the East some lessons. The East, they felt, dare not be allowed to birth another Napoleon. The horror of the Battle of Borodino and the smell of Mother Moscow burning were still too fresh in Russian minds, even if these new foreigners could not understand.

Around their province of Bessarabia, even more turmoil was brewing. Russians saw the scattered Jews as low-bloods, and feelings were whipped up to show them as the enemies they supposedly had become. The newspaper, *Bessarabian*, carried an article reporting that a Russian boy had been killed by Jews to get his blood for making matzo, Jewish bread. Hatred flared. Russian police and bands of soldiers attacked Jewish *shtetl,* settlements, scattered in the area. Riding through, sometimes in dark of night, sometimes broad daylight, the soldiers and police dismembered people with their swords, raped, killed, broke wagons, torched buildings, and rode away, laughing. It was the sport of kings in the hand of cowards. But who could oppose them? They were the law! Say anything to higher authorities and two nights later your whole village was torched and left for wolves and vultures. The Germans got the message.

Several young Jewish girls escaped into the night from one such raid in a neighboring *shtetl* and wandered, barely half alive, into Klostitz. When the dogs barked, Karolina got up, looked out the window, saw their slumped-over forms like wounded ghosts walking, and quickly pulled them inside. Barbara woke as well, and together they held the two, let them sob for what seemed an hour, then heated some milk, doubled up the other daughters in bed, and gave the two a bed together. They could not talk. For two days, they huddled on the bed in curled up balls. Nights they cried out in their sleep, waking up terrified and shivering until Karolina and Barbara sat on the bed and gently rocked them, rubbing their backs and stroking their long, knotted hair. Their clothes were tattered, and as with young women the world over, it did not take a lot of imagination for Mother to figure out at least part of what must have happened to them.

Each day Karolina and Barbara spent several hours just sitting on the bed and holding the two terrified young women, gently rubbing their backs, occasionally singing a German hymn, brushing their dirty matted hair, and washing their faces with a warm washcloth. When asked to the table, the two just shook their heads so Mother took porridge to them, then chicken soup, some bread, and cheese. Finally, the third day, Karolina again asked their names.

"I'm Deborah," one whispered.

"I'm Miriam," whispered the other. "We're sisters."

They said where they were from, and then, after Christ and the boys had all left the house, Mother asked, "Can you tell us what happened?" There was a long silence, so long that Karolina became afraid when she saw them shudder, their eyes wide as they looked at each other to see if it was safe. Slowly, in broken pieces, Deborah began:

"A group of soldiers . . . broke into our house . . . during the night. They were all drunk . . . Father and Mother got up and lit the lamp."

Miriam's hands clasped, her knuckles white. She shot a terrified glance at Deborah then down at her hands: "The soldiers . . ."

". . . Our parents . . ."

". . . gone . . ." The words were so soft that Karolina wasn't sure she heard right.

". . . They grabbed us . . . ."

With that horrible moment still too fresh, the two girls clung together and broke into wrenching sobs that shook the bed. Karolina and Barbara wrapped their arms around both and held them, feeling the pain through their quivering skin. After a long time, the heartbroken sobbing stopped, and all four were exhausted.

Then, with her eyes pinched shut, Deborah reached up to hold Karolina's face and choked out, "There was so much blood." Both girls were left torn and bruised, and now they shuddered as the horrible remembrance swept over them again with almost unbearable pain and guilt.

"Maybe we should look at you," Karolina said, "to see . . ."

"No, no," both girls cut her off, afraid to have strangers look at their shame. "No, don't."

"I'll make us some hot soup," Karolina whispered, kissing each forehead. "That'll help."

After several spoonfuls, Deborah looked at her spoon and shivered. "Their breath smelled like pig manure." The memory made her gag, like setting her teeth into a mouthful of *gefilte fisch,* gone bad, and both girls again broke into sobbing.

Mother and Barbara wanted to say something, but now was not the time. Words were done. Time only for rocking back and forth, for holding them in silence, and for a moment letting them be innocent girls again, children of loving parents who adored them, though innocence and parents were both forever gone in senseless brutality.

That night Karolina was finally able to learn where some other relatives of the girls lived, and the next day Christian hitched up the team and, with Karolina and Barbara along, drove them to that *shtetl.*

"What's going to happen to those poor girls?" Barbara asked on the way home. Her parents could only shake their heads.

"And who will be next?" Karolina wondered.

"I don't know," Christian replied. "I just don't know anymore."

Not long afterward, a delegation of proud military with much gold braid on their shoulders rode into town, sounded trumpets, and announced:

"The motherland is being attacked and threatened by yellow hordes to the East. Now our beloved Tsar Nicholas has asked his loyal German citizens to join him in fighting our enemies. Lists will be posted on the schoolhouse door. Those named must report to army headquarters in Ovidiopol within one week."

The village was stunned. Young and old together could only look into each other's faces and drop their jaws in disbelief. For over one hundred years, since Czarina Catherine the Great had issued her manifesto of invitation in 1763 and invited them, five different czars had kept covenant and allowed their German citizens freedom from military service in the Russian army.

"Will the tsar break his sacred promise to us?" Gottfried asked.

"I guess he has," Christ replied. "First taxes, now this."

Two days later, the dreaded list arrived, nailed like Luther's 95 Theses to the schoolhouse door. From every house, feet tramped to read.

Gottfried's name was not on the list, nor any cousins. But John's name was, along with several other young men from the *dorf.*

A slow walk home, and no word was uttered. John sat down at the table, head in his hands. Sister Barbara wrapped her arms around his shoulders, held him tight, tears rolling down her cheeks, his, and the whole family's.

"How could this happen? What now?" Christ shouted, pounding his fist on the table. "Why didn't God step in and stop all this?"

Karolina broke into the little huddle and hugged her son's shoulders in a fierce mother hug, sobbing bitterly, *"Nicht mein Johannes, Treuer Gott, nicht mein Johannes,* Not my John, faithful God, not my John."

The girlfriends, Fredericka and Wilhelmina, heard the news, and in minutes, they were also at the house.

By now they had grown close enough so they were Ricka and Mina, "Reeka" and "Meena" as they spoke it.

Ricka pulled a chair next to John, and for a long time they sat wordlessly wrapped in each other's arms. John inhaled the special smell of her hair, a scent he had grown to love so dearly, as hot tears ran down their cheeks, knowing a bitter separation would keep them out of each other's embrace for a long time to come. Around the room, more tears silently dropped on the board floor as every person knew what pain was soon to wrack their beloved's hearts. No one knew what to say until with silent sighs they glanced once more at the brokenhearted couple and slowly drifted out, leaving John and Ricka gazing into each other's eyes, wishing all this were not true, knowing it was only too terribly, frightfully real.

But John was now firmly fixed as one of the czar's freshly chosen ones.

Three days, and another message on the schoolhouse door tersely commanded:

> *All new soldiers report here*
> *To leave at sunrise*
> *On Monday morning*

These were days of desperate uncertainty. Some pundits applauded the 1880s as tremendous days of limitless progress for all humanity. Surely true for a few at the top of the food chain, but sadly, much of humanity "sat down by the rivers of Babylon, and there they wept," as the '80s spun into days of great upheaval, and now the '90s were ending in harsh, even more trying times. Fear and worry were the daily bread not only of the Osters but of many a soul across the land.

Maybe their new pastor had a prescient understanding when he said in a sermon, "The final century of the Second Millennium has the hopeful ring of a cracked bell."

Chapter 16

Letter from America

Everyone in the family was excited when an envelope arrived from America. It was a letter from Daughter Katherina:

Lieber Vater und Mutter, Dear Father and Mother,
Thank God we made it safe to Amerika!
Our journey across the ocean was blessed with good weather, so we were thankful. But 17 days on that big water seemed like it would never end. I cannot tell you how big that ocean is, it just goes on and on, sunrise to sunset and back to sunrise, nothing at all but water. We both spent two days being so seasick we thought we'd die, but then it got better.
We landed in New York and saw that big statue in the harbor. It was a nice welcome to our new land.
New York was very confusing. Every language from the Bible is spoken there, and all at once. Everyone is shouting, and all are in a hurry. Your nose is filled with a thousand smells, many of them not so good. We stood in line after line so long and answered so many questions. But then we finally found someone who spoke our German, it felt so good, and they directed us to the trains.
Three days we rode on the train, slept sitting up, ate bread and sausage, bread and sausage.
In Chicago we changed trains again and rode another 2,000 kilometers north and west to North Dakota, our new home. Herr Wiedrich, whom you remember, picked us up with his wagon. We rode all day, up hills and down, across prairies with no end, the sun always to our backs.
There are no roads, only wagon trails across the grass. We saw many white skulls that Herr Wiedrich said were buffalo bones that were shot by hunters a few years back. At night we stayed in a little town where some more kind German people took us in and fed us good warm food.

The next day we set out when the sun came up and drove till late afternoon when we got to our new home. It is called Krem and was just started a few years ago. Nearly all the people in Krem are Germans from Russia, so it is nice to visit with all of them.

Life for us here is much like it was for Grandfather Heinrich and Grandmother Anna Marie when they first moved to Russia almost a hundred years ago. We are having to start with almost nothing to build our life here.

We are feeling well, and miss you so much. Please write to us and let us know how you are.

Euere Katherina,
Your Katherina

Chapter 17

Your Left, Your Left

The rising sun kissing the schoolhouse door on Monday morning found the Russian army wagon, with driver and four-horse team, parked outside the school, driver smoking and waiting.

Karolina wrapped bread, cheese, and sausages in a bundle, knowing that food on the trip would probably not be the best. There was no need to take extra clothes since they would most likely all be thrown away once the recruits were processed. The Russian army was not known for its great generosity of provisions.

Families came with their recruits, and the morning stillness was broken by sobs as tears flowed and hugs could not let go.

Ricka buried her face in John's chest, trying bravely not to cry, but tears streamed down her face as she whispered, "Oh, Johnny, hurry home. I'll pray for you every night."

John and the others climbed on board, sitting on benches along the sides of the wagon box.

Reverend Mueller had also gotten up early to shake their hands and bid them Godspeed and farewell, and now, standing on the schoolhouse steps, he raised his right hand and silently blessed them with the sign of the cross. A dozen throats responded with a resounding "Amen."

The driver shoved his hand-rolled cigarette between bearded lips, snapped the reins, and army life was just a ride away.

Heading east over the steppes on the long road to Akkermann, they passed through other villages and picked up more draftees until their wagon was full. At each village, when they jumped off the wagon, tantas came out and gave them *blachinda* and bread, along with *kvass* to drink. Beer would have been better, but on this trip, it was forbidden.

Soon, more wagons joined them, forming a mournful caravan. To this band of young men, many away from home for the very first time, it felt closer to a funeral than to a rite of passage into supposed manhood. They sang no Russian army ditties, no familiar German folk songs. They watched the hawks circling in the sky, listened to the steady drumming of the horses' hooves and the creaking of harness leather, and grew to hate the dry wagon axles moaning for grease.

At dusk, they bivouacked outside a village. Somewhere along the route, their caravan was joined by a mess wagon, and now expectations ran high.

"Our first meal on the tsar," said John to his new comrade, Georg Hoffman, whom he knew from their village, though they had never been friends.

"What do you think they'll feed us to make us feel good about losing our freedom?" whispered Georg.

Hopes were soon dashed when each was handed a spoon and a tin bowl into which the cooks plopped a big spoonful of gruel and a crust of bread and told them to sit on the ground wherever there was room.

"This is it?" a pained voice muttered. "When do we get supper?"

That was it. There was no more. Whoever had bread and sausage left over from the trip was lucky and now was the time to break it out. With a lot of sharing and passing, at least nobody went to bed totally hungry on his first night as Russian Army.

Another full day's dusty grind and they arrived at the old fort in Akkermann, hard by the shores of Dniester Liman (bay), a forty-kilometer-long thumb of water jutting northwest out of the Black Sea's western side, down from lustrous Odessa.

Up at dawn the next day, they stood on the dock and looked across Dniester Bay. Thirteen kilometers away, they could see the eastern shore of the bay, but looking to the northern horizon, they could see no land. Shortly, they boarded shallow-bottom ferries for a two-hour journey across the biggest water any of them had ever seen. The Dniester River, beginning in Romania's high Carpathian Mountains and surging 850 miles south by east, channels copious waters into Dniester Bay. Still, the bay is not large, as great waters go, but for these *dorf* conscripts the white-capped water was enough to taste the bitter dregs of seasickness in a big way.

"Man, I never knew land could feel so good," muttered ashen-faced John when they finally reached the opposite shore.

They landed at Ovidiopol and were driven to the army base outside the city. The young men were quick to discover that this was not their father's house, and most of all not their mother's kitchen!

Escorted to quarters, they were fifty men to a barracks, assigned a bunk and lined up to receive uniform, boots, and caps. Some pieces fit, some didn't. Georg slipped his boots on and muttered, "These lousy boots must have been captured off some dead Mongol. They wouldn't even fit my donkey!"

A shrill bugle sounded, they ran outside, and their world spun upside down before the last note died. Screaming, obnoxious drill sergeants were all over them, eyes ablaze, tongues stabbing, and switches striking everywhere.

From then on, life was lines: forming lines, standing in lines, waiting in lines. And marching: marching in lines, marching in formation, marching with heavy packs to build endurance. Every day, "Your left, your left . . ." For young farm men, this basic training was strenuous but also exhilarating. They quickly proved their mettle, showing their worth to the officers.

Like basic training of every army in every land, these days were intended to break down individuality and instill total submission to authority.

"What else you learn?" barked the drill sergeant. "You'll learn to take orders! Got that *Kartouschki?*"

"Yes."

"You got that *Kartouschki!*"

"Yes, sir!"

The Russian officers assigned to these new Germans saw them as totally inferior beings, little more than alien scum, so they were not "private" or "soldier." They were "*Kartouschki,*" from *kartofel,* potato eaters.

They spent the next six weeks in grueling basic training: calisthenics, close order drills, sprints, lifts, crawls, and distance runs. If any man lay back, even a little, a sergeant was beside him with a stinging whack across his back or rump or legs, occasionally across his head to get his full attention. While the almost constant yelling by the officers made it immensely stressful, for most of these young draftees just pulled away from heavy farm labor, the physical rigors were the easiest part. They prided themselves on their strength and stamina. The mental side was the more demanding. *"We're not gonna let 'em beat us down"* became their silent motto. One of their numbers came up with a signal gesture: "Pucker your lower lip out." When that was flashed from any one to another, they were wordlessly urging, "Don't let 'em get to you!"

Though hard-pressed and dog-tired through all this, John grew terribly homesick. He had never been away from home this long. Now his heart ached for his precious Fredericka. Twice he managed to write her and twice received answer. She scented her paper to send special love, but it nearly broke John's heart with loneliness. Lying on his bunk at night, he closed his eyes and traced every line of her face, every curve of her body, felt her fingers riffing through the back of his hair, and smelled the delicious perfume of her special scent.

Her arms were again wrapped tightly around his shoulders, his around hers. The ache inside felt like it was going to blow his heart into two. He was glad it was night so no one saw the hot tears coursing long and silent down his cheeks until he fell asleep.

When the czar traveled, his personal priest accompanied him, but for these lowly draftees there were no chaplains to lift their loneliness or see to their spiritual needs.

The Russian officers were officially Orthodox, but they were not generally known for their fervent religious piety. Sundays were given more to St. Vodka than to St. Paul.

For the recruits, Sundays, at least, were days of quiet, sleeping late, until seven in the morning. After breakfast, John joined a group who gathered in a corner of the barracks for quiet worship time together. One of the men managed to bring a small Gospel of John from which he read a chapter, and then they softly sang *"Jesu geh voran,* Jesus Still Lead On"—which to their amazement they learned that no matter from which village they came, they all knew it from confirmation classes in church. Back then it had been a painful bore which their pastors made them memorize. Now it became the cornerstone of their spiritual building. After the song, they prayed the *Vater Unser,* Lord's Prayer, and their souls were ready to face the officers for another week.

Some of the draftees from the Catholic villages also met in small groups to say the rosary and pray the Our Father together in faithful devotion. They missed the familiar Latin of the Mass, but this would have to do.

Monday morning, sunrise, the dreaded bugle sounded early reveille, and they sat down to another tasteless breakfast of gruel, black bread, and thick coffee. Then sergeants barked to line up for an hour's marching. They hated the Russian marching ditties they had to chant, but it did help to weld them into a more efficient marching machine. *"They're not gonna beat us down!"*

Chapter 18

Letter #2 from America

Lieber Vater und Mutter:
God is taking good care of us here. If it weren't for Him, we would not last long in this pilgrim land, for here we are pilgrims indeed. How we long for the good things we had in Russia, that are only a dream now. We can't grow apples here, or pears or apricots, because it gets too cold. When I close my eyes, Mamma, I can just smell your wonderful fresh baked apricot kuchen again. Oh, how good a piece of it would taste right now. Some here have planted plums and grape vines, but they will take a while to grow, if they make it at all.

It is taking some time to get used to measuring everything different than at home.

Instead of grams and kilos it is now ounces and pounds. Instead of centimeters, meters and kilometers, now inches, yards and miles. Liters are quarts and gallons. Celsius is Fahrenheit.

Canning vegetables and meat is a real chore to figure out. But with help from my good neighbor women, I am getting used to it, and so is Adam. I think he is getting it better than I am.

We are thankful for our good friends and neighbors here. There are about 80 souls now living in Krem, around 20 houses so far. The houses in our town are all built of wood and are very small but they keep us alive in the heat and cold.

Yes, it does get cold here, much colder than at home. Several weeks ago the temperature got down to 38 degrees below zero. When it gets that cold, I stay inside and we have to burn lot of wood in the stove to keep from freezing, but Adam still has to go out to feed the animals.

The big difference here is that the farmers do not live together in town like at home. The law here is that all farmers who got homestead land free from the government have to build a house and live on that land. So you have farmers living all around our whole area, each one on his own place with just his family.

I talk to different farm women when they come into town, and some of them are terribly lonesome. Many of them only get to town every few weeks, some even less, and I think some of them would really like to go back to Russia if only they could do it.

Papa, you and Mamma should really think of coming here too. Our town doesn't have a good leather and harness repairman, and you are so good at it that you would have a wonderful business. We have several carpenters, a blacksmith, wagon repairman, and a good flour mill. But no leather and harness man, and no good shoe fixer either. They just got a school going, and there is talk of a minister coming to start a church for us. I hope he comes soon, because I sure miss church and good strong singing. Anyway, Papa and Mamma, life is hard here, but our coming here is the most wonderful thing that ever happened to us. It is so peaceful. We go to bed every night without worrying about the police or the army riding through and shooting up the village. No one is being persecuted. Our people don't have to fear the government or neighbors who didn't want us in the first place. I think we found what Grandfather Heinrich and Grandmother Anna were looking for when they moved to Russia many years ago. I wish you could be part of it too.

I saved the big news for last. Are you sitting down? Adam and I are going to have a baby. It will come in the spring, in about four months. We are so happy. I feel good most of the time, but I get so tired. I can't keep up. There is no doctor here, but several women are good at bringing babies into the world, and they have said they will gladly help me.

That is all I can think of to write. God be with you all. Please write as soon as you can and tell us what is happening at home.

Eure Katherina

Chapter 19

Army Life Intensifies

Monday, after their march, the captain barked, "Company G, fall out. Line up." He ordered them into squads, and Sergeant Tamarov marched their squad to the supply depot where they were each given their first real rifle, a single-shot bolt action M-1870 Berdan.

The sergeant held up one of the rifles and shouted, "We call this a 'Berdanka.'" The rifle's nickname, ending as it did with a feminine "a," was perhaps no accident. "She" was meant to be the soldier's sweet mistress, his day's best soul mate, and his night's most ' cherished companion.

"*Kartouschki,* from now on this will be your best friend in the whole big world," announced Tamarov.

"Love it. Rub it up and down like it's your best girlfriend."

"Learn to shoot it until you can shoot the balls off a wolf at hundred meters.

"You will learn to plug your enemy with your first shot. If you miss, he'll take you out before you get off another."

Then he had a small table brought out, ordered the men to sit down, and proceeded to take the Berdanka apart. He pulled the bolt, released it to slide out of the chamber, and dismantled the rest of the rifle.

"Watch!" he said. "Your life depends on this!" Carefully he assembled it, again broke it down, and once more assembled it, sliding the smooth bolt into place with a satisfying click.

"Now, *Kartouschki,* shoulder your rifles and march to the mess hall."

"Lay your Berdanka on the table and break it down like I showed you."

The men were all thumbs, and a few were able to do it on the first try. But after some choice Russian swearing and grabbing at a lot of rifles, jerking parts every which way, Sergeant Tamarov noticed the beads of sweat on a lot of foreheads and decided to give them a fifteen-minute smoke break.

Calling them back, he told them, "You will break your rifle down and reassemble it ten times every day this week. Next week you will be blindfolded and do it all without seeing.

"Remember, if you're attacked in the dark, and your gun jams, you don't have time to find a light!"

Every day, they did their rifle drills, and after that, Sergeant Tamarov shouted, "Shoulder your rifle and line up to march!"

As they fell into step, Georg muttered to John, "Hey, this is all right. Now I'm starting to feel like a soldier." But after several miles of rapid march, their exciting rifles didn't feel quite so light or so good.

John screwed up the courage to ask Tamarov, "How much does our Berdanka weigh?"

"10 *Funt 3, about a quarter pood* (9.5 pounds)!"

After five fast kilometers of marching, it felt more like a full *pood.*

Already their breech-loading Berdanka was obsolete in most of the world's armies, but to these draftees, it was real military and certainly a giant step up from the ball-and-powder guns that some of them knew from home.

To Tamarov's great surprise, the entire company passed the blindfold test, so he again marched them to the supply depot and had the quartermaster's assistant supply each with a bayonet for his rifle.

Tamarov held his bayonet high and with a cynical smile announced, "Your Berdanka is your mistress! This is her little sister!"

"Treat them well," he added, "and they will give your hours of pleasure!"

The men stared openmouthed into his face and did not see the humor in his remark.

"This little beauty," Tamarov continued as he slipped its collar over the barrel of his rifle, "is three *pyad* (twenty-three inches) of solid polished steel. You notice how it locks over the end of the Berdanka barrel."

Running his finger softly over the sharp edge, he continued, "This is an 1870 SKP Vintovka, made for your rifle. Notice the blade is designed in a cruciform shape." Pointing it at them, he said, "See?

It doesn't have two edges, but four, with indented sides for better ripping action when you run it into your enemy's belly."

Seeing their grimaces, he knew here was a lesson he wouldn't have to repeat so he quickly built on it, "The slotted sides let the blood out quicker, and you notice the tip is flattened from four back down to two sides to make it even deadlier!"

The next month was spent in bayonet drills. At the first day of drills, Sergeant Tamarov introduced them to their new drillmaster. Slightly portly and with a red nose from a lifelong companionship with Sister Vodka, the grizzled veteran promptly raised his Berdanka with fixed bayonet and spoke words the draftees would never forget: "You will learn to master your bayonet! Or you will be dead!"

"Do you understand, *Kartouschki*?" he continued.

"Yes, sir!" the men shouted, as one determined voice.

"Your Japanese enemy," he continued, "is learning to use his bayonet right now, just like you are," the DM continued. "And if he learns better than you, he'll run his point through your belly and out the other side."

"Pray that you die fast, or you'll spend three days in agony with your guts hanging out," he spat out as he finished.

Still standing tall and military straight, he commanded their absolute attention. "Remember three rules," he bellowed in a deep military bass:

"Step, stab, and pull!

With your rifle on your right side, deflect your enemy's bayonet.

Remember to keep your left hand on the middle of your rifle.

Then *step* ahead, into your enemy.

Lead with your left foot. Use your right foot for power.

Stab, fast and hard, and lift with your left hand.

Force your right hand down hard on the rifle butt to lift the bayonet point and rip his guts harder.

Finally, *pull*.

Get your bayonet out of him and rebalance, because there are probably two other slant eyes coming after you by now. Screaming helps, too."

Then he ordered them out on the drill field, which had been set up with straw dummies on posts. They lined up and for long hours ran at the dummies, stepping, stabbing, pulling, all with screams, and returned to the back of the line.

Finally, the DM called them together and bellowed, "For the sake of St. George, *Kartouschki,* remember, all this stuff has to happen in one blink of an eye. Go any slower and your enemy'll beat you and you'll have a belly fulla steel. Got that?"

"Yes, sir!" came the shouted reply, putting a new sense of urgency into their motions.

"Now, get back and show me you heard what I said!"

The next day he put them into live drills.

"Pair up," he shouted, "and give each other three *arshin* (seven feet) of space."

Most of the day they practiced, deflecting, parrying, and measuring their stab to reach but not puncture the other. Most of the time their stabs stopped short of flesh. Some blood flowed.

After eight hours of bayonet drills, the DM marched them to the mess hall for the usual misery dinner of borscht, sausage, and dry bread. Bolting it down, they were more than ready to fold up, but Sergeant Tamarov had other plans. Instead, he took them on a ten-kilometer march, returning to barracks by moonlight. Dog-tired, they stripped off their boots and nothing else, crumbling into their bunks, dirty, sweaty and totally wiped out.

For John, it didn't help when he found a letter waiting for him.

Chapter 20

News from Home

Lieber Johann, Dear John,
How terribly much I miss you. It seems like years and years since we have been together. Your letters mean so much to me, but sometimes, it seems like when I read your nice words it makes me even more lonely for you.

Things in Klostitz are mostly the same, though we hear about Jewish villages being attacked and the government police riding around the country bullying people whenever they want, even in our villages. The men are also bringing back talk of the Tsar going to war against the Japanese in the East, and that is terribly frightening to me, with you in the army. I pray to God that it will not happen.

Your parents received a letter from your sister Katherina in Amerika, and she is pushing them to think about coming to Amerika too. She says life is wonderful there and very peaceful. Your little sister Anna tells me that they are really thinking about it and so is your brother Gottfried.

Sister Mina and Gottfried are also thinking about getting married. I am glad for them. Wish it were us.

I miss you terribly. I wish you were here so I could hold you for a long time and just lay my head on your chest and close my eyes with your arms around me. I send you all my love and a big, big hug and kiss.

Your Ricka

Chapter 21

Them's Real Bullets

John lay in his bunk, his mind reeling with a thousand rattled thoughts tumbling over each other: *what if his parents decided to move? Would he ever see them again? Would Ricka really wait for him until he was done with his army duty? If they got married—when they got married—should they head for America, too? Would the tsar get them into war? Would he survive the war if they did?* These questions and more thumped against the walls of his brain.

When he was awake, the questions jumbled. When he dozed, they jumbled even more. Finally, the bugle sounded reveille, and he again belonged to Tamarov and their grizzled DM.

More bayonet drills.

"Snap to it, *Kartouschki,*" shouted the DM, "or you'll all be dead. Your enemy won't ask if you feel like fighting today! He'll come at you and let the Russian soil drink your German blood!"

That got some energy into their paired bayonets.

After a morning of drills, they were again lined up to march.

Put a fifty-three-inch Berdanka on a sixty-four-inch soldier's shoulder, tip the rifle with a twenty-three-inch solid steel bayonet, and as the bright Russian sun glints off the highly polished steel stretching eight feet into the crisp morning air, it gets the world's attention. Join a hundred of them together in close order formation, and you had an awe-inspiring sight. Put five companies of hundreds together in perfect regal lockstep, their steel tips rolling in the air like waves of Black Sea water rushing toward shore, and an enemy commander might just be moved to calculate his losses.

Though the lowly draftees could not understand, that was precisely the point of their marching and their drills.

When they marched out of the base on the roads around the surrounding countryside, they owned the road. Any civilians or animals on the road had better have the sense to get off quickly, or Sergeant Tamarov, marching with the lead rank, barked, "Ten . . .

shun! Lower bayonets! Prepare to attack!" Anything on the road was soon off the road, and their march continued. It gained neither admiration nor affection for the army, but the army's bigger concern was putting the fear of the czar into all the populace. After all, "Everything we do is in the name of the tsar, Father of all Russia!"

While there was a measure of satisfaction in doing well in this daily grind, it got to be more and more just that, a grind. Tempers began to flare, fights erupted, and morale seemed to be getting lower by the week.

The officers sensed the unrest and decided it was time to go to live ammunition. They lined the men up, and each was given a small cardboard box with ten .42 caliber shells for their Berdankas. On the practice range, targets had been set at fifty yards, and Tamarov and the other officers lined them up, a squad at a time, each man sliding one shell into the chamber, firing, then going to the back of the line.

"Squeeze your rifle butt tight against your shoulder, and grip your gun tight," bellowed Tamarov, "or it'll knock you on your ass! And remember, them's real bullets."

John squeezed it tight, but it still smacked hard against his shoulder, and the loud crack rattled his ears. But it felt good, and inside, he felt a smile rippling around in his gut. As each man fired and came back to the end of the line to reload, they looked into each other's eyes and saw a new glint. That night, the camp seemed much more relaxed and satisfied.

"Kinda feels like we're real soldiers now," chirped one of the recruits.

Once a month the officers ordered pails, and each company was given a turn to wash their underwear and socks. After every twenty men, they could change water.

When John complained about the long time between washing, one of the officers heard him and laughed, "Hey, *Kartouschki,* wait 'til winter. You'll put on your long underwear at the first hard freeze, and you won't ever take it off again until spring thaw!"

Their army grays were not washed unless they became terribly soiled. "A little dirt makes your uniform warmer in the cold weather," was the rule of the day. It looked like they'd be plenty warm all right.

Chapter 22

Letter #3 from America

Lieber Grossvater und Grossmutter,
Congratulations! Yes, you are Grandfather and Grandmother for the very first time. God brought our little Johann Adam into the world on March 23, and three Sundays later we had him baptized in church.

We are all doing well, but Mamma, I never get any sleep any more. I'm sure you know what I'm talking about.

In your last letter you asked about the Indians here and if they are still wild.

They are not wild any more, but they are very shy, and the women in the stores don't look at us. Their skin is reddish in color and they have high cheekbones with round faces, kind of like the Tatars from the East at home, with long black hair and black eyes.

At those words, her mind went back to the mental pictures she and all her people in the old country had about American Indians. They were wild, savage in appearance and action, dressed in loincloth and waving bow and arrows. How different was the reality she met in her new world as the Indians here came driving—fully dressed—in wagons to Krem from Fort Berthold, the reservation on the Missouri River, four miles away. While the adults spoke little or no English, the children went to school in a small Indian community of Rhee and learned to speak English.

Tapping her pencil on the table, she smiled to herself when she remembered how frightened she was of the first Indian people she met. Some white settlers still talked of the terrible battles that were fought between the Indians and American soldiers in this area not too many years before, and it left her nervous. Now she saw neither guns nor knives, and they were not the least threatening.

Writing of the women's eyes took her back some weeks to a conversation with her husband, Adam, when he mentioned talking with an Indian man and his son, and they told him that one of their big chiefs was buried on a high hill several miles from Krem. Now it reminded her of the women she saw in the store, wearing moccasins covered with the most beautiful beadwork patterns of every color, and she couldn't help wonder if the chief was buried with lot of beads as well. She had asked Adam if they could find the grave to see what kind of tombstone might be there, but he quickly told her to stay away from the place. *I'd still like to go, but I better listen, she thought.*

I've spent several days writing this, between feeding little Johann and trying to get some work done. He is growing and can cry very loud already. Adam says he will be a cowboy, yelling after the cows running over the prairies.

I still hope you will think about coming here too. This is a new land with so much happening, and we are so happy. Johann wants to cuddle up in your arms and smile his big smile at you.

Eure Katherina

Chapter 23

We Gotta Run

Sergeant Tamarov, much to his surprise and dismay, discovered one day that he had taken a certain liking to his bloody Kartouschki. They were sturdy, took orders, and were by and large rather intelligent, and he could depend his life on them. They were now well-trained fighting men through and through. He never had to worry about turning his back on them, like with some Russian units.

So now it was doubly difficult to get the news. The high brass far away had made a decision to move this entire German brigade further east, to the base at Sevastopol, in the Crimea. They were scheduled for a 250-mile overland march, which would include transporting all their supplies as well.

In a meeting of all the officers, Sergeant Tamarov raised a question: "Why do it this way? I just don't understand this at all."

"That's the word that's come down from headquarters in St. Petersburg."

"But why march them on foot all that way around the Black Sea when the army could get a steamship and sail them across the sea in just a few hours?"

"The communiqué we received," the captain responded, "simply said, 'This decision is made in order to insure the soldiers' total physical and mental preparation for whatever the future may hold for our beloved Mother Russia.'"

Whatever, thought Tamarov. But inside, he wondered if perhaps this was a move to show these rather unwelcome Germans that in high places they were still considered foreigners and they had better learn their place in this society.

On top of that, he and the other present officers would all stay at this base, and an entire new set of officers would now take command of the German brigade.

When the captain assembled the entire brigade, Tamarov and the other junior officers felt a sense of loss and puzzlement. Certainly, the czar, with all the resources of giant Mother Russia at his disposal, could afford to transport a few hundred highly skilled fighting men, as part of his well-oiled military machine, to a new base of operations in a way much better than this.

But the decision had been made, and there would be no negotiation. March the four hundred kilometers on foot it was, and marching four hundred kilometers on foot it would be!

They would have two more weeks at Ovidiopol, and then they would ship out. For both the men and their Russian officers, it was a confused and unsettled time. Training of some sort had to continue every day, but no one's heart was in it, neither officer nor soldier. There was no heart, nor energy, nor desire to fight about anything. Nobody really cared. The attitude was, "We can't do anything about it, so shut up and do what you're told."

So it hit John doubly hard when he read his next letter from his beloved Ricka. He lay in his bunk and unfolded his letter for what, the fifth time? He couldn't stop reading: *My Dearest John . . . Your parents have decided to go to Amerika to join your sister Katherina. They will also take little sister Anna along with them. They have most of their papers done and will leave as soon as they can get everything put together. They have sold the land and all the machinery and tools. Gottfried is to keep the house and animals for now.*

Gottfried and Mina got married several weeks ago and are also thinking about leaving for Amerika. Peter Dschaak has spoken for your sister Barbara's hand, and they will probably get married in several months. Oh, Johnny, everything is so confused. I wish you were here. I send all my love and a big hug. Your Ricka.

The next day another letter arrived from his mother, telling him much of the same.

For John, his whole world was suddenly turned upside down. Questions tangled themselves in his mind like spiderwebs on the *buryan*, tall weeds: *will I ever see my parents again? Will my brothers and sisters all be gone too? When I get home, what will happen to me? What will I do? Will Ricka still be there for me?* Everything was a terrible blur. During daylight, he was in a daze; at night, terrible things chased him through dark, scary places.

Before they knew it, the two weeks at base were finished, and they were ordered out, on the 250-mile march to Sevastopol. The

Black Sea was said to be beautiful, a vacation spot for the high and mighty of this world, including the czar himself. But for them it would be a Sea of Torture. Marching sunup to sundown, it would take them several weeks.

The last day at base was spent packing their few belongings and saying good-bye to their officers. With these toughened troops and their officers, there was no show of emotion. But when they shook hands, they looked into each other's eyes for a long time, and the handshakes were grips of steel. Their souls spoke of kinship and respect that would long be held deep.

At high noon, they were assembled at the flag stand on the parade grounds. General Uleshenko was sent down from army command in St. Petersburg to perform the formal ceremony of transfer. The small band played the czar's military salute, their plain green colors were struck, and their new brigade colors raised. Deep fervor swelled in the men's hearts as General Uleshenko proclaimed: "You are now designated as the 143rd Infantry Brigade, 2nd Army, Southern Forces, of our Blessed Tsar Nicholas's Grand Russian Army!"

Their new colors showed a triangle of three snarling black wolf heads with brilliant red eyes on a solid field of green, surrounded by a border of three-inch gold tassels. It was meant to represent the fierce fighting wolves on the vast, grassy southern steppe, which was the land of their birth.

A number of men were called up for promotions to private first class and for awards in shooting and bayonet. John received a medal, the Sharp Shooting Award, for his accuracy with the Berdanka.

Following a stirring bugle call, General Uleshenko presented their new officers. That led to salutes, formal bows, more salutes, and then a round of long, involved speeches, as sometimes happens in high places. The following day, the Odessa *Peoples' Free Press* would report: "It was a grand spectacle and a historic moment in which our newest citizens from the West can take just pride." It was a proud moment, indeed, and every soldier felt several centimeters taller. Yes, he would gladly serve his czar. Little did they know that the sweet taste of belonging would too soon be flavored by the bitter herbs of despair.

Another rousing bugle sounding "Charge," and the General announced, "Your last breakfast here will be at 05:00 tomorrow morning. You will be lined up and ready to march at 06:00. Troops dismissed! Fall out!"

They marched out promptly at 06:00, while Sergeant Tamarov and the grizzled DM stood on the edge of the field and silently saluted them. Without an order, every man in the ranks saluted back and marched, eyes ahead, but many moist.

The corps of new officers had, of course, also become familiar with the term, "*Kartouschki*," and now felt that being assigned to this brigade of potato eaters, as they thought of them, was a step down in their career. Thus, it was no surprise that as they rode their spirited thoroughbred horses alongside the recruits, they would soon show them that service meant duty, loyalty, sacrifice, and obedience! These officers meant to impose their will on the innocent conscripts and break any foolish notions they might have about being as good as the regular Russian Army.

An hour on the road and the new captain barked out from the head of the ranks, "All right, *Kartouschki*, time to move your sorry tails. Double time!"

Half an hour of running pace with full packs and Berdankas in arms, and men began to lose step and break ranks. Immediately, whips came out and sang in the air, smacking backs, as officers rode down the line, showing no mercy. Several men collapsed, others staggered to the side of the road and vomited. Finally, as the captain galloped to the rear, he realized that the ranks had broken and pushing them further would be counterproductive. He ordered a half hour rest, and all of them collapsed at the edge of the road. Canteens came out, but many overdrank, and the water turned their stomachs even more. Retching could be heard all up and down the line.

John looked up and saw several officers riding by, a half-snarling smile on their faces, and felt a look of loathing being cast over him. He hated these arrogant fools, and to Georg, crumpled on the ground beside him, he whispered, "Man, I'd like to put a bayonet up those stupid Russki's rear ends!"

"Careful," Georg whispered back, "the ground has ears."

By nightfall, they had passed the outskirts of Odessa and camped to the north of the city.

The next morning they returned to normal marching, the men sore but feeling stronger again. Now they were moving north, along the flat plains reaching out from the shore of the Black Sea. After a short noon break, however, the captain again ordered, "Double time!" It went the same as the day before.

By the third day, morale reached low ebb and the officers sensed it. An officer in the supply train found a willow grove and cut several dozen willow rods, four and a half feet long and finger thick. He passed them out among the riding officers who now used them with genuine glee. Welts were left across dozens of backs and necks; blood flowed, but there was no break in the marching.

During the march, Private Gustav Wiedeman, who hailed from a *dorf* close to Klostitz, collapsed, and the line was halted. Two officers dismounted and flailed him with their willows. His body twitched from their blows, but when he didn't answer, one officer kicked him in the stomach until he let out a horrible gasp and stopped moving. The other officer, angry at Wiedeman's silence, stepped in and kicked him full in the face. A sickening crack rang out as bones shattered, and blood gushed out of his ears and nose and gaping mouth, eyes frozen wide, and he saw no more.

Several men started toward their comrade, but the officer shouted, "Drag him off the road and leave him. His marching days are done!"

The captain ordered the stunned men to move out and make camp on the outskirts of Nikolajew, now 125 kilometers into their march. Supper that night was moldy bread, a wrinkled potato, and thin borscht. It tasted even worse when word passed around camp that another man from a different platoon had also been kicked to death and left by the roadside.

In the dark, John and Georg stretched out on the ground and wrapped up in their blankets. Their minds reeled with the bestial brutality of what they had witnessed, and sleep was far away.

"I can't believe they kicked Wiedeman to death," whispered John, "like a bunch of damned murderers."

"Or make us leave him out there," Georg answered as softly as he could, "like a dead cow."

"I don't know about you," John responded after a long silence, "but I can't take this anymore."

"I know," Georg answered in quiet whisper. "I feel the same way."

"What do you say we pull out."

"Like when?"

"Tonight."

"You mean now?"

"Ja, soon as the camp is asleep."

"You're not serious."

"Never more serious in my life."

"Run? Tonight? What if they catch us?"

"Gotta make sure they don't."

"But how?"

Another long silence, both men thinking, weighing, and calculating.

Finally, after more thinking, John whispered slowly, "In an hour or two, everyone should be out . . . Everybody's tired, even the officers."

"But they got sentries posted."

"Ja, but I'll bet they all got a big gourd of vodka tonight to shut them up about what happened back there."

"We'll have to leave everything."

"We take nothing, just our canteens."

"If we start soon, we'll have quite a few hours before they know we're missing."

"I'm scared. I feel like a kid stealing candy, but I'll go if you go."

Their hearts were pounding so loudly that both were sure the sentries could hear the wild thumping. Their breathing turned short and rapid, and they tried not to blow out any sharp breaths to keep from attracting attention.

The moon, flirting with dark clouds, was a night short of full, and when the long arms of time had finally dragged it up the sky, John carefully rolled back his blanket and rose up on one elbow. Slowly turning and looking around, he saw no one moving. Snores came from different places, but all else seemed quiet.

"Come on," he whispered, "if the sentries stop us, we'll just say we couldn't sleep, and we'll come back."

They got up, and in the dim light took several careful steps around sleeping figures, and headed toward the edge of the camp. Just as John had guessed, the sentries were well vodkafied, out colder than all the rest.

As soon as they were clear of the camp, they picked up the pace, walking, then jogging as long as their bodies would go, along the road they had just traveled a few hours ago. The whole night they moved, meeting no one, stopping only short minutes to catch their breath.

Running on the clear road, John stammered between breaths, "As soon as it's . . . a little light . . . we'll have to get off the road . . . and hit some back roads . . . . They might send some riders looking for us."

At first light, they veered off on wagon roads, still heading west and south. Shortly, they came to a small village that somehow had a familiar look to it, and suddenly, Georg held up his hand and stopped.

"Sh-h-h."

"What?"

"*Gott hilf uns,* God help us. I think I heard somebody talking German."

They followed the sound and quietly walked up to the house, where indeed a man and a woman were speaking German, getting ready for the day.

Georg knocked very softly, trying not to frighten the people inside. Soon the door opened, and a terrified German farmer asked, "*Ja, was wollen Sie,* what do you want?" Their army uniforms told him something terrible was about to befall him and his family.

Quickly explaining what had happened and what they were doing, they asked if the family had some clothes they could have. In minutes, the mother had fixed them a quick breakfast with a tall glass of cool milk, and the man dashed next door and found two sets of clothing that fit well enough to turn them back into bona fide farm men going to work on a relative's farm down the road.

Giving their rescuers a quick hug and "*Gruess Gott,* praise God" and taking the lunch the mother had quickly put together, they set out on a more casual but long-strided walk toward home. Down the road a ways, they turned to look back once more and saw smoke curling from a chimney. Their uniform and army canteen were already ashy history.

"I wonder," Georg said, "if the buttons burned?"

John smiled and picked up the pace, to make them look like workers eager to ply their forks to help their unfortunate uncle.

"If they stop us," Georg wondered, "what do we tell them happened to our uncle?"

"Poor Uncle Friedebert broke his leg falling off a hayrack."

Each German village directed them on to another, and at each, they were led to a house that took them in and fed them. As darkness fell, they spent the evening hours telling their story of army life and how the Russians were treating their comrades. In a number of villages, their hosts called in some neighbors, all equally disgusted with the treatment being given to their people. The response of a number of fathers was, "I'm taking my family and getting out of this land as quick as I can. We have to get to Amerika before our sons are pulled in too."

Several times, along the way, a small unit of mounted troops went by them. Thankfully, they were usually moving at full gallop, raising a cloud of dust. These arrogant henchmen of St. Petersburg—"army crooks," the German settlers called them—came down the middle of the road and anyone who didn't move out of their way felt the sting of their whips as they flew by.

One unit slowed down and gave the two walkers a long stare.

John looked at the ground, heart pounding thunder in his ears, and, moving his lips as little as he could, whispered, "Keep walking, look down, don't slow up."

Georg's bladder was on the edge of letting go, and he couldn't breathe but kept moving in the tall grass alongside the dusty road.

"Ja, Ja," he muttered through clenched teeth, afraid to look up.

Finally, the soldiers spurred their horses, yelling over their shoulders, "Stupid dirty farmers," and galloped on.

"*Gott im Himmel*, God in heaven," said Georg, finally taking a deep breath, his whole body now trembling in relief, "I haven't been that scared since the teacher caught me peeking in the girl's outhouse in school."

"Ja," John replied, "that was too close."

After eight days of steadily heading west and south, staying well clear of Odessa, then west around the long arm of Dniester Liman, they reached home. Klostitz had never looked so good. John shook Georg's hand, and they each headed for their own home. Even the dogs in John's neighborhood remembered him and barked with tail-wagging recognition.

Knowing that his presence would be a shock, he knocked on the door of his parents' house, and as Brother Gottfried's wife, Mina, answered the door, she let out a short, surprised yell, "*Ach, Lieber*

Gott, dear God" and dropped the plate she was holding. Her face turned an instant white as if an ancient ghost had blown rancid breath in her face. Gottfried came rushing to the door, afraid it might be the dreaded Russian police, and reached out to pull John into his arms. Quickly pulling him inside and slamming the door, he ran off a string of questions: "But what are you doing here . . . ? Why are you home . . . ? What happened . . . ? Are you all right?"

John was desperate to see his beloved, but for now he just nodded his head and collapsed on a chair.

Chapter 24

Letter #4 from America

In America, Sister Katherina was becoming increasingly concerned about the prospects of her family obtaining decent homestead land if they were, indeed, planning to emigrate as she hoped they would.

When she picked up a recent issue of their German newspaper, *Der Staats-Anzeiger*, her pulse jumped as she read, "More immigrants are pouring into the area west of Bismarck with each passing week. The railroad cars pulling west are filled with people seeking a better future in the new world. The hard work and thrift of German settlers coming out of the turmoil of present day Russia will do much to change the face of North Dakota, and indeed America, and make it a better place for all of us."

"I'm afraid," she told Adam, "if my parents don't decide soon, it will be too late."

The next week another article followed: "Many thousands are fleeing Russia and settling in western North Dakota, South Dakota, Iowa, Kansas, and as far south as Texas. Still more are choosing to settle in Central Canada and South America. While many are coming to take up the US government's offer of homestead land, others are fleeing the persecution at the hands of Russian authorities who seem to harbor a sense of vengeance against both their German citizens as well as Jews."

One afternoon, Adam walked to the tavern, and when he came home, he was all excited. "There's talk going around about a railroad line being built up here from the south," he told Katherina.

"That would sure change life around here."

"Sure beat the steamboat or the wagon train."

"I just gotta write my parents," she replied. "I don't know how we can convince them to come over here and get away from the trouble back there."

"And they have to move quick if they want any kind of land," Adam added.

****

When Katherina's letter arrived in Klostitz, Mother Karolina panicked, "Something terrible must have happened to the baby. Or maybe the Indians attacked."

Quickly Christian read the letter to the fearful family gathered around the kitchen table:

Lieber Grossvater und Grossmutter,

It has not been long since my last letter to you, but I am very concerned and must write immediately.

The things we hear about life in Russia sound like it will only get worse for you, and you may have to suffer great hurt if you stay there. Please, please think about coming here to be safe.

Every day more people are arriving here, and the good free homestead land is being claimed very fast. Soon only poor land will be available. I beg you to think it over and come here as soon as you can.

Baby Johann is changing every day. I think he will be a big man, like his father. He has dark hair and is just beginning to smile. Those smiles light up my heart.

He is always hungry and never gets full. But at least he sleeps for longer stretches now so I can get some sleep too.

We worry so much about you and are afraid of what might happen to you if you stay there. Again, I beg you to come here and be safe. But remember, things are happening so quick around here that it is terribly important for you to move fast before the best opportunities are gone.

Baby Johann would be so happy to have you hold him and sing to him. We miss you and hope you will come.

Eure Katherina

Chapter 25

Amerika? Dah

John pulled off his shirt and started a quick rinse at the washbasin as Mina tore off her apron and laughed, "I have to get over first and warn Ricka, or she might die of shock!"

"Good idea. Tell her to start puckering. I'll be there in three swishes of a cow's tail!"

When John arrived, Father Boeshans winked at Ricka, took his wife's hand, and walked with her to the neighbor's house. "Let's give the young ones a little time to be alone with each other," he told Mrs. Boeshans.

A flood of tears flowed as Ricka rushed into John's arms and breathed into his ear, "As long as we live, I'll never let you out of my arms again!" They kissed so hard that their mouths hurt, but they couldn't stop. Never in all life had anything felt so good or hurt so sweetly. For a long time, neither moved nor spoke. Kisses were enough.

When John finally pulled his head back, he saw questions written all over Ricka's face so he gently pulled her face to his chest and quickly told her enough details to explain why he was suddenly back home. She asked no questions, letting him swiftly lay out what was on his heart. The rest could come later.

After another long, intense kiss, with their hearts still pounding hard, John said, "Let's go tell your folks to come home, then we'll quick walk to my place and talk more with Gottfried and Mina."

John was still frazzled, afraid that the military police would try to hunt him down and take him in as a deserter, where he'd most likely end up being shot.

"I think we ought to move fast," he said. "Gottfried, are you two still thinking about going to Amerika?"

"Yes, but we haven't done anything about it."

After talking about their options long into the night, John said suddenly, without fanfare, "Ricka, would you want to get married and head out for Amerika?"

Ricka was caught by surprise, but with a happy laugh, she jumped into his lap and squealed, "I thought you'd never ask! You can be so slow!" Once more, with fierce embrace, she kissed him.

In a short while they decided that Ricka and Mina would go to their parents tomorrow and make wedding plans with Reverend Mueller for a small family wedding in two weeks, while John and Gottfried would saddle up at sunrise and ride to Odessa to file for emigration papers. The hundred-kilometer ride would take about two long days.

"We could take the *Eissenbahn*, train," said Gottfried. "It would be easier than riding all that way."

"It sure would," replied John, "but I'm scared about the train. The army might have police on it, looking for some of their missing boys."

"Guess you're right. Not worth taking a chance."

On horseback the next day, they continued reviewing plans. Their younger sisters would stay behind for the time being: one to be married in the near future and another to live with their oldest sister and her husband. Youngest brother, Friedrich, meanwhile, had struck out on his own after their parents left for America and married Natasha, his Russian girlfriend, for which the parents disowned him.

The next months were going to bring a great many changes in the family, and the plan was for all of them to head for America as soon as money could be scraped together to pay their way. Friedrich alone would remain in Russia, much to the regret of the brothers and sisters.

Two days' hard riding brought them to the outskirts of Odessa, where they found a *Gast Haus* and an innkeeper that provided partial directions to get to the Customs Office at the port in the city.

The next morning, they set out to find the Customs Office. Riding through the city to the waterfront, they passed the palatial Primorsky Stairs that stretched almost five hundred feet down to the waters of the Black Sea.

"Remember Herr Goethe told us about those stairs?" Gottfried said, shaking his head at the sight.

"They're even bigger than I thought they'd be," replied John.

Finding a livery, they stabled their horses and walked the long colonnade to the government offices.

Still several streets from the consulate, they encountered a huge line of people. Hearing German being spoken, Gottfried approached one of the men and asked, "What are you lined up for?"

"To get emigration papers."

"Been waiting long?"

"Since this morning. We aren't even close yet. They're in no big hurry in there."

With little hope of getting into the office, the brothers decided to find a room nearby and get there by sunup the next morning.

At first rooster crow from somewhere close by in the city, they were up and by sunrise, stood in the queue at the Customs and Immigration Office of Odessa. Already they were thirtieth in line, with John anxiously looking around for army or police officials who might be looking for AWOL soldiers.

After a frustrating wait, they found themselves across the counter from a rather pompous civil bureaucrat who from his appearance most likely loved his house, his table, and his vodka, in no particular order. His face was locked into a perpetual scowl on which the smile had been frozen off.

When he was done fiddling with his tobacco-stained fingernails, he raised his meaty jowls and lifted his hooded eyelids just far enough to give them a cursory glance through the haze of smoke from his dangling cigarette, his expression saying, "How many of these lousy Germans am I going to have to mess with today?"

He needed no sign to see why they were there or where they wanted to go.

"*Amerika?*"

"Dah, yes."

"*Kahk vahs zavoot,* what's your name?"

"Minyah zavoot, My name is Johannes Oster, O-s-t-e-r."

"*Johannes. In Russian that's Ivan, you know . . . Zhynah,* wife?"

"Dah." *Well,* he thought, *she will be in a few days.*

"*Imya,* name?"

"Fredericka, F-r-e-d-e-r-i-c-k-a."

"*Deetya,* children?"

"Nyet, no."

After a number of added details, John was finished, and Gottfried went through the same procedure. Finally, the process finished, Mr. Scowl collected the entire sheaf of papers, thumped them thrice on his ancient desk to straighten the pages, rifled through them once more and slammed an oversized stamp on six different spots, and then finally showed them where to sign.

"OK, boys," he said, "that's it," and waved them away from the counter.

Before they left, John asked, "Can you tell us how long it might take to get the papers?"

"Usually four to six months."

They came prepared for such an answer, and both reached into their pockets. Each pulled out two five-ruble silver pieces, and reaching across the counter to shake Scowl's hand, each slipped the two fives into his palm as well.

"Any chance it could be worked out a little faster than that?" asked Gottfried.

Suddenly, Mr. Scowl, with the biggest smile they had seen in the entire Customs Office, reached down for the stack of papers, thumped them six times with a second stamp, and replied, "You should have the papers in about a month. Two at the most."

"*Spasiba,* thank you," John offered, returning the smile.

"*Spasiba balshoye,* thanks a lot!" Gottfried added with a nod and a slight bow.

Walking outside, they both continued to keep a sharp eye out for teams of army or police. John had hoped that the bloated Russian bureaucracy would continue their ways of not letting the left hand know what the right was doing, and thus had not gotten any lists of AWOL soldiers to the Customs Office or port authorities, much less to the regional authorities around home. So far it appeared that he was right.

Then, casually looking back, they noticed two soldiers fall in behind them, maybe ten steps back, watching them with animated conversation.

John's mind nearly exploded as he sucked in his breath and whispered, "Oh no."

"Let's turn the corner up here," he continued, trying to appear calm.

Making a left turn, they kept walking, trying to look interested in store display windows. Gottfried glanced out of the corner of his eye and stammered, "They're s-still coming."

John's forehead ran beads of sweat, and his armpits put out musk. He saw himself filthy dirty, bound in chains, beaten to death with fence posts by guards whose fangs dripped blood, and heard himself screaming for mercy until all screaming ceased.

"Let's turn right at the next street," Gottfried said, even more nervous as he saw John's eyes, wide with terror, "and if they're still following, maybe we can walk into a store and go out the back."

"Ja, if we're lucky. Maybe we can get to our horses and get out of town before they catch up with us."

At the corner, they turned right and walked past several stores. Slowing down to look into a store window, they glanced back and saw the soldiers, still busy in conversation, going down the previous street and away from them.

"*Danket dem Herrn,* Thank the Lord," said John, letting out a huge, whistling sigh of relief. "I don't know when I've ever been that scared in my whole life."

He wiped sweat off his forehead, and Gottfried noticed that his hands were shaking like tall prairie grass in a north wind.

"Hurry up," Gottfried said, "let's get to the horses before anybody around here gets ideas."

As they started riding, they noticed the majestic 150-foot spire of St. Paul's Lutheran Church, not far away, stretching into the Odessa sky. Reverend Mueller had fired their imaginations about this splendid new church as they were growing up.

"I know we have to get out of here," John said, "but I think we should stop at St. Paul's Church and thank the Lord again."

When they got to Lyuteranski Prospekt, Lutheran Street, they saw the church just two blocks ahead, and quickly tethering their horses, they climbed the long flight of outside steps leading into the church.

Stepping quietly into the beautifully ornate church, with its majestic vaulted arches, lit only by the dim light coming through the long, stained glass sanctuary windows, they were awestruck by the magnificent, gold-trimmed baroque altar of white marble. Now it was softly colored by radiant reds and blues and yellows from the stained glass windows of the apse, portraying Jesus along with the Gospel writers: Matthew, Mark, Luke, and John.

"Boy, it almost feels like you can reach out and touch God here," whispered John as the stillness surrounded them.

"Seems like Jacob's ladder reaching up to heaven," Gottfried whispered back as he looked up, awed by the immense height of the huge sanctuary.

In the reverence of this holy place, the dreaded police seemed continents away.

Kneeling in a pew, both men prayed the most fervent "thank you" prayers of their lives. John coughed as tears ran down his cheeks. "Oh God, thank you, thank you," he breathed over and over again.

Treading on silent soles, they turned to walk out, and looking up, they were astounded by the brilliantly decorated ranks of pipes on the huge rococo organ in the rear balcony above them.

"Ei," John whispered, "a little different than our little St. Johannes at home."

Carefully closing the great ten-foot-high outer door, they returned to the horses, mounted up, and broke into a slow gallop heading out of town. They rode in silence, but as they reached the open countryside, they could not contain their ebullience, and both let out a whoop that could be heard for half a kilometer.

"I can't believe it," shouted John, riding close to his brother and punching him on the arm hard enough to knock Gottfried askew in his saddle.

"What a day! God is watching over us," replied Gottfried, "that's for sure!"

Both pulled their caps down and settled into the saddle for the long ride home to Klostitz; John couldn't get there fast enough.

Chapter 26

Letter #5 from America

Dear Brothers and Sisters,

We are so thankful to God that Papa and Mamma and Anna arrived here safely. They are living with us for now until their house is finished. It is crowded in our house, but they are enjoying little Johann, and it is good for him too.

Papa made the long trip to Bismarck (that's like Klostitz to Odessa) with some neighbor men and bought some machines to start up a shoe and harness business. There is a lot of work, and people are already calling him almost every day to fix things or make something for them. My Adam is helping him build a small shed behind the new house for his shop. Building a house and shed is keeping them busy. A carpenter is helping them some, but the rest they are doing themselves.

I hope John is getting along all right in the Army. I still think it is not right for the tsar to draft our men into the Army, but what can anyone do?

Every week another family is coming from Klostitz or other Russian villages to live here in Krem. It seems like all of Russia is moving here. We can hardly keep up with learning names as new houses are getting built in every part of town. Of course, there is plenty of room here. There are also many people taking up homestead land west of here.

Mamma and Papa said that the rest of you are also thinking of coming here. I hope you do. This country is so peaceful and full of hope and people are so good to each other. Now we have our own school and a Lutheran church with our own pastor, so we have everything we need right here. Mamma and Anna and I baked some prune and some custard kuchen yesterday, and we have it almost eaten up. The men are always hungry and never seem to get enough sweet stuff. It is nice to see them happy when they are working so hard.

Your sister,
Katherina

Chapter 27

How Big Is This Ocean?

Gottfried and John were overjoyed when they finally saw Klostitz in the distance and, spurring their horses, rode in at full gallop.

After hugs, Mina had some bad news.

"Word came here that the Wiedemans, in the next *dorf*, are on the warpath."

"Why?" Gottfried asked.

"'Cause they think John should have helped their son when the Russian officers kicked him to death."

"What?" John shouted. "What do they think I could have done?"

"Well, they think the rest of you should have stepped in and saved him."

"I just hope the idiots don't go to the police and tell them I'm here, or I'll be dead."

That thought left a lump in every throat and a new urgency to get things done. The next three weeks were a furious blur of activity as the Boeshans family orchestrated a beautiful short-notice wedding for Fredericka and John. Then Gottfried and John made arrangements to sell the parental Oster house, family home for the better part of the 1800s, to an elderly couple and all the family animals to neighbors. The sturdy milk cows and hardworking horses, each with a precious name of its own, the pigs, rabbits, a few sheep, chickens, geese, were all petted, fed once more, and neighbors came by, one by one, to lead them away. "Schepp," faithful dog and family friend, brought tears to the family's eyes as another neighbor came with a wagon and loaded him up, puzzled and bewildered, on the way to a home he didn't know and where he didn't want to go.

For these brief weeks, John and Ricka continued to live at the Oster house, along with Gottfried and his wife and the two younger sisters. It was a houseful, but John and Ricka were more wonderfully happy than they could ever have imagined. Soon, so soon, they would be in a new world, living a whole new life.

"Ei," Ricka cried in exasperation, "everything is such a *verhoodle*, tangled mess."

After one of those frenzied days, John and Ricka needed a moment alone and went walking in the dark through the silent village streets they had known all their lives. A sudden moment of loneliness struck John as he thought of how soon all these familiar sights and smells would be only distant memories. Walking hand in hand, they were both enraptured by the great expanse of stars above them. Stopping for a moment, Ricka sought out the Big Bear and the bright North Star, asking, "Johnny, do you think we'll see our North Star in Amerika too?"

"I hope so. It would be a nice way to sort of tie our old life and our new life all together, wouldn't it?"

After several agonizing weeks, a courier arrived with their passports and emigration visas. To their surprise and relief, everything was in order. Early the next morning Gottfried boarded the train for Odessa to buy passage to America for the four of them. Before he left, they had decided that it could be dangerous for John to go along, since the army might still be looking for him, so Gottfried would go alone. With the sale of the house, their meager furniture, and the animals, together with John's carefully hoarded, puny military pay, Gottfried had enough money for tickets and some left over to begin life in America.

Next day, he was back, and all the tickets were secured. As Gottfried walked in the door, he held up the package of tickets and shouted, "October 29, our Lord's year, 1902, will be a good day indeed!" They had space reserved on the steamship, *S. S. Armenia*, for its next passage to America.

In a moment the whole house was in an uproar as all jumped, hugged, cried, laughed, and shouted, all talking, no one listening. They were about to face life-altering changes!

The following days were spent getting two round-topped steamer trunks, one for each couple, and making the terrible decisions of what to take and what to leave behind.

Mina and Ricka both folded their favorite dresses, including their black wedding dresses, which they could also wear in America for church and for funerals. They carefully packed featherbeds, winter coats, doilies, lace handkerchiefs, and embroidered sets of dish towels, some cherished gifts from Mothers and from their weddings, and some items they had made themselves for their "hope chests." Stockings, underclothes, white gloves, bonnets, crocheted shawls all went into the drawer that would fit on top just before the cover was closed. Black lace-up dress shoes went in. Their Bibles, catechisms, and the hymnals they had received from their parents as confirmation gifts were slid into corners.

And there were arguments! The men wanted to take tools, but the women wanted to take more cooking utensils and extra clothes. Finally, with most of the disputed items left behind, the trunks were locked, tearful farewells finished, and they boarded the train for Odessa.

The small port was a virtual anthill of screaming, cursing, shoving, anxious humanity. Before they were allowed to board, each was put through a free, perfunctory medical exam conducted by steamship doctors, the reason for which was rather simple: any immigrants who were turned back or rejected at Ellis Island had to be returned to their place of origin, free of charge, by the steamship company.

Finally, they were put aboard a rusty Greek freighter, stopping again at Yevpatoriya (Eupatoria), Crimea, for more supplies, then a five-day sail out through the Black Sea, across the sparkling Mediterranean, up Europe's Atlantic coast, and docking at Hamburg, Germany. Hamburg's modern dock held the *Armenia,* which would be their fifteen-day home across the fearsome Atlantic.

The port was filled with a number of steamers, flying the flags of the world. Beside the rows of steamers were giant derricks loading tons of coal and great sling-nets of supplies, their gangplanks sucking in thousands of people and every imaginable form of freight, from cows to whiskey to French designer clothes and sable-fur hats from Russia for America's elite.

The *Armenia,* at 5,500 tons and 390 feet long, was a very average steamer. Her fiery coal boilers breathed through just one funnel and turned her great single bronze screw to plow the Atlantic's waves at fourteen knots an hour.

Gottfried led their party of four on board, all filled with an immense sense of excitement, picturing their wonderful new life and being reunited with their parents and sisters. But reality would soon be painted with a wholly different palette of colors.

They were immediately ushered down two sets of stairs, into the bowels of the ship, to what was euphemistically called "steerage." It might more properly have been called the ship's basement, below the waterline. A ship's steward stood at the bottom of the stairs separating them, men and boys to the huge right-hand room, women and children to the left.

As their eyes began to adjust to the dim light, Ricka quickly noticed the stifling, low ceilings, and looking around at the walls, exclaimed, "There are no portholes. We can't see out at all."

"And no doors or windows," added Mina, "to let in fresh air."

"Oh, man, there are no rooms down here," was all John could get out. "This is like the army barracks again!"

"We're in trouble now," whispered Gottfried. "This is *not* what the girls wanted!"

The four had reservations, but to their great dismay, they discovered that only meant they had a bunk assigned, one of 550 double-deck bunks arranged in two rows along the outer edge of the two large rooms, with two more rows down the middle of each. These two rooms lay side by side in the back half of the ship, each 150 feet long and barely 20 feet wide. A row of five weak new electric light bulbs ran down the center of each room, putting out dim yellow light that stayed on day and night. Mattresses were single-bed-sized sacks filled with oldish straw that gave off fine dust, enough to choke on as passengers sat on them. On each bunk lay one blanket to cover up and a life jacket that doubled as pillow.

Their trunks had been loaded a deck further down, so all they had were their canvas bags of food, a few toiletries, and one change of clothing.

"Where do we store our bags?" asked Mina after they found their numbered bunk.

"You put them on your bunk," snapped a woman already in place, "and when you sleep, you put them down on the floor at the foot of your bunk."

"But aren't there bugs?" inquired Ricka.

"Who knows? Who knows."

"If there are, what can we do?" added another voice nearby.

Mina had just recently discovered that she was pregnant, so wishing not to strain herself too much, she claimed the lower bunk, while Ricka slowly climbed into the upper. Both curled up on their fluffed-up old straw and wept bitterly.

After a few minutes, Ricka dried her tears, but her sister was still softly sobbing. It brought to Ricka's mind a heartbroken ancient lament that poured out of the souls of a captured Jewish people carried off to bloodthirsty Babylon. She climbed down and taking Mina in her arms, softly whispered, "Do you remember that Psalm we learned in confirmation, Psalm 137?" And quietly she recalled those haunting words which eternally resonate with suffering people of every time and every place:

> "By the waters of Babylon we sat down and wept
>   when we remembered Zion.
> We hung our harps upon the willow trees.
> Our captors demanded of us a song,
> But how can we sing a song to the Lord
>   in a foreign land?"

"How can we sing about this, dear Lord?" Mina muttered softly. "How!"

"The Lord is strong. He'll see us through!"

Their announced departure time was 16:00 hours on this fourth day of November. By 15:45, they heard muffled metallic sounds as the heavy gangplanks were cranked back to the dock and the mooring lines cast off from bow, mid-ships, and stern.

Soon the harbor was filled with a low, penetrating "Wu-u-u-u-u" hanging in the air as the *Armenia's* captain ordered the ship's great steam whistle sounded for a full ten seconds. Two minutes more, and promptly at 4:00 p.m. all on board could feel a slight shuddering as tugs slowly eased the ship out of its berth and into the harbor. Now the funnel belched thick black smoke as the steam turbines cranked power to the twelve-foot screw, and it began to churn Elbe River and soon North Sea water.

For the Oster party, as for all the steerage-class passengers, there would be no storied standing at the rail, waving fond farewells. There was only profound silence as one thousand and one hundred steerage passengers, crowded together in two stifling rooms, were each left to wonder just what the coming days would hold.

Once the ship was underway, passengers could move around so the men walked over to the women's side and sought out their wives. Ricka and Mina both jumped into their husband's arms and broke into tears.

"We're never going to make it through this," sobbed Mina.

"Oh yes, we will. It'll be rough, but we have each other," replied her husband, bravely trying to sound reassuring.

Other couples also found each other, some weeping, others laughing, and some singing old songs that brought back memories of happy days gone by.

As John held Ricka, he heard one of their favorite songs and hummed along. After they all relaxed a bit, he held her at arm's length for a moment and with a smile announced, "You know, I'm really getting hungry. We got anything to eat in our bag?"

Their fifteen-dollar ticket each for passage was serious money— for the average working man the princely sum of two months' pay. Many an immigrant could not raise that money and had it sent by some benefactor in America for whom he then had to work as an indentured servant until it was paid off.

That fifteen-dollar ticket also included no food. With no dining hall for steerage, all passengers were required to bring all their own food for the entire voyage. So now the women opened their canvas bags and spread out their first on-board supper: dried sausage, black bread, cheese, and some dried prunes for sweets to finish it off. They would save the boiled eggs, dried figs, and brick of halvah for later days. Each item was carefully rationed, to have enough to last the entire voyage. Sitting cramped together on Mina's bunk, they bravely made the best of it until John wryly observed, "Well, the first-class passengers are walking around up on deck right now, sipping Cognac and watching the land of our fathers fade away."

"But are they really having a better time than we are?" asked Ricka, trying to bring a little cheer to their meager feast.

"I hate to say it, but maybe they are," replied Mina.

"But I'll bet they aren't any happier than we are!" added John with a smile, and with that, they were all moved to laugh. Suddenly, the ship's dark hold didn't seem quite as dark as before.

By the second day of sailing, the routine of the ship had settled into place, and steerage passengers were allowed on deck. But their assigned deck was the lower back third of the ship, which caught a strong amount of swirling fumes and fine sooty ash from the smokestack, making it disagreeable, even irritable. Fifteen minutes on deck and many passengers began coughing and wiping runny noses. But at least they could see the sky and soak in a bit of salt air and glory in the vastness of the ocean. Some smoked, some chewed snuff and enjoyed spitting wads over the railing, watching it catch air and sail. Others chewed little bags full of sunflower seeds.

By now the rolling ocean also rolled the ship with it. Mina felt ill in the morning and now the added rolling suddenly turned her stomach. She jumped up from her bunk and headed for the toilet, Ricka racing right behind her. A few feet before she got there, her stomach convulsed, and she vomited in huge splashes. The aisle between bunks was splattered, her clothes were splattered, and the stench was awful. Several nearby women grabbed a scrawny mop from the latrine and tried to clean it up, but did little good. Mina made it to the toilet, embarrassed, even more sick, smelling awful, and threw up twice more. Ricka put her arm around her shoulders and supported her while she cried all the way back to her bunk. She would spend most of the rest of the voyage in that bunk.

She tried to reach the toilet on time, but there was only one located at the far end of each of the two rooms, four toilets for one thousand one hundred people, each with two sinks and three stools. There would be no baths on this voyage. Worse yet, there would be many more accidents and considerable seasickness, each one adding a bit more to the overpowering stench that hung like moldy garbage in a smoke-filled room. Add to that the smell of sweaty bodies putting out sour odors, latrines overflowing with bloodied women's items, copious amounts of garlic (Germanic medicine for all seasons) consumed and belched out, food of all sorts starting to go bad, infant diapers changed, and a picture emerges of truly revolting, nauseating overload. Multiply that by two days of sleet-driven North Atlantic winter storms, the ship pitching and yawing, and things got to the point where even the dingy deck with stack gases swirling seemed a relief. The several hours when each group was allowed up top to walk and flex their bodies transported them just to the east of

Eden. Out of Eden, certainly, but close enough to buoy their spirits for a little while. The constant cloud of smoke shrouding steerage below, especially on the men's side, was enough to gag the stoutest of heart until even the soot on the deck felt good.

John, always curious, had been talking to a steward, and later one afternoon as the four were walking on the frigid deck, he remarked, "You know, this ship only has room for twenty first-class passengers."

"Guess it isn't a champagne cruise," replied Ricka.

"Yeah, it's a borscht run," he laughed.

"We're not much more than some rich ship-owner's cows!" lamented a disheartened Mina.

Of the 1,100 steerage passengers, 137 were Germans bailing out of their settlements in Russia. The rest came directly from Germany and a dozen other nations, with languages and dialects that made steerage a constant carnival of sound.

Days were spent with little groups gathered telling tales of their experiences with the Russians, singing hymns and sentimental songs of home, playing cards, laughing, shouting, retelling stories the grandfathers told about pioneer life in Russia, and occasionally screaming in outrage when someone crossed some invisible line that another had drawn.

Nights they took off their shoes and slept in all their clothes, wrapped in their blankets. Prayers rose out loud from many a bunk and many more silently from a host of others. This hole of a place was not good, but it was leading to glory. They didn't dare let go of that wondrous hope.

"How big is this miserable ocean anyway?" cried Mina when they reached their bunks.

Sunday, November 9, dawned crisp and cold, but Captain Falk had announced a brief worship service on their deck, and it was crowded on the sooty planks. They huddled shoulder to shoulder against the icy cold. With a booming baritone voice, the captain read several Scripture passages in German, beseeched the Almighty's blessing on ship and man, led them in the Lord's Prayer, and with a final "Amen" it was over.

The following Thursday was a heavy day. One of the infants on board had died, and they gathered on deck again for an agonizing funeral. The crushed mother wailed at losing her child and her hope and finally would not let it go when the officers reached to place it on the "death plank" to slide it over the side and commit it to the sea. Her husband and the captain both wrapped their arms around her shoulders, spoke gently and lovingly to her, and finally she let the dreaded act be finished, turning her back so she didn't have to see the awful thing take place. That moment lived in the memory of every person present that day, and they would tell it in every village they'd inhabit.

The next day Gottfried and Mina sought out the distraught parents and tried to console them. He briefly shared the heartbreaking road their family had walked when Aunt Natalia's little boy had died and how hard it was for her. It didn't end the mother's grief, but at least she knew that here were kindred spirits that understood her bitter suffering in this lonely hour.

Several more people died from various causes on that voyage. It was a sad part of life.

Wednesday, November 19, they berthed for half a day in Halifax, Nova Scotia, and the next day they sailed past the magnificent 305-foot Statue of Liberty and docked in New York's bustling harbor. John and Ricka breathed a silent prayer of thanks to God, as did many a believing soul on board. The beautiful statue, "Mother of Exiles" as some called her, was only a teenager, barely sixteen years old, but already she was the majestic symbol of hope to all who experienced her. The whole ship crowded to see her, to feel her magnetic welcome, to hug each other and rejoice at the privilege of being able to reach this magic moment and join the great host of "huddled masses yearning to breathe free." A great many of these steerage folk had walked the harsh road of heartbreak much of their life. These were "the tired, the poor," the oppressed and downtrodden, the left out and left behind ones whom she beckoned. For them the flaming torch of Lady Liberty was much more than alluring sculpted metal as they now arrived by the boatload at her door. A thunderous shout arose, every throat exploded with joy, and hearts even out here on harbor water already felt at home. Joyous tears streamed down many a face, and their dancing was infused with new life as they beheld Liberty "lifting her lamp beside the golden door."

Chapter 28

America the Frozen

The exhilaration over the statue waxed thin, however, when they were unloaded and ferried to the noisy confusion of Ellis Island to be processed into America. Before disembarking, all were given an inspection card listing their name, age, sex, birthday, place of origin, preliminary medical condition, and final destination. Now they were taken to the main floor of the immigration building for cursory medical exams. With two thousand people to be checked that day—some days up to three thousand—everything had to be done quickly. Some doctors were stationed on the balconies looking for obvious defects or strange behavior among the throng, while more were stationed at dozens of tables to check for a range of contagious diseases, mental illness, and dreaded trachoma, eye disease.

From here they were ushered, thirty at a time, up the stairs to the great Registry Hall for final processing. This stage also included a battery of twenty-nine questions, including among other things, whether they had ever been in prison, in an almshouse (poor house), or had been a polygamist or anarchist. "Why'd they want to know all that stuff?" Gottfried wondered out loud.

Going through this immense swarm of activity, with ears tuned to sounds around him, John commented, "Did you notice how many of those inspectors and doctors spoke a whole bunch of languages?"

"I asked one," replied Gottfried, "and he said he spoke seven different languages. And he wished he knew more."

Five endless hours later, they were finished and moved on to Money Exchange, to turn their rubles into dollars, and then to the Railway Ticket Office to purchase fare to their American destination: New Salem, North Dakota.

Now, reunited again with their trunks, they were shuttled to the rail station to finish the final leg of their lengthy journey. After finding the right train, they found a bite to eat, boarded the train, and soon heard the conductor shout his hearty, "All 'bort." They didn't understand this new language in their new land, but the bustling around them seemed to say, "We're moving out!"

They had heard lot of Russian and German being spoken, but they had no way of knowing that as part of the 1,900,000 immigrants from Russia, they would be the largest of all groups to arrive during these years in America, second only to Italy's 2.5 million going through the Ellis Island facility. The Ellis Immigration Center was a scant ten years old, but already it was playing a vital role in America's future and in the future of many of its citizens in coming times.

Four days and four nights, they rode the hypnotizing rails, watching their new country speed by as the thick black train-smoke trailed past their windows. They ate, slept propped up against each other on the hard slat benches, prayed, and wondered about their new home. Sitting on the hard wooden seats, Mina's back began to ache until she could hardly stand it, but she tried her best not to show it. Walking in the aisle helped, but only for a little while.

"You know what I like best about this train?" asked Ricka.

"What?" Mina wondered.

"Two toilets at the end of every car!"

"And I like the good smell on here. No stink! Isn't it wonderful?" replied Mina.

They laughed, but all shared in feeling huge relief from the misery of the awful stench on board the *Armenia,* a smell they would remember to the end of their days.

Through Pennsylvania they rolled, Ohio, through the jumbled stockyards of Chicago, and on ever westward. In Minneapolis, they lay over in the depot for the train to the frontier and saw a pair of cities in their infancy. Soon after that, the landscape turned to frontier as evidence of human population became more scarce with every hour on the thumping rails. Cropland became more plentiful again through the flat plain of the Red River Valley, but climbing out into the rolling hill country, they were taken aback by the miles and miles of nothing but wild, dried-up prairie grasses bravely poking through the snow.

"Look," said John, waving his arm in an arc, "there are absolutely no trees here."

"And the farms look awfully poor," added Gottfried.

It was a somber moment until Mina chuckled, "Not much flowing milk and honey either."

In that stark instant, they all realized that this magic land would not be coming to them begging to pour all things bountiful into their laps. What became of them here, and how life would treat them, would depend on them rolling up their sleeves and applying themselves with every ounce of their being, willing often to forgo common pleasures and soft tranquility and denying themselves many a creature comfort just to survive.

The further west they rolled, the smaller the cultivated fields became. Some farms had wooden houses; some still had sod houses with several more sod buildings for animals. This was not the cultivated Russia of home. This was the frontier in all its bleakness. As they stared out of the train windows, ever pointing west, conversation became less and less enthusiastic.

Mina's swelling discomfort grew ever more intense, along with a rolling sense of homesickness. "Oh, Gottfried," she begged, clutching tightly to his arm, "I hope we didn't make a big mistake!" He looked at her pale visage and could not bring himself to utter any lighthearted words of encouragement. All he could do was hug her tight and look back out at the frozen, snow-covered prairie grasses sliding by the window.

It also didn't help that their first experience of this new land happened in late November, the bleakest, darkest time in North Dakota. Heavy, swirling storm clouds swept the frozen layer of snow covering everything they could see, few animals were about, and no people to be seen anywhere along their route. One farmer in a wagon stopped at a rail crossing as they passed by and cheerily waved to the train, but that was scant comfort in introducing them to what was supposed to feel like home and didn't. This frozen tundra was far from the Promised Land, the virtual paradise of which they had dreamed and Katherina had pictured in her letters. Would they survive this harsh land? No one spoke it, but suddenly, it did not seem an idle question.

At a distance from the train, small houses dotting the prairies showed chimneys hoisting white smoke into the frigid winter air, prompting Mina's further discomfort: "How are they staying alive here in all that cold, and what are they burning for fire if there aren't any trees?" A question no one could answer, but causing several nearby passengers to cough in discomfort as well. Several train cars were filled with New Salem-bound passengers, and many were beginning to ask themselves if this was indeed the greatest move they could have made, or the worst.

Gradually, the train windows began to freeze over until they could no longer see out. Ricka and Mina felt claustrophobia set in. For the men, the frozen windows turned off the visual misery and left them with cheerier thoughts of soon meeting their loved ones again.

"I don't know," Mina whimpered, "but I think they should call this 'America, the frozen.'"

Some of the passengers laughed, but it was a hollow laugh.

Several more stops in small stations for coal and water, and before long, the rhythm of the chugging train began to slow. Its piercing whistle shrilled across the prairies, and the conductor came through announcing, "Next stop, New Salem." Then, with a jaunty smile, he added, "For some of you this is home!"

At the word "home," Mina's heart sank. She couldn't hold back the tears, softly crying, "Are we home or are we in hell?"

Chapter 29

There's No Sound Out Here

New Salem had 353 souls and a Main Street. That carefully platted street ran east and west alongside the railroad and hard on the trail of the immigrant wagons forging west. New Salem touted itself as "The Little Princess of the Northern Pacific Line." Its city newspaper proudly hailed it, "The most progressive city west of the Missouri River."

The jewel in its diadem was the stately Salem Hotel. Its Eastern investors, aware of the exploding land boom in the area, widely advertised the region's excellent game hunting for prospective, well-heeled Eastern and European sportsmen, and the city as a rail hub for the flooding tide of immigrants. And in the center of this cornucopia was their prairie showpiece.

The ultramodern Salem included the advanced technologies of electricity and running water, with indoor plumbing. Since the town yet had no electricity, they built a small generating plant of their own, big enough to power the hotel and several adjacent businesses on Main Street.

As the new settlers stepped off the train platform and took their first steps on North Dakota soil, they were struck by a cold blast of air that almost took their breath away. Clouds of breath hung in front of every face. They could not have picked a worse time to arrive here—except maybe December or January or February.

But all that was quickly forgotten when they saw Father Christian and Brother-in-Law, Adam, waiting nearby to greet them. All of them ran into a jumbled group hug, so totally happy to see each other again.

Father Christ stood tall, belying his years. At sixty-two, he had already outlived the average life span of the time by fifteen years. His full beard was streaked with more white than when he left Russia two years ago. Now it was also flecked with tiny icicles, with his breath freezing on his face.

He and Adam were both wearing ankle-length, long-haired, buffalo-hide coats, black and heavy. Their tall, stand-up collars could be pulled up to cover most of their face. Heavy rabbit-fur caps with earflaps folded down and tied around the chin. Fur-lined leather mittens with long leather gauntlets covered their wrists when they were holding the reins to drive. They were a picture of Eskimos come to Dakota.

After the stationhands unloaded the trunks from the train to the station platform, Adam pulled the sled around, loaded trunks and bags, and all six climbed aboard. Since it was mid-afternoon, too late to start the long two-day journey home, they drove to the Salem Hotel, where a young bellhop met them. He was splendidly dressed in a fire-red, brass-buttoned jacket with gold braid on shoulders and sleeves, flat-topped matching red bellboy hat set at a rakish angle and held snugly in place with a gold chin strap.

To their surprise, he addressed them in their own tongue as he loaded all their belongings on several luggage carts and hauled them inside.

The desk clerk, at their request, set them up with three rooms.

As Gottfried filled in the forms, Mina turned to him, "Oh, Gottfried, that bed is going to feel like heaven tonight."

"I think any bed would."

Christ and Adam would share a regular room, with bath at end of hall, for fifty cents.

John and Gottfried decided to splurge on their wives after the harsh times they had so bravely endured. They spent an additional quarter each and got "Empire Rooms" on the second floor, with private bathrooms.

While the desk clerk pointed the two single men to their room down the hall, the bellboy picked up some of John's and Gottfried's heavy bags and led them toward the second-floor stairs, calling over his shoulder, "I'll bring the rest up in a few minutes."

Ceremoniously unlocking the first door, he pointed the four newcomers inside.

With a slight, knowing smile, he pushed a button on the wall, and the room exploded in instant light.

"*Euer licht,* your light," he announced.

"Just look at that," Ricka delighted. "It's like a miracle."

"Guess I can throw my matches away," John replied.

"And God said, 'Let there be light,'" Gottfried added, as the thought popped into his mind.

They had seen the bright lights on shipboard and on Ellis Island, and now they were fascinated to see how they were switched on.

The bellhop had made the impression he wanted and now squared his shoulders and led them into the spacious bathroom.

Without a word, he reached up toward a white ceramic box on the wall and pulled a fobbed chain, releasing a scary whoosh of water into the white ceramic commode.

"That thing could suck you right down," said a startled Mina stepping back, even though they had been introduced to indoor plumbing on the *Armenia.*

With an all-knowing smile, the bellhop turned away, and Mina rolled her eyes as John looked at her and shook his head.

The bellhop, clearly enjoying himself, next stepped over to the huge, five-foot-long white enameled, cast-iron bathtub.

"*Heisz,* hot," he said, turning the left knob and pointing to the gushing water. "*Kalt,* cold," he added twirling the right.

"Bigger than any I've ever sat in, that's for sure," beamed Ricka.

"Look at those nice legs," Mina embarrassed the bellhop, but she was pointing down at the bronze lion's claw feet on the tub. "I feel like I'm in the African jungle."

"You're gonna be as fancy as the tsarina," Gottfried laughed.

Finished with his initiation, the young bellhop walked to the door and stood facing them. In the strained silence that followed, no one knew quite what to say, until the men finally caught on and each gave him a nickel tip for his efforts. He squared his shoulders, raised his chin, and walked out of the room.

The gesture was not lost on them, and as he closed the door, John muttered, "The damned little general."

"Guess he figures we're just simple Russians," Gottfried added, trying to diffuse John's irritation.

"Maybe we should go down get something to eat," Mina said, her little passenger seemingly kicking for food.

The hotel menu featured esoteric delights for the elite who passed that way. But it also included familiar *fleisch kuechle* so they felt right at home. Hot *knoepfle soup* and strong coffee never tasted so good.

After supper, both women grabbed their husbands' arms and hurried upstairs. Squealing with delight, they ran back and forth to each other's rooms.

"Isn't this just the most fun," Ricka laughed, "that you've ever had in your whole life?"

"I feel like the tsarina's sister, come for her first visit," Mina replied.

In minutes, they settled into their own rooms and quickly undressed, ready to climb into the comforting womb of hot, soothing water.

For Ricka, the first thing was washing her hair in the sink. She undid the bun and shook her head, letting her waist-length, silky tresses unfold. John watched it sensuously slide down her back, curling like the snake of Eden, inviting him to eat. As she bent over the sink, working her hair, all her luscious, freed-up curves bounced in fluid motion.

"Oh, Ricka . . .," John stammered, heart hammering, breath coming in short gasps, and couldn't finish the sentence.

She turned her head and, with a smile, slowly winked at him, her teasing almost turning him insane, and gloried in the moment. *This is such fun,* she thought, beaming brighter than the bulb in the ceiling.

Finished with her hair, she cooed, "Can you help me into the tub?"

He lifted her lithe body, kissing her neck, and felt an animal inside him tearing at its leash and wanting out, but knew how much she was anticipating this bath. As he slowly lowered her into this dew of heaven, she surrendered to the soul-renewing waters recharging everything within her.

She let out a long sigh of joyous celebration as she reveled in the luxury of that cleansing. After three weeks of no baths, with hair gone total grubby, she felt dirty inside as well as out. Now in this healing pool of Siloam, she felt clean even from the distasteful dirt inside.

Glancing to the foot of the tub, she noticed a vial of vanilla-scented bath oil and poured it in. After several swishes in the water, she was enveloped in such rich, aromatic bubbles that she felt transported to a distant paradise. Minutes of this decadence felt like an unforgettable season spent with the Queen of Sheba herself.

"Oh, Solomon," she demurely whispered.

"What?" John asked, puzzled, as the remark sailed right over him. He knelt beside the tub, totally enthralled by the delicious sight of his new bride. Letting his eyes feast on her at bathtime proved a never-ending delight. Now his excitement triggered raging juices with the zing of a summer lightning storm crashing up and down his body. Hearing her splash and giggle in pure delight, like a schoolgirl after the last bell, cranked his heart to pounding passion.

Softly splashing bubbly water over her and gently caressing every curve of her wet body took him to heaven. Teasing her with smiley tickles made angels sing. The aroma of each other suddenly became more alluring than the rich bath oil. Their hearts raced faster than they had ever known, even on their wedding night, which seemed so long ago.

Ricka's face flushed with the electric force of desire rising through her body. Slowly, she raised one leg sensuously out of the water, toes extended, lowered it back into the steaming water, and seductively raised it once more, waving like a scarlet battle flag calling for an all-out charge against the cannon. She gazed into John's rapturous face, and seeing the hunger in his eyes, caressed his chin and floated her fingertips like a butterfly across his eyelids. Brushing her tongue over her upper lip, she fluttered her eyes and broke into a girlish giggle. Feeling the flames raging in him suddenly made her whole body shiver.

John could take no more. He stood up and gently lifted her out of the tub, standing her full like a princess, on the floor. He threw the large white hotel bath towel around her shoulders and, opening it in front, knelt with his arms around her, kissing every inch of her voluptuous body he could reach. As his lips soothingly brushed her skin, she threw her head and swirled her long vanilla hair around his face, then bent over and enfolded him like a hungry mamma bear with a big salmon.

Groaning, her body on fire from his touch, she dug her hands into his hair. In a fumbling instant, she tore off his clothes, and they went tumbling in bed. In that sweet twinkling when all time stood still, they rolled together, touching and exploring every part of each other's body. His mind almost blew its boundaries as his hands glided up and down her warm, smooth firmness.

"Your skin feels like you just bathed in fresh cream," he whispered with his lips to hers, his hands gently exploring every circle, every valley, every route to glory.

Finally, virile energy spent, they lay back, wrung out, the riot in their souls all stilled, their hearts in blissful rapture.

"Oh, Johnny, I felt like I was inside your skin," Ricka murmured after a long silence, "like I actually became part of you."

"I'm gonna remember this night 'til I die," he whispered in reply, pulling her close.

And Adam knew his wife, strangely scrolled across his mind over and over as he closed his eyes. *Yes, Adam, so did I, and it was good.*

Ricka wriggled tightly against him, her head nestled into his shoulder, hair fanned across his face, as they drifted off in pure angelic joy, and pleasure danced with blessedness.

When he woke in the morning, he hugged her awake and whispered, "That was a quarter well spent!"

She threw back the covers and jumped into his arms, smiling the biggest smile he had ever seen on her face. Suddenly, she slid her cheek past his and gently bit his ear. "Hey," he yelped in mock pain, and they tumbled together, riding the rails to glory land one more time. At breakfast, they were all smiles.

In the adjoining room, with Mina's condition, all her desire had frozen and fled. Gottfried's hopeful quarter had yielded only a good bath and a long night's sleep. The next morning they were both grumpy.

Unfortunately, the little delights of this night—light at the push of a button, a flushing toilet, and a self-filling bathtub—were wonders these pioneer women would never experience in their homes, as long as they lived.

At the first glimmer of dawn, they were up for a quick breakfast. The liveryman brought the horses from the barn at the rear of the hotel and helped them hitch the team, and they loaded up for the forty-mile journey home. Christ and Adam had brought along a set of heavy coats, caps, scarves, gloves, and overshoes for the newcomers, and they stuffed themselves into all of it. They had also loaded the thirty-inch-high sled box with fresh straw and extra heavy blankets, and now the hotel brought out four smooth prairie stones, the size of angel-food cakes, which had been heated on the stove, and these would keep their feet warm, at least for a time.

The sled was pulled by two horses, with two more trailing, so they could change off and keep the teams fresh. Half an hour into the high hill country north of town and all they could see were more hills and deeper ravines. A few shivering houses off in the distance were puffing smoke into the sky, bravely bracing their thin walls against the awful cold.

To the untrained eye, there was not a hint of road here. Yet the horses knew and needed no reins to guide them.

Mina, sitting with Ricka in the back of the sled, found herself in a mighty struggle to keep her breakfast sausages down. Any moment they could come shooting up. Finally, she drew her legs up, bent her head down, and wept. It was all too much for her. When Ricka inched over to hold her, Mina softly sobbed, "I wish I were home in our beautiful *dorf* at Mamma's table."

While the women huddled together for warmth under their blankets in the deep pile of straw, the four men were standing in the front of the sled, with Adam driving. John and Gottfried found themselves strangely filled with exuberant ardor as they gazed out at the endless panorama of nothing but white stretched out before them. Lay your eye along the top of the horses' collars and gaze into that infinite horizon, and suddenly you realized that there was nothing between that point and you. Each row of hills hiccupped softly and stretched out to another.

"Isn't this great?" Gottfried shouted over the steady tinkling of the harness chains and the rhythmic, plopping hooves of the trotting horses.

"Sure feels great to me," John replied, grinning into the icy wind.

Adam and Christ smiled, "It'll get even better. You'll see."

To the men, the great silence of the majestic emptiness surrounding them was a rare moment of communion. Both God and the hearts of the others felt so close, all so wonderfully bound together. As the frigid north wind streamed past John's face, suddenly it seemed like his mind left his body and melted into the vast earth around him until he and it were all one.

In that mystical moment, the ugliness of his Russian army life and all the nauseous stench in the hold of the *Armenia* were gone, and pure unspoiled beauty flooded his soul. The memory of those things of the past would still remain. But their power was broken, and he felt the deepest sense of tranquil freedom he would ever know. This was pioneer life at its finest, the idyllic stuff that Currier and Ives would immortalize.

Unfortunately, in all their enthusiasm, the brothers had not bothered to look back at the huddled women. For them, it was a different story. Mina raised her head, and as she looked over the edge of the sled, her eyes grew wide and she whispered, "I'm afraid there are wolves out here, and they're going to attack us."

"Sh-h, Mina, there are no wolves. Don't be scared," replied Ricka, trying to comfort her.

"I can't help it. I'm so scared. And how do you know there are no wolves?"

"We'll be all right. You'll see."

"Do you think my baby will be all right?"

"Dearest sister, you're going to have a strong, healthy baby!"

"I'm so glad my baby wasn't born already," she added, beginning to sob. "I just know it would have died on this trip."

Ricka hugged her more tightly and said, "You'll be fine, and the baby will too!"

Mina put her head down and said no more. The welcoming openness of the virgin prairies could not lift the pressure that seemed to be squeezing all joy out of her heavy heart.

John looked back at the women with their heads down in intense conversation and remarked, "Looks like the women are enjoying it too."

"Bet they're talking about their new houses," replied Gottfried.

And both smiled, so glad that in this exhilarating, brand-new day in North Dakota, they understood their wives so well.

Over those long, slow miles, Christ and Adam filled them in on where land was still available for homesteading, what crops grew well here, prices for grain, cost of horses and machinery, and the essentials of making it in this new world.

All that day, the sled runners silently swished across the snow-covered ground as the horses continued an easy trotting pace. The treeless high hills and long valleys flowed by without end. Occasionally, a dry creek was outlined with small, struggling trees, and once they saw two white-tailed deer racing away in the distance. Several times they stopped for a few-minute break.

"Listen," Ricka said suddenly, cocking her head during one of the stops.

"What?"

"There is no sound. Absolutely no sound."

"Out here," replied Christ, with a faraway look, "you can hear your heartbeat."

One of the horses briefly snorted and shook its harness. But after that they were again swallowed up in the eerie, total stone-silence of these vast prairies. Adam smiled, clicked the reins, and kept the sled moving again until the sun reached its zenith, when they stopped to feed and change horses. It also gave the women a chance to stretch and unwrap a quick bite of bread and sausage for all to recharge. They also passed around the jar of apple juice the hotel kitchen had packed for them. Here and there a ragged, unpainted, little pioneer house was spitting smoke into the air, but none sat next to their unseen trail, and no people were about. Late in the afternoon, the scudding clouds finally broke, and the stinging wind slowed to a rippling breeze with less bite.

As the weakened winter sun bent to kiss the upturned lips of the immense western horizon, they finally saw several men off in the distance, moving about to do the milking and feed their animals. The faraway yelping of a few dogs came as a welcome sound to break the day's silence. By nightfall, they made it to Stanton, the first thirty miles of their long trip, where they would stay the night with friends.

The next day they finished the final ten-mile leg to reach home in Krem.

Sweet tears flowed when they reached their parents' house. There was no aromatic bathtub waiting for them here, but the enfolding love of family warmed them much more deeply and made them feel like they belonged. It was too new to be home, but yet it was home. Their hearts were surely, safely, finally home!

For the rest of the winter months, John and Ricka stayed with Father, Mother, and Anna in their little house, while Gottfried and Mina stayed with Sister Katherina, her husband, Adam, and their children. The hope was that Katherina could take her scared new sister-in-law under her wing and perhaps slip in some subtle lessons and hints about motherhood, especially motherhood in this new German-American wilderness.

With new immigrants arriving almost every week, John and Gottfried were anxious about getting land, and the euphoria of arriving in America soon wore off, replaced with worry about their future. The third day after arriving in Krem, they were back on the sled with Christ and Adam, heading west and south to lands the two early settlers had already scouted out. All day they drove, stopping on high hills to look over areas that showed some promise.

Late in the afternoon they found it: two quarters of land just a mile apart, each with high grazing land for cattle, falling away into flat valley land they could break up for raising crops. Each had a perfect little hill at the valley's edge for a house and barns. If it were still available, this would be home.

Arriving back in Krem, they could hardly contain their excitement at having found their acres of blessing and bubbled the good news to the wives and the rest of the family. But that night the two men tossed, waiting for first light when they would again set out in the sled, this time to the land office in the county seat at Stanton, ten miles away, to file their homestead claim for a quarter of land, 160 acres each.

They answered the questions, identified the land exactly on the map for the legal description, and signed their names. Each paid their $18 filing fee, agreed to erect a building on the land, and were the happy recipients of a piece of the US government's land offered free to willing settlers.

Back in Krem, the men dropped into Huber's Beer Parlor, and all the talk involved acres, miles, feet, and bushels. They felt lost, and when they got home, they asked Adam to work them through this new world of measurements. He sat them down with pencil and paper and started in.

"Now, remember, a mile here is about 1.6 kilometers in our German measurement."

"And in Russian?" asked John.

"Well, a mile would be roughly 1.6 *verst* too, same as in kilometers."

"Good. Now how about land?" asked Gottfried.

"Remember, in Russia our families were each given about *forty dessiatines* of land. That's about the same as 36½ German *hectares.*"

"And what's one *hectare* here?"

"One *hectare* would be two and a half acres here. So they got around ninety-one acres of land back in Russia," replied Adam.

"So with 160 acres here, the American government gave us quite a bit more land than the Russians did," mused John, feeling a bit smug.

Now Adam reached up on a shelf and took down a wooden ruler. "This is called one 'foot' long," he said. "It's about the same as one Russian *fut*, and in German, it's one *wurst*."

"Funny," Gottfried replied, "one ruler is the same as a sausage."

"Ja, and three of these make a yard," Adam said.

"But isn't a yard what's around your house?" asked John, trying to remember some of the talk he had heard.

"Same word, but used different," answered Adam.

"Don't know if I'll ever make an American," was all John could reply.

The rest of the winter months dragged terribly. They spent long days in Christ's shoe and leather shop. They learned the rudiments of making shoes and crafting harnesses and bridles. They shoveled snow, curried and fed the horses, and cleaned the barn. The women worked together cooking and baking, cleaning, washing, darning, and learning new measurements as well. They visited neighbors, played cards, sang songs, and enjoyed going to church. They spent happy hours sharing news about the old country and hearing stories about the new.

But the days of joy also carried a certain edginess that made them all a bit guarded with each other as conversations easily led to inane disagreements that got loud before they were able to back off again. Casual remarks that were suddenly snapped at each other made them aware of the pressure of all this togetherness. When John groused at Mother Karolina for moving his boots away from the warm stove to a cold spot beside the door, Ricka interjected, "You should have moved them yourself."

"You shut up," he shot back, "and stay out of it." Through the rest of the night, it was icier inside the house than out.

Several sunny Sundays after church, they filled the sled with straw and all ten of the family piled in for a three-mile drive down to the frozen Missouri River. The women were terrified at going out on the ice. But after the men chopped a hole in the ice to show that it was two feet thick, they relaxed and came out to watch the men trying to catch fish through the ice.

One large, long-whiskered catfish was all they could catch. Its huge black head and fat yellow belly looked like supper, but when they grabbed its writhing body and felt its slippery, scale-free skin, no one wanted to clean it.

"Johnny," called his father, Adam, "come and hold the fish."

Six-year-old Johnny had been squealing and running in circles all over the ice, and now when he touched the squishy fish with one fearful finger, he let out another shrill squeal and ran off again. His father took the hook out of the toothless mouth and slid the fish back down the hole.

In the midst of all this excitement, Mina glanced back at the riverbank and suddenly turned pale. Following her openmouthed stare, they saw a small group of Indian men standing there, watching their every move.

"Don't look at 'em," Adam whispered, "just keep doing what you're doing."

The women drew closer together and said nothing. Several minutes later, the Indian men silently turned and walked single-file back up the riverbank.

After everyone finally relaxed again, the women unwrapped several fresh-baked cream-cheese-apple *kuchen*, which everyone devoured in a few minutes' time, and soon they were back on the sled, driving home.

Then, a few weeks more and changes began to take place. Almost imperceptibly, winter began to lose its stranglehold on the land, the days grew minutes longer, and the snow began to melt into crystallized puddles. Emerald Spring was making ready to fold four eager new children to her ample breast.

It wouldn't be long until Gottfried and John could test themselves against this strange new wilderness and turn it into the paradise of their dreams.

Chapter 30

Plowing Barbed Wire

When the life-giving sun had finally thawed the top layer of earth, John and Gottfried got up at first light of day, eager to get started. Earlier, they had removed the steel-rimmed wagon wheels and slathered the axles with heavy grease. Last night, they loaded the wagons with a four-foot double disc, a sod-breaking plow they borrowed, a single harrow, shovels, rakes, and sacks of wheat seed, along with hay and oats for the horses. Now they lifted up the wooden chest of food the women prepared and along with Christ and Adam, headed for their homesteads some thirteen miles away. Each found a strong team of horses to purchase and another to borrow, so they were ready to break the tough sod of their new land and prepare it for the first civilized crop the land would grow.

At home, before they left, Gottfried said, "You remember our homestead papers said we have to break up at least ten acres of land for crops?"

"We have to find the right ground," John answered, "to break up at least two ten-acre pieces each."

"Let's see," Christ figured, trying to remember all the conversions. "If you take a piece half a mile long, you get an acre every 16½ feet wide."

"So on a quarter mile, you need it three-three feet wide for an acre," Adam chimed in.

"That means 330 feet wide to make 10 acres."

This whole "acre, feet, mile" business was still awkward for them since they were still used to thinking of *dessiatines* and *hectares* for land and *versts* and kilometers instead of miles.

John tried to remember and did some quick conversions in his head. "That should come out to about 440 steps long and 110 steps wide."

Now standing on the high ground of their new land, they found two promising plots. They walked down and stepped off two ten-acre plots, pounding in fence posts to mark the boundaries. After unloading the plows, they harnessed up the teams of three and started the backbreaking work of taming their wild sod. Already they were struck by the constant blowing wind that swept across these rich prairies, seemingly without ever letting up.

Christ went with John and Adam with Gottfried as they set to work wrestling the sharp steel lays of the breaking-plows through the wire-hard roots of the greening buffalo grass.

One man handled the horses' reins, while the other manned the jerking handles of the plow. The verdant grasses had grown here for countless centuries, and now they stubbornly fought the proud steel plow every inch of the way. It seemed like every root joined every other in conducting all-out war. It was resistance to the death. You could hear them pop when they finally yielded and were turned upside down on the black earth. It was going to be an intense struggle, made more difficult by rocks that bounced the plow out of the ground every few feet.

"This stuff is like plowing barbed wire," John stammered.

A hundred yards into the first furrow and John already felt his muscles tighten. His lean, conditioned army physique was hardly a match for this perverse sod.

"Holy buck wheat," he puffed, "I don't know if we're going to be able to do this."

When they finally reached the quarter-mile fence post, he felt exhausted.

"Here," said Christ, "you take the reins, and I'll plow." But both knew he would not make it back to the start of the furrow. Even the horses felt the effort and snorted as they leaned into their collars, straining to move the little two-handled toy that had turned monster behind them.

Halfway back to where they started, Christ's years betrayed him, and he called out, "Whoa." His muscles quivered and could take no more.

"You take it, Son. I thought I could still do it," he said. "I can't."

"That's all right, Papa. I don't know how long I'll last either."

Somehow they managed two more furrows and then collapsed on the ground, both too tired to move. After lying on the grass for a while, they unhitched the horses to let them graze and got out the food box. Simple bread had never tasted this good, nor water this sweet. For all their aches, they had broken up exactly a fourth of one acre!

After a short nap, Christ rode one of the horses over to Gottfried's, to trade places with Adam and give John a little more help. The rest of the afternoon, both teams struggled to keep going until, when they finally quit after sundown, their hands were raw even through leather gloves, and every muscle in their bodies screamed abuse.

Christ dug a pit, piled up rocks, and started a fire to cook some supper. They ate it but tasted mostly nothing. Even their taste buds were shut down from exhaustion. After supper, they tethered the horses and let them graze, while all four raked up piles of dry grass and piled them under the wagon as mattresses for a night's sleep.

They had no medicine for tired, achy, protesting muscles, no relief for throbbing backs. Lying on the ground, Christ said it first, "Ei, yei, yei, everything hurts tonight."

"If we had some horse liniment, I'd take it right now," Gottfried added.

"Could have at least remembered some schnapps."

Chirping black field crickets finally sang them to sleep, as did the tired horses crunching mouthfuls of grass as they grazed contentedly nearby.

It wasn't long, however, before a lone coyote sent up a long, mournful howl from atop a hill across the valley, a mile away. That shrill howl somehow made the hair on their arms stand up and broke any threads of sleep. Shortly, a second coyote on another hill set up a barking howl in reply. A moment later, a third joined, the trio now talking coyote in sharp staccato cadences. Even the horses stopped grazing and turned their heads to listen for any critters that might be circling close in.

By now, the night was pitch, coal black. There was no moon, and the millions of stars yielded no light at all. Ears were their only eyes now.

Suddenly, a shrill howl sounded close by, too close. An echo followed, making it sound closer yet, maybe right on the hill above them. Straining for any sound, John whispered, "Hey, that sounded like a critter's teeth snapping."

All four sat up, now not only awake but more than a bit unnerved. Gottfried got up and hustled all the food items into the wooden chest, afraid the hungry coyotes would close in, trying to snatch food for their young back in the dens somewhere in these hills. Their sharp noses could smell alluring garlic sausage from a long ways off.

They brought no gun, no long knives, so John grabbed two shovels off the wagon, and these would be their defense in case the snarling thieves formed a pack to attack them.

Adam and Christ got up and gathered all the nervous, snorting horses, tying them to the wagon. Neither man nor beast had much experience with this kind of thing, and neither knew quite what to expect from the other.

John thought of the stories Grandfather Heinrich told in Russia, which was also wilderness area when the German settlers first arrived there, and how wolf packs had hunted their animals and on occasion attacked people, killing several. He began to wonder if that experience would be repeated here, this time with them in the center of it.

Full half an hour the unnerving barks and long, drawn-out howls continued, far away, then close, far again, close, in awful rhythm. Then suddenly, there was a howl on the other side, from the broken sod close by. Their silent stalkers were encircling them! How many, no one knew. Now both man and horse made ready for battle, hearts thumping, sure they would be attacked at any moment. The horses snorted and stamped and jerked their heads against the halter ropes. That meant something was nearby, maybe a number of somethings.

Finally, John slammed his shovel against the rim of the wagon wheel, steel on clanging steel, and the sharp report shot into the dark. Instantly, the barks and howls ended. Hopefully, the "shot" had scared the unseen graybacks off into the night. A few more minutes of holding their breath, and all seemed quiet. The horses shook their heads once more and relaxed, as if to say, "It's over." For now the danger seemed past.

Adam staked the horses back out on ropes around the wagon, and the men lay down once more, confident that the horses would serve as first-line sentries if any intruders should come near. The howlers opened up again a few more times across the valley, but finally, they were silent, and the men drifted off to sleep. But between aching muscles and riled-up minds, sleep came in fits. Wrapped in their blankets, they tossed and snored through the short night.

Long before the blowing east wind could push the morning sun into the sky, a coterie of resident yellow-throated flickertail meadowlarks were at their posts, each on its own jutting rock in their avian homestead. With glorious gusto, they sang their melodious "Ode to Morning," which some Grandma Meadowlark must first have trilled, then taught many, many years ago. Their joyous symphony would get the dullest bell to ring. These were the early ancestors, the great-grand-birds of modern North Dakota's official State Bird. This day they would be busy lining their nests in the prairie grasses, soon to lay their beautiful brown-flecked ivory eggs to bring in tomorrow's choristers.

The men stirred, hoping that nature's own alarm had somehow been set on fast time by mistake. They ached too much to do anything very quickly.

Finally, Christ's crackling fire and boiling coffee with thick bacon slabs and bread dipped in the hot, sizzling bacon grease got them going again.

They hitched up and set the plow into the wiry, tangled roots again. John winced in pain the first time the plow hit a rock and jerked to the side. Controlling it was a huge effort this morning. Even the horses seemed to have lost their energy, stepping slower than yesterday. But a hundred yards into the furrow, and horse and man seemed to run on reflex, mindlessly hanging on just to keep going.

All day they endured. And the next. Those wretched little lines of upturned earth were only a fourth of a mile long, 1,320 feet, a mere speck in this glaciated valley. But don't tell that to these four: the pain in the birthing of this virgin field bespoke the vast estates of Czar Nicholas himself. Two and a half days more, and Saturday noon they laid the plows over on their sides at the end of the field and loaded the wagons for the return trip home to Krem.

"You know," said Gottfried, thinking out loud on the way home, "maybe best we don't say anything to the women about the coyotes."

"Well, Katherina will probably ask," replied Adam, "because she's heard them around home."

"We'll just say, ja, we heard some a couple times," answered Gottfried. "That's enough." He didn't want Mina panicked more than he feared she already was about this new world.

They were so exhausted, their bodies one big ache, that while Adam drove, the other three stretched out in the wagon box and slept. Soon Adam sat down in the box, holding the reins, and fell asleep as well. Several times he woke up, looked around, saw he wasn't needed, and returned to peaceful slumber. Luckily, the horses knew the trail and finished the trip home by themselves.

When they walked into the house, Ricka ran to give John a quick hug, as Mother Karolina asked, "Well, how did it go?"

John held out his blistered hands, "About this good."

"Oh, that's terrible," responded Ricka. "Let me get something for that."

As she softly rubbed some ointment on his swollen hands, he continued, "It was much harder than I thought it'd be. We wrestled those miserable plows for six awful days, sun up to dark, and all we got done was about six acres." Shaking his head, he looked at the floor and added, almost under his breath, "A lousy acre a day is all we can get done." The rest could tell the disappointment in his voice.

The women had a wonderful-smelling supper on the table; tomorrow would be church, and maybe the world would look a touch brighter again by next week.

Church was special because this would be Easter Sunday. For these sturdy frontier folk, this was the highlight of their entire year. Not only would it bring the retelling of the great good news of a sorrowful cross and a mighty resurrection from the dead, but as they sat in church, next to the still-young cemetery just outside, they were only too aware that the sod already held several young mothers and little babies who had died way too young. This day then, more than any other, reminded them that they were not without hope, that beyond the harsh life on these uncompromising prairies, there was planned for them a sure and certain life of joy where tears would finally be over, where death would be no more, and life would shine eternal.

But this glorious-messaged day also had a flip side: the marvelous opportunity of every woman to dress up, both herself and any daughters she might have, in the best finery they could put together. Some labored long, pedaling their Singer sewing machines by kerosene lamp to craft a new dress, and some spent days pouring over the latest offerings in the fashionable collection staring out from the spring Sears and Roebuck catalog and ordered their best. Completing their ensembles with colorful hats, white gloves, lacey everything, ribbons abounding, they were a feast to the eyes and brought delighted smiles to every glad worshiper packed tightly into the little church. They sang their hearts out, the pastor preached with gusto, the good news came alive—but the day's finery was the dessert that made it perhaps most memorable of all.

The dozens of children were especially antsy during the pastor's hour-long sermon in church, impatient to get home to the many-hued Easter eggs they had dyed and the little baskets of fruit and chocolate candy, which the fabled Easter bunny left during the night.

After church, the men talked to a neighbor who piqued their interest. He had a relative south of town who ordered a breaking plow from the Sears and Roebuck catalog, and with it, he could break three acres of sod a day.

After their sumptuous Easter goose dinner and a long nap on the sunny ground outside, it was time to walk around the neighborhood and compare further notes, and by then, the women were calling them for yet more goose and ham, bread and cake before they scattered for home.

Tomorrow would be Easter Monday, and by long tradition among these Lutheran believers, a second consecutive day of worship, remembering with sacred memory the one empty grave which triggered their faith. After church, they loaded up the women and rode out to see this new invention, which they also heard about in Russia but had never seen. While the women visited in the house, the men walked out to see this new sod-breaking plow. It still had only one cutting blade to turn the earth, but it had a heavy steel frame on three wheels and a lever to control its depth, from four inches to twelve. It even had a molded metal seat, letting the driver ride in near ease all day long.

On the way home, they made some quick decisions. "How about when we're done breaking the ten-acre pieces," Gottfried said. "Let's stop for now, and then maybe we can order one of those new plows together."

"Sounds good," John answered. "Then later in the summer, we can break up a couple more pieces for next year."

Things were moving now. When they returned to their land, they were pleased to see almost the entire valley abustle with activity. During the winter months, all the surrounding land had been claimed for homesteads, and now on every quarter of land new pioneers were busy as well, starting to break the sod for small start-up fields. The valley had been claimed by Kellers, Eisenbeises, and Rickers. The high country behind them was claimed as well, a Renner, a Wiedrich, a Huber on every 160 acres, Germans all, and all from Russia as well, eager for a new life.

This week they finished breaking their ten acres and then walked behind the team over every foot of it a second time, pulling the double disc to break up the clods of sod and finally a third time, raking it with the four-foot, steel-toothed, wooden harrow.

Two more weeks and the biting north winds lost much of their sting, while the smiling sun grew longer teeth each day, warming the good earth enough for planting seed.

Now it was time for the men to return to the new fields. They decided to join forces, and all four would line up, each with a sack of seed slung over his shoulder, to walk abreast and hand-broadcast the precious golden kernels of wheat seed over the blackened earth. Covering a strip of four feet each—step, throw seed, step, throw seed—they could plant half an acre with each pass, one acre each time around.

After completing this slow, wearying task, each field had to be gone over a fifth time, harrowing it again to rake the seeds into the soil and protecting them as well from birds and little critters of the earth.

The next day held a more joyous promise. They drove all around the lower hills at the edge of their valley, surveying each rise to find the best spot to build a homesite. Several times over they drove it, looking from every direction.

"We want enough ground," said John, "for a house and maybe several barns in a few years."

"And think about the terrible north winds and blizzards in the winter," Adam added. "Lots of snow around here."

"Remember summer, too," Christ chimed in. "It can get awfully hot, so you gotta be able to catch some breeze or you'll cook."

"And once in a while," Adam warned, "prairie fires come roaring across these prairies so you have to be able to protect your place from that."

"Hey, water," John declared, "what about water?"

After half a day of driving and talking and weighing, John found his magic carpet. Here on a gentle rise that topped out with a small flat plateau, he and Ricka would raise their family. Here they would become American, and here they would build America as well.

Thank you, Lord, he smiled to himself, *You've been so good to us.*

All that remained was to check if there was any possible source of water close at hand. They had heard that a neighbor a mile to the east had "The Gift." He could "witch" for water. When they drove to his place, he dropped everything, more than happy to oblige. Within an hour, he was crisscrossing John's chosen building site. Using both hands, he held his two-foot long, forked willow divining rod straight out in front of himself, walking back and forth over a hundred-yard area. All eyes followed his every move when suddenly the rod dipped.

"Look at that," exclaimed John, "that thing didn't just wiggle in his hand."

"Yei, it went straight down, right now," muttered Gottfried.

"Well, here it is," said the neighbor. "You've got a little stream of water running right through here, coming down from the hill back there. From the way the rod is dipping, you should hit it about ten to fifteen feet down." John laid a rock to mark the exact spot.

Amazed, John offered him *"Viel mal dank,"* many thanks, and a promise of supper when they had the house built. When Gottfried asked him, the man was kind enough to do the same at his place. This was neighborliness at its best, brother helping brother. Already, this felt like home.

Back in Krem, John tore open the door, ran in, and shouted, "You're not gonna believe this." The stunned women held everything in midair, afraid to ask, but he hurried on, "A guy found water on our place with a stick!"

Quickly he rattled off the entire amazing episode and added, "Tomorrow we're gonna head back and dig a well. Then we can get started on the house."

Ricka let out a little squeal and ran to throw her arms around him. "That's the best news I've heard in weeks!" she exclaimed. Then moving back a step, she patted her stomach with both hands and, with a big, wide-eyed smile, added, "It's time all right."

It took a moment for John to understand what she was saying. Then he scooped her up, swung her around, and bounced her lightly several times on the floor. "Oi," was all he could get out, but smiling just as big, "Ei, yei, yei."

Karolina grinned from ear to ear. "More grandchildren, more joy," she said softly.

The next morning the men were back on the trail again. This time they were going with picks, shovels and spades, ropes and pails, along with a big ladder that Adam hammered together. On the rear of the wagon box, they also piled lumber and nails to build a box over their new well.

An early lightning storm pushed through during the night, and this morning the men were struck by the distinct smell of ozone still hanging in the air. Overnight, the world had also changed color as well. The soaking rain brought new life to the great green carpet of buffalo grass, which began to stand tall, with its own special green-grass smell, still waiting for its namesake to come and graze its tender shoots. Sprinkled over all the hills, as well, were beautiful, waving, clusters of rich purple crocuses with brilliant yellow stamen that could fill even the most jaundiced heart with new serenity.

On a nearby hilltop, a mallard duck uttered a single quack, swooped out of the sky, and flew sharply into the grass, making ready to lay a cluster of eggs in her new downy earthen nest. Several great red-tailed hawks were circling overhead, riding the currents, waiting for a careless mouse to come out for breakfast. "Just look at all that," John said as he watched this panorama of nature unfold, "could heaven be any more beautiful than this?"

They barely arrived at the spot on John's place when he was already off the wagon and swinging his pick to get the hole started. If there were no water here, he would have to start looking all over again for a place to put down roots. An artesian spring a mile away had promise, but it was too far to haul water from there every day.

Before long, the sod was stripped, and he had spaded two feet down. But then, bad news. He hit blue clay, almost as hard as solid rock. It could not be cracked or broken into chunks. Every cantankerous two-inch chip had to be chiseled out with the sharp steel pick. Half an hour, and he was beat. Gottfried took a turn and then Adam. Four feet of battering, smashing, pounding the pick, and no end in sight. Silently, each began to wonder if this was all going to be for nothing. By now they were down deeper than their heads, and in that tight hole, sweat rolled off them in streams almost bigger than the river they hoped to hit beneath their feet.

"Let's go another foot," said John, "and if we're still not through the clay, let's move."

They had battled for every chip of clay they loosened.

Then suddenly, the pick stuck in the clay. Wedging it out, John discovered that they had broken through and something softer lay below the clay. The digging grew easier, but now they had to scoop every shovelful into three-gallon buckets and have the men on top lift it out with ropes. They slid the ladder down, and an exhausted John slowly climbed out of the hole.

By now it was almost dark, time for cold food and recharging worn-out muscles. Tonight, two would sleep in the wagon and two on raked-up grass on the ground. No one wanted to say it out loud, but in each mind, the threatening coyotes seemed only yards away. Thankfully, all the night's mournful howling stayed in the distance.

Up at dawn, they were soon attacking the stubborn hole again.

Finally, eight feet down and not a drop of moisture. Nine, then ten feet, and nothing but dry, pebbly sand.

John rested a while and then slowly began climbing out of the hole. By now every muscle was shouting angry things at his head. This was like breaking sod all over again. "And I thought the Russian army was tough," he called out halfway up the ladder.

Adam tucked a chew of snus into his cheek, in no hurry to get down the steamy hole. As he stepped off the bottom rung, there was a sudden shout.

"Hey!" he cried out. "It's wet down here."

"Hallelujah!" Christ shouted. "Time for the rock."

Adam dug out another foot of mucky sand that was starting to seep more water and climbed up the ladder.

In the meantime, while the three younger men finished digging, Christ had taken the wagon up to an outcropping of sandstone shale rock on a nearby hill and gathered a load of it to line the edges of the hole to keep it from caving in. Eons ago, nature had laid this sandstone down in neat, thin layers, and now they were tailor-made for pioneer building materials. After they had thrown several dozen sandstone rocks into the hole, John climbed back in to brick up the walls of the well. Several hours more by each of the men, and they had a well.

They lifted the canvas-wrapped, gallon clay water jug out from the shade, pulled the cork, and passed it around. A short rest on the ground, enjoying bologna sandwiches more than they ever thought they could, and they walked back to look down the hole. Its shiny bottom reflected their faces. Sure enough, it was filling with water. John had a well!

They hammered a box together to cover the well and hitched up the team to do the same project at Gottfried's place. Another day and a second well was done.

Now it was high time to start building houses, and the trip back to Krem was filled with good-natured jostling and easy laughter.

"This rock-tough country might turn out all right after all," John reflected.

"Sure, hope the wives think so too," replied Gottfried, only half-smiling.

Chapter 31

Soddy on the Prairie

Constructing the house would finally involve the whole family. The men hoisted up a keg of spikes to nail the roof timbers, loaded the whole family on two wagons, along with a week's worth of food and cooking utensils, and headed for their homestead. Ricka, Mother Karolina, and Anna would all help in building their new house.

This was the first time that Ricka would get a glimpse of her new home. When they got to the land and stopped beside the well, she looked around and was shocked to see absolutely nothing—no other houses, no animals, no sign of civilization except some teams breaking sod across the valley. She was used to houses surrounding them on both sides, with more behind them in the old country. She knew her sister would be living just over the hills less than a mile away, but she couldn't see that place either. Her heart sank, realizing the terrible loneliness that would hang like spiderwebs around this place for the rest of her life. This was not the close-knit neighborhood she had envisioned in her dreams. But she knew her beloved John was enthralled with this place, so she swallowed hard and began unpacking the wagon. She felt like throwing up, but she hoped it was the new life inside her speaking, rather than her sharp disappointment. *This new house will be no Salem Hotel North,* she thought, *but I better make the best of it. I'm not the only woman in these parts. We're all in this together.*

Before they began doing anything else, John suddenly shouted, "Wait." With the rest wondering what had happened, he purposefully walked over and pulled up a bucket of cool water from their new well. He lowered the tin dipper into the bucket, filled, and handed it to Ricka.

"Here, Lady of the House," he smiled, "you get the first drink."

"Goodness," she laughed, "is that some good tasting water or what!" and passed the dipper all around.

"I think it's even better," Anna added, "than our water in Krem."

Then, getting down to work, the men staked out the exact sixteen-by-twenty-foot area for their one-room house. They hauled several wagonloads of sandstone from the nearby hill and carefully bricked them down for a foundation. Halfway through, they left it for the women to finish while they set to work on their second structure, the outhouse.

They dug a five-foot pit, a good distance from the well and a quick jump from the house, then began building the little all-weather outhouse, a modest one-holer with seat room for catalog paper or a pail of not-so-delicate corn cobs.

After the women had fixed an ample prairie supper, the men lifted the box off the wagon frame and turned it upside down on the grass. This would be the roof over the women's heads, their storied mansion for the next few nights, and their protection against all that the dark might hurl against them. As they wrapped themselves in their warm blankets, they were thankful for the comfortable layer of straw they brought along for a prairie mattress. The men would sleep across the open end of the upside-down wagon box to safeguard against invading creatures of the night. Let the coyotes howl their mournful cry and the rattlesnakes rattle nearby, their grassy fortress was secure. In this grand canopy of silence, they felt utterly safe, yet a little shadow flitted around in each heart, leaving them feeling somehow less than totally protected on that grass. Only God could provide that, and to God, each heart silently turned in the pitch-blackness before they fell asleep. Even Pushkin's fables of make-believe in czarist Mother Russia could hardly match the complex mini-drama that was quietly playing out on this little spot of earth, so far from anywhere, but to this family the new center of the world; drama played out here by these strong-willed pioneers bent on creating a new life for themselves and their children's children. They were quietly, wordlessly, writing a drama all their own.

During the night, John woke up and was totally amazed. He gently brushed Father's arm and said, "Sh-h, Papa, look up." As they both looked up into the northern sky, they were treated to a breathtaking display of swirling, moving, dipping colors. The northern lights were beaming up a brilliant show of radiant greens, blues, purples, reds, shooting high, fading, and bursting back again.

"Should we wake the women?"

"It's so beautiful, but let's not. They'll never get to sleep again."

"Yeah, I guess they'll have plenty time to see them over the next years."

Over early breakfast, they described the thrilling treat they had received during the night. The women were disappointed but glad to be able to sleep the night without being disturbed more than by the strange, weird dreams they all seemed to have had and shared this morning, over laughs and strong coffee.

After breakfast, the men found a smooth strip of grass next to their seeded field and put the breaking plow in to turn over strips of sod. Then they cut the strips into eighteen-inch bands, lifted them into the wagon, and hauled them to the house site.

After a full day of cutting and hauling, they were ready to lay the first strips on the sandstone foundation. Laying the strips crossways and packing them airtight, they would have eighteen-inch-thick walls in their fresh sod house, their "prairie soddy," ample protection against winter's blast and summer scorch. Finally, one foot of sod wall was raised and done. So were they, after this long, punishing day.

The next day, they just began working when a wagon approached from the east. Their neighbors had heard a soddy was abuilding, and they came to help. They came, children and all, with practiced hands and hearts full of warm enthusiasm, ringing in distant songs as they came.

After introductions, Ricka felt embarrassed, saying apologetically, "I'm terribly sorry, but we don't have much extra food along out here."

"Oh, that's all right," laughed the neighbor. "I shot a coyote on the way over, and I thought maybe you could roast that for dinner—if that's all right?" Seeing Ricka's stunned look, they all quickly headed for their wagon and brought out two woven baskets and a gallon jug of cider.

"I only had two canned-peach kuchen, with the meat and bread and stuff," added the wife, "so that will have to do."

"That's so good of you. Thank you!" Ricka exclaimed, relieved not to eat coyote, and gave her a hearty hug. Already these lonesome prairies didn't feel quite so lonesome.

The neighbor headed back to the wagon, volunteering over his shoulder, "I brought another sod-bustin' plow," and with that, he was up on the wagon, heading out to join the men in breaking more sod.

With extra hands, the walls kept rising.

The next day, they were amazed when two more wagons rolled in, with more food, more help, and more neighborly enthusiasm. By nightfall, the walls were nearly finished. One more day, and Ricka would have a house. They left framed space for a south-facing door and two small windows, on the east and south sides, away from the screaming winds. The following day, they had the sod up to a full seven feet and hoisted the two-by-ten-inch stringers across, cut them into the sod, and nailed the low rafters into place. With some rough roof boards they brought along from the sawmill in Expansion and two layers of tar paper nailed down for waterproofing, they were ready to hoist up two more layers of sod, which would serve as shingles for the roof. By sundown, one last day, the soddy was enclosed. One more night under the wagon box and by first light tomorrow, they would head home to Krem. It couldn't come too soon for the women.

"I don't know when I've been this dirty," said young Anna, "this totally pig-dirty!"

Ricka was ready for a bath, but a bed would feel even better. "My back sure aches," she said, looking at Karolina, who understood totally what she was talking about.

"What I wouldn't give to be back in the Salem," Ricka muttered half under her breath.

"What?"

"Oh, nothing. It's good to be home again." She suddenly thought, *Wait a minute, out there will be home now* and gave a slight shudder as that strangely uncomfortable thought passed through her mind.

"We'll soak you good and hot in the tub," added Karolina, one mother to another-to-be, "and you'll feel better again."

A day home and the men returned to the soddy, this time with a door, windows, trowels, and pails. They spent the rest of the day carefully hanging the door, then nailing in the windows, and packing the frames with hemp to seal them. The eighteen-inch-thick walls gave them good room to get the frames adjusted and tightly seated.

The next day, they mixed mud and powdered lime and plastered the inside of the grassy sod walls to a smooth finish. In a week, when it was dry, they would return and mix several gallons of water, more powdered lime, and laundry bluing, and paint all the walls, leaving them a beautiful soft blue—which in many a first sod house would outlast its pioneer owners. In the absence of easily available and affordable "boughten paint," this distinctive "blued" blue was to become the soddy hallmark of the day.

The final step to make it livable came when they nailed a perpendicular pole onto a two-foot board and made a tamper, with which they tamped the dirt floor, sprinkled water, and tamped some more, until the dirt was hard and level and smooth. This would be the floor for their cooking and eating, their living and sleeping. *On this floor our first baby will be born and walk its first steps,* Ricka thought. *God help us.*

Chapter 32

Bless This House So We Can Live

The week back in Krem was a whirlwind. They had to hunt furniture and cookware, get some animals to raise, and find seeds for their new garden.

But there was one big problem: no money. Their funds were about exhausted, and while Father wanted to get both his sons started in their new homes, he didn't have that kind of money either. His harness shop was enough to make a living for his little family, but not enough to finance two others.

They huddled together in worried discussion.

"We could both hire out," Gottfried spoke up, "and make some money that way."

"But then," John replied, "we wouldn't get our own places up and running."

Finally, Christ said, "You know, Peter Miller in Expansion runs the sawmill, and he has a little money. I've heard he's made some loans to a few people around town."

"Well, we've bought plenty lumber from him. Maybe he'd help us."

"Worth a try."

The next day, the three drove the few miles down to the sawmill in the nearby settlement of Expansion and found Mr. Miller. After explaining their situation, he agreed to help both with a loan. They'd have to sign a two-year note at 10 percent interest, and Christ would have to cosign. "That's kinda tough," he said, shaking his head, "but what else can we do?"

After they all agreed, Miller took out his pencil, wrote out three slips, and each one signed.

Now everything turned to sprint speed. John found a farmer willing to sell three cows with new calves and another who let him buy six sows. Ricka and Karolina found a friend who gave them a good deal on two-dozen chicks, four hens and a rooster, along with three white geese. They also rounded up a supply of garden seeds. Between trips to their small village general store and a fast overnight trip to Stanton, they found the furniture and machinery they needed to get their new home started.

The brothers decided to join in buying a horse-drawn haymower with a six-foot sickle blade, and an eight-foot dump-rake for making hay. Then they ordered one of the new sod-breaking plows from Sears and Roebuck. These were the machines they felt they had to have this first summer if they were going to make it.

Moving to their new home would mean two more thirteen-mile trips. This seemingly simple operation suddenly had nothing simple about it.

On the first trip, the men loaded up fence posts to build fences for their animals, rolls of barbed wire, staples to nail the wire, a new black kitchen stove, and sacks of lime to paint the sod house. Finally, using planks and ropes, with two horses pulling, they wrestled the haymower up on the wagon. Behind the wagon, they hitched the dump-rake. The second wagon was loaded with lumber. Now they were ready for their long, heavy journey.

Arriving at the new soddy, John and Christ quickly set to work bluing the four walls. Then they unloaded the wagon and started pounding in fence posts. With the posts in place, they nailed up three strands of barbed wire to make a fence for the cattle. Then they nailed up a smaller, four-strand fence for the pigs. Two full days of backbreaking lifting, pounding, stretching, pulling, and they were both exhausted.

"I guess we can rest up on the drive home," said a tired John as they climbed back on the wagon and let the horses do the work.

At last, preparation was done. The next trip would mean cutting the cord. No more falling back on the parents. Now they were on their own, cast adrift on the prairies. They would make it by themselves or go under.

They loaded John's wagon with their simple furniture, sacks of flour, sugar and salt, canned meat and vegetables which Karolina, Katherina, and concerned neighbors had gathered up, cookware, dishes, sack of potatoes, a tin of eggs, several smoked hams and bacon slabs. Then they piled on firewood, a covered box with the two-dozen chicks, and a crate of geese. Finally, they added a seat on the top of the very full wagon, and with considerable effort, Ricka climbed up beside her husband. On her other side, their excited new dog, *Schutz,* jumped up and settled in.

John named him *Schutz* because it meant "the protector," and he was already part of the moving, pioneer family.

With this one single wagonload of stuff, they would have to survive. There was no easy wild game, no food delivery service to call if they started running low. They were finally ready to plant their homestead in this brash new world.

Father Christ followed in another wagon loaded with the pigs, a crate of chickens, and three little calves. The cows would trail the wagon, in motherly concern for their braying little ones.

After miles of riding in silence, John heard a soft sob beside him.

"Ricka, what's the matter? Are you sick?" he asked. "Should we stop?"

"I'm not sick. I'm just scared."

"Of what?"

"I'm afraid of being alone so much. And what if something goes wrong with the baby? Where will we get help?" It was a paralyzing fear that made her tremble in the warm sunshine of the day. John pulled her close to himself and held her so tightly that she wheezed a little.

"I know," he said, "it's kinda scary all right." Then after several minutes of silence, he continued, "But don't you think God will take care of us out here, like he took care of me in the army, like he did on the ship, and all the way here? I'm counting on him!"

"I guess so," she answered, but it was a very soft reply, less than totally convincing.

As she stared vacantly across the rolling hills, she noticed the beautiful clusters of flowering purple crocuses. Then her ears became tuned to the procession of brightly trilling meadowlarks, and her spirit began to lift with new hope. The faint aroma of wild onions, growing in the prairie grasses, wafted through the air and filled her with a sudden, strange desire to do some serious cooking for her man.

When John turned to look at her again, he saw the slightest smile on her face.

"We're going to have a good life out here. You'll see," he said. "And you mean everything to me. Always remember that!"

She made no reply, but the way she nestled tighter into him gave him good answer. *Schutz* perked up his ears and cocked his head to look at them, glad from the feelings he was picking up.

When they got to their new house, John took Ricka's hand and led her to the door. He put his hand on the handle and bowed his head. "Oh God, you've been with our fathers and with us all our days. Bless this house so we can live as your children, always. Amen."

"Amen," she added. "God will be in this place. I know it."

They drove the cows and pigs to their fences, turned the geese and chickens loose, took the chicks inside, and carried in all the furniture and food.

A quick bite of food and a cool drink of sweet water from their well, and Father left with his team for home, where by now he had gotten terribly behind in his orders at the harness shop. Now, come what may, his "kids" were on their own.

They placed their furniture, and it didn't take long. Table and four chairs close to the black cookstove, cupboard for dishes and pans close by, washbasin and stand with a small mirror beside the door. On the far side of the single room they placed the bed, steamer trunk beside it, with a small wardrobe next to that. John nailed up a few simple shelves to set things and drilled in a few pegs to hang things, and that was that. Home sweet home!

As it grew dark, John made sure he was in bed first. This natal night in their pristine new house let loose a virtual flood of amorous feelings juicing through his veins, and he was ready. Unfortunately, the long, heavy day plus her little passenger had worn Ricka down, and her back ached something awful, with nothing to take for it.

When she crawled into bed, John smiled and reached for her. Just four words and he knew his ship would not be sailing out of the harbor that night.

Feeling dejected, both soon fell sound asleep. Somewhere during the black of night, John felt nature's call, and walking outside, he noticed the wondrous northern lights dancing in all their royal glory. He walked back inside and gently nudged his wife, "Ricka, I want you to see something."

She woke with a start, looking down immediately to the dirt floor, afraid of what might be streaking around down there.

Gently, he took her hand and led her outside. Before they even reached the north side of the house, she let out a gasp, "Oh, they're beautiful."

"Oh, just look at that," she continued, squealing in delight. "Look how they keep moving. And just look at all those colors." She put her arm tight around his waist as both stood transfixed by the spectacular heavenly dance unfolding before them.

After long minutes of joyous silence, she looked up higher in the sky.

"And look up there. There's our Big Bear that we saw at home."

"And the North Star, just like we saw it on your front porch," he replied. "Remember?"

Seeing those very familiar heavenly bodies brought a warm feeling but with it also came a strange twinge of loneliness.

"I wonder if Mom and Dad are all right at home in Russia."

"Sure hope so. Maybe they're looking at the Big Bear tonight too."

The comforting stars made her feel connected and, somehow, contentedly at home.

Back in the dark house, she jumped into bed with a girlish giggle and threw her arms around John. The sudden ferociousness of her lips on his told him the new house would be properly dedicated this night after all.

Up at dawn, she had her first job for him to do.

"I have to get a garden in. Think you can dig up a space close to the house," she asked, "and close to the well too so I don't have to carry water too far?"

John spaded up a piece of ground close to the house that was worn bare from all the building activity and now yielded more easily to his spade. Several hours and that job was done. Now it was time to get pounding on a small shed with roosts for the chickens that were running loose in the yard. Not only would they need protection in bad weather, but they were a most inviting target for the daring coyotes, which were always ready for an easy feast during the night.

While he was building the chicken coop, Ricka gathered up her seeds, put on her sunbonnet, and started planting her first garden. She finished two rows of radishes and was starting a row of beans when she happened to look up toward the high hill that rose just to the east of the house. There, on an outcropping of sandstone rock, stood a solitary large, gray coyote. He didn't move a muscle, just stood there silently staring at the scene below. This virtual feast had piqued the wild one's well-honed nose and now he came to check it out. Shudders ran up and down her spine, and for a moment, her voice failed her. Finally, her frozen throat opened up, and she let out a bloodcurdling scream, "John, come quick!" and pointed up the hill.

For a moment, the wily creature didn't move. But when he noticed John suddenly running across the yard, he took one step back, then slowly turned and loped away, over the hill. By then, *Schutz* had also spied him and gave furious chase, with his most ferocious barks. Once on the hilltop, he saw the chase was futile and came running back to lick her hand, wagging his tail as if to say, "I protected you good, didn't I?"

After John and Ricka talked a few minutes, he returned to his building, satisfied that everything was over. For Ricka, it wasn't. She laid down her hoe and seeds and went into the house. For a moment, she just sat there. Then the tears rolled and she sobbed, great, body-shaking sobs that almost made her vomit. Loneliness swept over her like a heavy black wave back on the ocean and then fear gripped her so strongly that she couldn't stop shaking. Her insides were a huge jumble, and through her mind flashed an ugly picture of a pack of vicious, gray beasts circling and attacking her in the garden. She heard snarling howls and snapping teeth tearing bloody gashes into her, and it made her gag. Everything was coming apart, and she just wanted to run away from here as far as she could get. Maybe Sister Mina could help her. But she was back in Krem, too far away to hold her safe. And her husband didn't seem to understand how totally scary this terrible moment was. Finally, she collapsed on the bed and sobbed until she fell asleep.

After an hour of restless sleep, she woke up, and as she looked around, the strength of the thick, pale blue walls seemed to calm her spirit, and somehow her composure slowly returned. She didn't want John to see her in this condition, so she walked to the basin and washed her face. Looking into the mirror, she saw a disheveled, worried person looking back at her, and she began talking to her, *I can't let go like this. Other wives must go through this out here in the wilderness too . . . I don't want to be a fraidy cat and whine around my husband . . . I, I have to be strong for my John . . . He needs me as*

much as I need him . . . I can't let one measly coyote get me down . . .
I have to be strong for my baby and be a good mother.

The mirror made no reply, but after her little speech, she felt better anyway. As she reached to hang up the towel, something suddenly gave a little jump inside her. Like every mother in the world, she instantly knew the meaning. Her hands flew to her growing abdomen, and she bolted to the door.

"Johnny, Johnny," she shouted as she ran toward his little shed. For a moment, he panicked, afraid that something had invaded the house and destroyed her sanctuary.

"Oh, no, not another disaster," he muttered and shouted back, "Ricka, what is it?"

She ran up to him, grabbed both his hands, and held them to her abdomen.

"Here, feel, the baby's kicking."

He felt, bent his head, listened, but felt nothing. Seeing the fire in her eyes, he knew he couldn't let her down and maybe had to lie a little.

"Something going on in there," he finally whispered. And, for sure, that wasn't lying.

That night in bed, she turned her back and snuggled tightly against him, pulling his arm over to hug her abdomen.

"Hey," he exclaimed overloudly in the dark, "it's moving. I feel it too. Our little boy wants to come and ride horse with me." Surprised by his sudden outburst, she gave a little giggling shriek. *Schutz,* lying beside the door outside, heard the commotion and barked, checking to see if all was well in there.

"*Ja, Schutz, alles isch gut*, everything's fine," John answered in *Schutz's* mother tongue.

The day had seen an ugly streak cut through it, but it ended in wonder, and both slept like babies as well.

The next week the brothers worked together cutting grass to make hay on each farm. John put the horses on the mower, while Gottfried operated the dump-rake, pulling the mown grass into windrows. Three days to let it dry, and they stacked the hay into *kopitza,* little stacks, they'd haul home and stack in the yard later in the fall.

Gottfried's wife, Mina, meanwhile, had not come to live on their farm. Her baby was due any time, and she was afraid to be alone out there in that forsaken wilderness, going through a fearful first childbirth. She stayed, instead, with her sister-in-law, Katherina, and her family, who were not totally overjoyed at this arrangement but knowing her deep worry agreed to have her stay.

During these weeks, Ricka had Gottfried over for supper, at least every other evening, and it meant a great deal to both him and John. When she asked what he did for meals the other days, he just shrugged and replied, "Oh, I find stuff."

Finally, Mina's time came due, and a rider came, summoning Gottfried back to Krem. With the help of Mother Karolina as midwife, Mina delivered a baby boy and all was well. Two weeks later, after little Joseph Heinrich was baptized in church, Gottfried finally brought his bride to their new home. John drove Ricka the mile to his brother's place, where she would stay for three days to help Mina get on her feet and get things organized in her new sod house.

Ricka's infectious joy over those brief, busy days proved a contagious blessing for her sister. And knowing Ricka was living nearby and they'd be visiting each other regularly gave her a new sense of optimism and joy as well. This life was going to be very different, but still an exciting adventure. Mina began smiling again.

Chapter 33

Down and Dirty

The brothers now set to work cutting a trench into the sidehill of each farm for an earth-barn to house their cattle and horses. Gottfried loaded up Mina and the baby and brought them along to spend the day with Ricka, who had a glorious time carrying her new nephew around. Even *Schutz* bounded around, barking, and excited over this strange-smelling, squawky little creature that they were fussing over at his house.

After plowing up the sod, the men hitched their horses to a metal dirt scraper to cut a sixteen-by-twenty-four-foot trench. Slicing several inches of dirt at a time until the scraper was full, then dragging it around beside the trench to dump it, then back down into the trench took endless passes to get it done. The women brought out sandwiches and cool water to refresh them, but the work was terribly, oppressively, muscle-busting hard. A hot, strong west wind swirled the loose dirt, blowing into eyes, filtering down throats with every cut they made. Even the horses were hanging their heads in their harness.

"I thought breaking sod in the field was tough," said John, pulling out his red handkerchief to wipe the sweat streaming down his face, "but this is worse."

"Wish we could afford to buy enough lumber to build a regular barn," replied Gottfried.

"That'd sure be a ton easier."

For a week they wrestled the scraper, sunup to sundown, until finally the trench was finished.

"I can't believe how good it feels to be done," Gottfried sighed.

"But now we have to do it all over again at your place," sighed John.

"Humph," his brother snorted, "don't even talk about it!"

A day's delay after a welcome rain moved through, and they began at Gottfried's.

After they had Gottfried's trench cut, they drove across the valley to some unclaimed hill country that had deep ravines with large trees, and here, they spent more days felling several trees to use as roof timbers for their earth-barns. Smaller trees would serve as crossbeams and supports, with the branches stacked on tightly for roofing material. Still another day of trimming the trees and hauling them home, and they were ready to put a roof over their trench-barn. Then came the long, exhausting work of shoveling the dirt they had dumped beside the trench back onto the roof branches, and their barn was nearly done. Nailing together a wall for the front of the barn, a rough door, and two small windows, they were a little closer to being ready for the winter. Now all they had left was to build some mangers to put in hay for the cows and horses, with a few stalls to separate them, and poke several stovepipes through the roof for ventilation.

This grueling work was almost more than they could take, but it was a huge relief to have it done. They decided that it was time to take a break and loaded the wagon for a short stay with the folks in Krem. Grandmother was thrilled to hold her little Joseph, and even Grandpa took time to dandle him gently on his leg.

A long day of visiting and eating, with the men taking a relaxed afternoon nap on the ground outside, and they felt much better. It was a time for telling stories of life in the old country. Father Christian recounted Grandfather Heinrich's accounts of the monstrous snakes on the Russian steppes of the old country, around their Klostitz village, when they first arrived there in the early 1800s.

"Some of those snakes," Heinrich had said, "were as big around as a stovepipe and up to nine feet long." Everyone now wondered just how much the snakes had grown in a hundred years, but at any rate, they must have been big.

"I'm glad the rattlesnakes around here aren't that big," declared Karolina, "but you better keep watching for them, especially with the kids around."

John recounted some of his army life and told them, "The bastards beat us with sticks and marched us for days on nothing but moldy bread and sour borscht. And when one of our men fell down, the stinkin' officers kicked him to death and left him there to rot." The others could only shake their heads, glad they were living in a land of freedom.

The next day was Sunday, with church, and more visiting and eating. All the neighbors wanted the latest news of the newest homesteads, and they were glad to recount the bittersweet times. At night, a neighbor came over with a fiddle, and they sang the old familiar hymns they all knew by heart, until their voices began to crack. The joyous sound brought yet more neighbors, one with an accordion, and all sang their hearts out. Finally, the glad songs of Zion gave way to merry polkas, and happy feet would stay still no longer. Couples got up and the dance was on. This became the sweat of celebration as the young bounced and the heavier old glided together in mirthful rhythm. The simple night turned into a grand summer festivity that finally wound down with sandwiches and pickles, kuchen and cakes, and with a full moon high in the sky, their day came to a glorious, star-twinkling end.

In the midst of all the backbreaking labors, these courageous pioneers were confident that with God in his heaven, the morning stars still sang together, and there would be joy in the morning.

The following day they decided it was time to round up buckets and head for the Missouri River bottomland, where they would all pick chokecherries to make jam and chokecherry wine. The chokecherries, a little smaller than a blueberry, and with a large pit inside, grew wild on the steep sides of the deep ravines, going from green to red to purple-black when they were ripe. They had a delicious tart, bittersweet taste, but also a definite downside: eating them turned your teeth black as shoe polish.

Spreading out along the clusters of small-fruited trees, everyone in the small party kept shouting back and forth, "Got enough to fill the bottom of your bucket yet?" All knew that the others were also eating more than they were getting into the bucket, at least to start with, until their teeth started getting sticky from the dark deposit as they worked the cherries to spit out the pits. When their buckets were partially filled, they gathered back at the wagon. As Ricka set her bucket down and smiled, everyone roared.

"You look like you been chewing soot," teased John.

"And you look like somebody knocked out a couple of your teeth," laughed Ricka, as she saw his black-stained incisors, with everyone else's stained just as badly.

Only brushing with baking soda would clean those messed-up teeth, and it would take several days at that.

The next day, the women processed the cherries into pint jars of jelly, while the men hauled out gallon jars to turn their part of the juices into strong, sweet wine. Suddenly, the prospect of a heavy winter coming didn't sound quite as daunting after all.

Back at home, Ricka enjoyed seeing the strong stalks of her sunflower plants stretching higher every week, with their bright yellow faces smiling at the sun. She was busy again tending her garden and her chickens while singing her favorite hymns and collecting eggs in strange places where the chickens insisted on hiding them. But with her abdomen rounding bigger, it was getting more difficult by the week and energy harder come by.

The brothers, together with August Keller, had joined to buy a new McCormick "Daisy" reaper with a five-foot cutting sickle and a canvas conveyor belt that laid the cut grain down in a neat windrow. They spent a day hitching the horses to it and slowly driving it around the yard, figuring out the moving parts and where trouble spots might develop.

Every day they checked the wheat, and when the heads turned gold and the kernels hard, the three worked together, running the reaper first in Keller's ten acres, then Gottfried's, and then John's. After cutting each field, they got out five-tined pitchforks and went down the windrows, piling the cut grain by hand into waist-high *kopitza*, little pointed stacks, to finish drying.

To the relief of the whole neighborhood, several other Keller brothers had joined to purchase a huge Rumley coal-fired steam engine and threshing machine. It moved so slowly that you almost had to set up a stick to see if it moved at all, but move it did. Putting out great puffs of smoke, like a train engine, it had amazing power and easily handled threshing all the grain for the twelve neighboring farmers who joined in the cooperative threshing effort.

For several cents a bushel, the Kellers did the threshing, and each farmer came with a team and hayrack to haul the little *kopitza* on each little plot of land to the machine.

As the puffing steam rig set up on each farm, it became that farm wife's job to furnish food for the entire crew. Ricka became worried, afraid that in her condition she might not be able to handle that much heavy work. But before the Rumley began rolling, three neighboring women each told her they would be there to help and bring extra food as well.

Threshing those little fields that first year was quickly done. It took longer for the sleepwalking Rumley to move from farm to farm than to do the actual threshing. But the camaraderie among both threshers and chefs was worth its weight in golden kernels. It helped to form bonds that made the neighborhood into a band of brothers and sisters who would be there for each other, come what may.

When the last field was threshed, the brothers again worked together shoveling up the wheat where it had been dumped on the ground and filling their wagons to the very top of the box, a fifty-bushel load. At dawn the next morning, they set out with four horses on each wagon, pulling over a ton and a half, heading the nearly twelve miles to the village of Expansion, hard by the banks of the swift Missouri. From there, the wheat would be shipped downriver by steam barges to Bismarck and on by rail to Eastern markets. As quickly as they could, they shoveled the wheat back off the wagons into the grated elevator pit and headed for home, getting back in the dark of night on the prairie trail, which the horses had long ago memorized.

The next day they loaded again. The day after, they hauled. And once more after that they did it all again. During those long trips, there wasn't much to break the boredom but to chew pocketfuls of sunflower seeds and listen to the meadowlarks cheering them on.

On the last trip, the women went along as well, planning to stay several days in Krem for another visit and for making serious preparations for winter. These new soddy-moms had heard some gruesome tales about prairie winters out here, and their hearts were more than a little uneasy at the prospect of what might be awaiting them.

Chapter 34

Letter from Russia

When they got to Krem, Katherina told them a letter just arrived from the sisters in Russia and invited them over to hear what the sisters had written.

Liebe Katherina und alle meiner Familie, Dear Katherina and all my family,

It was so good to get your letter and hear how all of you are doing. With eight children your days must be very full. I imagine the children are very busy in school and helping you and Adam at home.

It was also good to hear that Gottfried and Mina and John and Ricka all made it safe to Amerika as well. It was very confusing here until they were able to leave, but I am glad they are all well, along with Mamma and Papa and Anna. I hope Mamma had a happy 63rd birthday in June. Tell her I thought about her all day.

Barbara and I have both gotten married, to the Dschaak brothers, Peter and Jacob. We wanted to wait and get married in Amerika, but the emigration papers are much simpler for married people, so we went ahead here. We had a double wedding, and the Dschaak family was wonderful in putting everything together so nice.

It seems like all the people from Klostitz and all the dorfs around us are heading for Amerika. I know not everyone is going, but it seems that way. The Russian police and military keep running all over the country and stealing things from people, beating people if they say anything. Jews especially are being beaten, villages burned, animals killed or stolen. No one gets paid for the damage, even though the dorf mayors have complained. The tsar and the government just talk and do nothing about it. They say it is too bad, and it should be stopped but no one is getting it stopped.

Sister Fredericka and her husband Konstentine and the children are also planning to leave for Amerika. His Stohler family has also been good to help us. We have most of our paperwork done, and all hope to come to Amerika sometime early next year. Hopefully, you can show us how to get started there.

We talked with Uncle Jake a few weeks ago, and he said that he and Aunt Natalia and their family are staying here and not going to Amerika. He thinks moving would be too hard for Aunt Natalia and might make her sick again. He does not want to take a chance.

John, do you remember Georg, the man who escaped from the army with you? One day soldiers came and picked him up, and nothing has been heard from him since. His family is worried sick over him. Doesn't sound good.

I know Papa has put Brother Frederick out of the family, but I will tell you he has now married his Russian sweetheart Natasha, and they are very happy. He was also recently drafted into the army and is serving somewhere far in the East. Greet all our family and hug them. We miss you so much and wait to see you again.

Your Louisa

Chapter 35

Digging in for Winter

The money from selling their wheat was a godsend for John and Gottfried. Cash in hand, the first place they went was to visit Herr Miller at the sawmill to pay him the first year's loan payment and interest.

With a cheery, "*Nu, Osters, wie gehts?* Well, Osters, how are you?" Miller got out his ledger and marked off their payment.

"I can't believe how good this feels," exclaimed John, "just to get that off our shoulders. Now we're half paid off."

"Already feel like a new man, a couple years younger!" Gottfried replied.

They also bought more lumber to build a granary for next year's crops and a small shed beside the house to store wood and coal to burn for the coming winter. Later, they found a pair of sleds, which they would need for winter transportation and for hauling manure out and straw in.

In the afternoon, they took several sacks of wheat to the mill to be ground into flour, bought supplies of sugar, salt, and other staples for winter, and drove around to nearby farms looking for two more cows to buy first thing next spring.

The following three days they spent at Adam and Katherina's, butchering their winter meat supply. To Adam fell the considerable task of assembling all the tables and scalding kettles, knives and meat saws, firewood, stuffers and grinders, and finally the two selected hogs and one beef.

The four families all joined, but it still turned out to be a massive job, with blood flowing, and innards and cuts of meat piled everywhere. Finally, all the meat was cut, some canned, some cuts smoked, others salted, some turned into several kinds of sausages, and some left fresh for immediate eating. With all involved in a huge cleanup job, finally all four families were more prepared for the months of winter just around the corner.

During the long ride home, Ricka felt the bumps and jolts of the wagon wheels on the prairie trail a lot more than she had before. For her, getting home couldn't come fast enough.

Once back on their homesteads, the brothers spent long days taking turns riding the breaking plow and turning over more sod for bigger fields next year. Before the ground froze, they hoped to have forty acres each to plant next year. Ricka, in the meantime, spent her days canning garden vegetables and digging carrots and potatoes. As she continued to grow more round, bending over was also getting considerably more difficult for her, but never once did John hear her complain.

While Gottfried had the plow at his place, John drove four miles down the valley for a load of coal from another neighbor, John Bauer. Bauer had discovered a little coal vein showing through on a sidehill of his farm and dug into it. The vein turned thicker as he got further in, and by now he had a regular cave dug in, bracing the entrance with large timbers and hauling the coal out by donkey and four-wheel cart. He was also employing dynamite to blast the twelve-foot-thick coal vein apart for easier handling, and it made for some high excitement in the neighborhood.

When John got there, he heard muffled pounding from deep inside but looking into the entrance, saw nothing. After long minutes of patient waiting, he saw coming slowly toward him a jet-black figure with tired white eyeballs and a bobbing light on his head, leading a weary, soot-covered donkey, straining to pull his heavy black burden out of the cave.

"Hello, Bauer," yelled John, catching himself shouting as if the coal dust had somehow turned his neighbor deaf.

"Ja, Oster," muttered Bauer, "dirty work in there, dirty, dirty work."

After they had loaded the wagon, Bauer asked, "Ja, Oster, have you ever helped shoot dynamite?"

"*Nei*," John replied, "I was around some big canons firing in the Russian army, but never dynamite."

"Pull your wagon down the hill and tie up your horses good, and you help me blow a shot."

When he came back, Bauer grabbed some tools and several sticks of dynamite out of a wooden chest and led the way into the mine.

John had no light so he stayed right on Bauer's heels down the damp incline. He could see absolutely nothing, only smell the heavy, sulfurous coal dust that made him cough and his eyes blink.

Suddenly, Bauer stopped and handed the dynamite to John, "Here, you hold this." John held it more carefully than a newborn babe, while Bauer used a sledgehammer and chisel to drive a hole into the black wall of coal. When the hole was a little over a foot into the wall, he reached for the sticks of dynamite and packed them in tightly with coal dust. After attaching the blasting cap, he ran a long fuse away from the dynamite, raised his right leg to make his pants taut, struck a "farmer stick" wooden match on his leg, and held it to the fuse, which lit immediately with a determined sizzling.

By the time he could say, "Don't worry, we have plenty time to get out," the sound of his words was already far away, as John, suddenly terrified at what could happen here, was wheeling his feet, scrambling faster than he had moved in a long time, hoping he wouldn't stumble in the dark as he ran for the faint spot of light up ahead. He stood panting beside the mine entry, when, it seemed like several minutes later, Bauer came shuffling out with a big smile on his face.

"I told you, don't worry," he exclaimed, pulling John away from the hole.

Just then the ground shook with a horrific, thunderous explosion, followed in a moment by a great cloud of dust blowing out, like some giant one-eyed Homeric Cyclops spitting an angry mouthful of bad mutton out of his cave.

John's knees were still trembling; his breath coming in short gasps, as he turned in time to see the horses rear up and nearly rip their bridle lines in unstrung fear, their eyes round as saucers.

"Whoa, Sophie, Whoa, Schwartz," John yelled to the horses. Then, "*Danke,* thank you, Bauer," he continued, "that was something all right."

When he got home with the load of coal, he was barely off the wagon when Ricka took one look at him and said, "Johnny, what happened. You look terrible."

After telling her the whole story, in minutest detail, he took a deep breath, "Boy, that was something all right. I'm sure not gonna complain about carrying coal in this winter."

Later, he sat down to read the *Staats-Anzeiger* newspaper they brought back from Krem. "Ach," he snorted, "there's a dumb story here that somebody made up about two guys named Wright trying to fly in the air in something they call an aeroplane. I don't think God will ever allow that to happen, do you?"

"Well, you just never know," Ricka replied. "Remember how we got light in the Salem Hotel just by pushing a button on the wall?"

"Humph, that's way different."

The next day John drove the team out to haul home the little hay *kopitza*, piles from the hay field and fork them into a rounded stack close to the earth-barn. After that, he hauled home several loads of straw from the threshed straw stack in the wheat field, a ready supply of soft bedding for the animals during the icy cold of winter, and stacked it next to the hay.

Last Christmas, Christ gave each of his sons a long, heavy wool coat for a present. Now, sitting on the breaking plow as the sky darkened and the north wind blew a fierce cold, that wool coat was a godsend to keep John from freezing into a solid lump. Luckily, the three horses on the plow knew the routine as well as did the driver, and for periods, he could wrap the reins around the depth-lever and sit with his hands curled up in his mittens. On occasion, he even managed to get off the moving plow and walk behind it. In those times he realized how attached he was becoming to his horses.

These horses are almost as good as a good wife, he said one day to himself. *Well, not quite, but still awfully good.* Walking on, he pondered, *With a good wife and these good horses, I'm a lucky man. One lucky man.* He felt like stopping and patting each of the horses on the nose but thought better of it and just kept walking, with the widest smile that no one but God could see.

When the unbroken sod showed a heavy coat of white in the morning and frost began to penetrate into the wiry roots, the men decided to stop plowing for the year and embark, instead, on a venture of a totally different kind.

"You remember all the buffalo bones scattered over the prairies when we drive around?" John said one day.

"Yeah," Gottfried replied, "lots of 'em still there."

"Remember, one day Adam mentioned that Peter Miller at the sawmill in Expansion buys bones and ships them east on the steam boat for making fertilizer?"

"Hey, tomorrow let's grab both wagons and make some money."

In the next week's cold, they crisscrossed the neighboring hills and loaded buffalo bones, heaping their wagons high until they became a virtual cemetery of horned buffalo skulls staring hollow-eyed back at the earth they had once roamed in such vigorous, snorting multitudes.

In a little over two week's time, the enterprising brothers had earned the princely sum of fifty dollars each, enough to buy several more cows next spring to add to their small herd. Soon they would be grazing on the very grasses named for the herds whose bones they were daily grazing around.

November brought dark, flying clouds, driven by harsh north winds that howled around the corners of their brave little sod house, sometimes strong enough to wiggle Ricka's flowered curtains. Gradually, November's rattling winds segued into December's bitter cold. By now they had added a pot-bellied heating stove, opposite the kitchen, and its red-hot grates stoked by chunks of Bauer coal kept the tiny thick-walled house rather comfortable, although the dirt floor never got warm. A woven rug beside the bed got them started in relative comfort, but after that, they either had shoes on or very cold feet.

Outside, the prairie birds were all gone, save for the little chirping, black and white snow buntings, and hearty sparrows. The creatures of the earth all burrowed down deep, save for the sturdy coyotes whose mournful howls rattled the air waves for miles across the frozen hills. The only other sound was the blowing wind that wrapped the earth in a snowy cotton mantle with ever-changing folds.

Ricka knew her time had almost come. Her back ached, her legs hurt, everything was uncomfortable and hard, and the baby was banging its cage day and night. Every week now Gottfried, Mina, and little Joe came to spend time with them, talking, playing cards, singing a few hymns and old folk songs. Other neighbors came as well, all checking, encouraging, and cheering the expectant couple. And since the coffeepot was always hot on the back of the stove, the night always ended with coffee and sandwiches and kuchen or cake for the road.

In late afternoon, John finished feeding chickens and pigs and was out feeding the cows and horses in the earth-barn when he heard a loud shout from the house. Only one thing could bring on that piercing shout, and he dropped his fork and ran. After checking to see that Ricka would be all right for a while, he saddled his fastest horse and flew the two miles to get the neighborhood midwife. Snow was driving hard across the open prairies, but John never noticed. The midwife and her husband were on their sled in a matter of minutes, while John raced back to be with his wife as quickly as his winded horse could carry him.

When Ricka went into serious labor, John hitched up the sled for the short drive to Gottfried's place.

"Mina," he shouted from his sled, "quick come with me and help us."

Shortly after they got back, birthing began, and anxious John and the neighbor went out to the barn, leaving the women to usher a new life into the world. *Schutz* went with his master, tail down, searching John's face to make sense out of the anguished screaming going on in the house, thinking the two of them should be doing something to help. John patted his head, "It's all right, *Schutz*," but neither was entirely convinced.

Ricka was brave and strong, but birthing is rarely easy, nor was it for her. The pain was almost unbearable, but she gripped the women's hands until they fairly broke and bit down on a rolled up dish towel until her jaws screamed back in agony. After what seemed like days, the midwife exclaimed, "Ach, the head is coming. *Schieb*, Ricka, *schieb*, push." When she had absolutely no push left, she felt a slithering motion, and the midwife gently pulled the little one out into its new world. The women finished cleaning and wrapping and laid the baby into Ricka's curled-up arm.

Mina opened the door and faced the barn, yelling as loudly into the howling wind as she could. A nervous John slammed the barn door, and in a flash, he and the neighbor were up in the house. The door being ripped open and slammed shut made the dimly burning kerosene lamp flicker and give everything in the house a ghostly appearance, especially the long spectral shadows of the women for whom John was so immensely grateful.

"You have a new son, John," smiled the tired midwife, "come see him."

His first thought was of Ricka, but when he saw her bravely trying to smile through her tears, he knew she was going to be all right, and he bent over and kissed her wet forehead. Only then did he get around to a good look at his new son. He had a hard moment trying to show excitement over this wrinkled, bawling little thing, but still he was thankful that all had gone well and that an heir had been born to his house. Quickly he folded his hands and all eyes closed as he led them in a prayer of thanks to God for being so gracious and caring to all of them.

The winter seemed to fly, as though it were blown by the great winds of the north. Between several huge blizzards, they were blessed with visits from a number of neighbors, with Gottfried driving their sled over every other Friday night and the other Fridays they loaded the sled and headed to Gottfried's. They had cards to play and songs to sing and baby Phillip to carry around, puckering his cheeks to see him smile, which he learned to do with infectious little giggles, much to everyone's delight.

The days soon settled into a routine and even the howling two- and three-day blizzards piling up six-foot drifts didn't seem to change things much.

Ricka was busy nursing the baby, cooking big meals, doing dishes, hand-washing clothes, sprinkling the hardpacked dirt floor with water, and sweeping it. John's days were filled with drawing water from the well, feeding the pigs and chickens and gathering a few eggs, milking the cow, feeding the horses and cows, hauling out manure, and bringing in more hay and straw.

Then one day it happened as John knew it had to sooner or later. Ricka was quietly singing to a contentedly nursing little Phillip when suddenly she jumped in her chair and let out a shriek, "Johnny, there's something up there." Following her wide-eyed gaze upward, the dim kerosene lamp revealed two bright, shining little eyes peering down from the rafters.

"Oh, it's only a little mouse!" he replied, but with the baby now frightened and wailing up a storm, John spent the next half hour swatting and banging at the little creature over almost every inch of the soddy, missing it with every exasperated swing of his broom.

Suddenly, it dashed under the bed, with John quickly down on all four after it, but it totally vanished.

That night Ricka hardly slept, sure that the thing was somehow, somewhere in her bed and was going to crawl up her nightdress. And when she did sleep, such bizarre, crawly things kept chasing her that she woke up even more tired. Morning brought no resolution, but she could only hope the little monster had somehow found a hole to crawl back out to its own world.

Then before they knew it, winter had lost its grip, the days became longer, and south winds brought welcome warmth. Snow banks gave way to puddles, and the tinkle of sweet water music gently echoed through the ravines as rivulets gathered to hunt out lower ground.

"I don't remember a time," Ricka told John, "when I ever appreciated spring even half this much."

Chapter 36

Snakes in the Grass

As the days warmed, they began to realize that in one short year's time their country had changed forever. All the land around them was now homesteaded, more sod was broken up, and the entire valley was bustling with farming activities. Fences were going up on the once wide-open prairies, and cattle were grazing on a thousand hills. In that one brief year, the age of hand labor was over, and the age of machinery had been ushered in.

When the prairie trails dried out enough for wagon travel, Ricka and Mina decided that four months cooped up in their sod houses was enough and they needed a change. Between cabin fever and a need to be with family and hear about the world out there, they needed to get out.

The brothers loaded John's wagon with straw for comfortable sitting, the women bundled up the babies, and they set out for Grandma's house. Seeing the purple crocuses bravely breaking out of the prairie soil and hearing the joyous meadowlarks, who had just flown in from their winter homes and were singing their hearts out, brought an overwhelming sense of joy and relief to all of them. "Oh, it feels so wonderful," Mina shouted, "to be out again."

Visiting the appreciative grandparents and seeing Katherina and her large, growing family cheered everyone's spirits. But it was also time for some serious business that would impact their future as well.

Grandfather Christ had developed a thriving leather business, and along with fixing shoes and fashioning bridles and harnesses, he even tried his hand at crafting saddles. Getting both the light wood and the heavy leather shaped and formed together just right and then embossing it for greater appeal was a real challenge, and he often spent long nights by kerosene lamp in the shop finishing his work. It paid off, too, with customers coming from long distances, even a few from across the frozen Missouri in winter, and paying hard cash.

With his many contacts at the shop, Christ also became a walking bulletin board, with a great deal of information about who had what to buy or sell, and many a customer turned to him for help in locating something they needed. Now he also knew where to point the boys when they wanted to buy more cows and another good team—emphasizing the "good"—of horses, along with a mechanical drill they wanted to buy together for seeding their crops.

Within two days, each of the brothers had his good team and three more cows, and the dealer was able to find them an eight-foot drill to plant their new ground into wheat and oats. It seemed strange to buy just one piece of machinery, but both brothers got along so well that they had the same goals and aspirations, and doing the work together seemed like the natural thing to do.

The trip home was like a band of gypsies moving through, pulling their drill behind the wagon and herding half a dozen bewildered cows and four horses. While John drove the wagon, Gottfried rode bareback on one of the horses to keep all the livestock herded together. A few cows started rambling across the prairie, but finally, he managed to get them all following the wagon, and after a mile, they got the traveling idea figured out, making a right lively little circus. An occasional "moo" from the cows and a snort from the horses even seemed to help lull the babies to sleep, and they were soon at home.

When the ground had warmed enough, John hitched up the team to pull the disc over his plowed land, then harrowed it, and finally filled the new drill with sacks of cleaned wheat seed, making short work of seeding his entire forty acres of wheat and oats for the year. With a double team on the machinery, even the four horses seemed to appreciate the ease of this work and stepped lively the whole day long.

When John got home and they sat at supper, he reflected, "You know, life here is really going to be different than anything we ever knew before."

"Why do you say that?" Ricka asked.

"Because all this machinery is making farming so much easier, and farms are going to be bigger than ever before, here or anywhere in the world."

"I can see that."

"In another few years we'll hardly know this country anymore. They'll have machines for everything."

On Easter Sunday, they traveled back to Krem. Along with special worship services, it would also be a special time to have little Phillip Heinrich baptized. Unbeknownst to them, John's three sisters and their families had also recently arrived in America. Now all were joined together for the festive celebration. Little Phillip, in the white baptismal gown that Grandmother had sewn, was passed around and cuddled until he wore out and fell asleep. After a big goose dinner, with dishes finished, the women set out chairs to do some heavy conversation, catching up on the old country, getting hints about the new.

The men spread out in the yard for their usual nap and then got serious about prospects for homestead land still available further west. They decided the three brothers-in-law would come to John's, and he and Gottfried would accompany them farther west to pick out land and help them get started.

They found suitable land and were soon busy filing their claims.

The next week John was back in the fields while Ricka returned to her garden, which had to be bigger this year, with another eater and more neighbors visiting as time went by. She wrapped the baby in warm blankets and laid him into a woven straw basket she had received as a baby gift from a neighbor. After planting more peas, she walked back to the edge of the garden to check on him. As she got closer, she suddenly froze.

Curled up against the warm sunny side of the baby basket was a venomous diamondback rattlesnake, coiled and relaxing. She called for *Schutz,* but remembered he had gone out to the field with John.

Ricka wanted to scream, but who would hear, and besides, it might spook the poisonous snake. Slowly, step by tortured step, she approached the reptile, her heart pounding furiously and hands shaking. The snake raised its head and watched her every step. As she reached to within eight feet of the snake, its tongue shot out, unblinking eyes ablaze, tail suddenly up and sounding its angry signature rattle, as if to say, "No closer."

She had been told that rattlesnakes could not jump at you, but she also knew that they could strike the length of their body. The problem was, with the creature coiled up, she couldn't tell how long it was, only that its unblinking, beady black eyes and flicking tongue looked terribly menacing. As she drew nearer, it again sounded its angry rattles and spiked the threat higher.

She didn't want to strike at the rattler with her hoe, afraid she might miss it and hit the baby's basket instead, tipping it over so the rattler could attack the baby. Her stomach revolted in terror.

Finally, holding the very end of her hoe handle, she struck the hoe on the ground several feet away from the snake. Almost quicker than she could see it happen, the snake struck the hoe, then instantly recoiled, rattling louder than before.

Ricka was beside herself. "If only Johnny were here," she cried through frightened tears. Her tortured mind went blank for a moment. And then she had an idea: she would tease the snake with a number of jabs near it, hoping it would either get irritated and crawl away or else become tired and perhaps slow down.

Three times she jabbed the ground near the snake, away from the basket. Three times it struck and recoiled, now rattling with rekindled fury.

Then the fourth time, she held the end of the handle with both shaking hands and jabbed the ground again, this time anticipating the snake's strike. As it rippled, beginning its strike, she snapped the hoe up and brought it back down in a flash, catching the snake before it could recoil. She stunned it enough to stay stretched out for just an instant and then struck again with every ounce of her strength, driving the hoe blade hard enough to sever the creature's body.

She picked up little Phillip, hugging him close to her chest, and ran screaming all the way into the house. She held him for long minutes and only began to relax when he wanted to be fed.

When John came home from the field, she ran into his arms crying, sobbing until her whole body shook.

"Oh, Johnny, I hate this ugly country!" she sobbed.

"Whoa, what's wrong?" John asked. "What happened?"

"A snake. A big, ugly."

"Where? What did it do?"

"It attacked me. It wanted the baby!"

"Maybe so, but probably it was just enjoying the warm sun beside the basket."

"I don't care. It feels like those animals are out to attack me."

"Well, maybe they think you smell really good, better than all the stuff around here," replied John, trying to lighten up the tense moment and at the same time letting his hand slide down her back, squeezing her bottom, aroused by the flames in her eyes.

"Johnny, what are you doing?"

He slid both hands down, massaging her hips.

"John, is that all you men ever think of?"

"Well," and thinking better of it, he let it drop but squeezed her more. "Well . . ."

Then he whispered in her ear, "And God looked and said, 'It is very good!'" as he pressed against her.

She knew where he wanted to go with this and knew it was his solution to the fear and the confused tension inside her. But for her, it was an insult, thinking a few moments in bed could solve the turmoil in her soul, and she wanted none of it.

"Time for supper," she shot back, turning away and walking to the stove, disgusted at his uncaring attitude.

Sleep that night was a miserable affair, with terrible things terrorizing her all night. Fortunately, during the night, it rained, so the garden was too wet to work the next day, allowing her to spend the day inside, cleaning, playing with the baby, and scrubbing clothes on the tin washboard to settle her mind again.

The rest of the time in the garden was peaceful, with no more snakes. Hoeing, she couldn't help but think, *How did the old folks put it, "As you cook the porridge, so you must eat it." Guess I'm on my own out here,* and kept swinging her hoe.

John returned to the field the next morning and pulled a furrow halfway to the far end when his heart suddenly felt strangely overpowered, and he called out to the team, "Whoa." When they stopped, he got off the plow and kneeling down, picked up a handful of the newly turned soil and held it to his nose, breathing in the full aroma of his rich earth, this little spot of earth he called his "Little Osterland." Gently filtering the dirt through his flexing fingers, he called out to the horses, "This is my home. And on this soil I'll die." The horses flicked their ears back and forth, not sure what he was talking about, but understanding his tone, and shifting their hindquarter weight to one leg, relaxed in the harness.

Then it struck him that this land under his feet and under his fingernails was not just property, not just a welcome homestead, but that this was indeed something more, something spiritual. For centuries, his people had been people of the soil, and here he was, continuing the tradition, but with a new twist.

This is like Father Abraham in the Bible, he mused, *and how God called him to leave his home and go to a new land of promise, "by the oaks of Mamre," in old Israel.*

He heard Pastor Mueller again telling the story in confirmation so long ago, *And Abraham built an altar there.*

Intense devotion gripped him, and he looked around for stones. Seeing none close by, he sank to his knees and prayed, "*Lieber Gott,* Dear God, this place is holy, like Mamre, and you brought me here to do your work. I lay it all into your mighty hands."

With eyes closed, he saw Father Abraham, in the heat of the day, sweating behind a hitch of oxen, and continued, "Use me and Ricka, like Abraham and Sarah, and use our children and our children's children to bring glory to your name. Amen."

When he got back up, he felt a new lightness around him and inside. He couldn't explain it, nor would he make a big deal about it to others. But when he got home, he told Ricka, "I had the strangest experience today."

"What happened?"

"While I was plowing out there, it seemed like God was suddenly so close to me that I could almost touch him."

"Really?"

"It was like the story of Abraham, and it seemed like God was telling me there's something really special about this place and about us being here."

Then, looking deep into her eyes to gauge her response, he continued, "I hope you don't think I'm getting funny."

She clasped his shoulders, "Dearest John, God must have something special in mind. Maybe he will raise our son or someone else in this place to serve him in a special way."

They held each other for a while and said no more. But Ricka held those words as a beacon in her heart to the end of her days as did John.

Chapter 37

Stretching the Horizons

On a warm spring day, after planting was done, a man rode into the yard. He was a farmer from several miles away, and he wanted to talk to both John and Ricka.

"You know," he said after several minutes' small talk, "we have a lot of children around our big neighborhood here, and I'm sure more will be coming, so we need to think about getting a school going."

They knew that was true, even though little Phillip was yet too young to worry about it.

"The county has drawn up a plan," he continued, "and all of us in this township are in one school district."

They both understood that their township, like all others in the state, was comprised of 36 sections of land, stretching 6 miles by 6 miles, with each section being 640 acres or four quarters of 160 acres each. And two sections in each township, sections sixteen and thirty-six, were set aside as "school land," which could not be homesteaded. They were reserved for school buildings, while the balance could be rented out for hay or cropland to make money for the school district.

The Mercer County Superintendent of Schools, appointed by the state, had full control over all rural schools in the district and had called a meeting for them to organize and select sites for all the schools to be located in their township.

Since their township was virtually 100 percent Germans from Russia, they were mindful of their Reformation heritage and Martin Luther's strong emphasis on education, and they named theirs the "Wittenberg School District," after Luther's town and university. And when Adam Keller donated five acres of land for a school in their designated area, their school, officially School #2 of the township, would become "The Keller School." For Gottfried's children, it would mean a one-mile walk to school, for John's nearly two miles.

By September of the following year, the county superintendent planned to have a one-room school built, equipment supplied, and a teacher engaged. After that, the school would be turned over to an elected township school board who would control everything for their school.

When they met to organize, they were told there would be one catch: the county would go through all the property records and issue a tax on every landowner to pay for the schools. The taxes would be an irritant, but they realized that this was also the price of the great freedoms they were enjoying.

In the meantime, Ricka continued to delight in her little son. She loved to sing hymns and time-honored baby songs to little Phillip and see his eyes light up, his tiny face reflecting her every expression, beginning to coo and voice sounds with different notes, his arms waving in the air with excitement.

Several times Ricka packed baskets of food and they loaded the wagon and drove out to help more new settlers build their sod houses. The hard work always turned into a time of joy as the labor turned into friendships with these new neighbors. Their valley and the surrounding hills became their new *dorf* that spelled a good life.

Between haying and harvest time, they decided to visit John's parents in Krem and were surprised to see how Grandmother Karolina had aged. She had shrunk several inches in stature and grown plump and her legs seemed stiff when she walked; she had developed a pronounced mustache along with long chin hair, and she never did anything without wearing her long *schuertz*, apron, and *deechle*, her grandmotherly three-cornered kerchief, tied at the chin. She smiled and hugged little Phillip until he almost squeaked and loved to have them visit, but she was definitely feeling her years.

"Mother's starting to age," observed John when they were driving home.

"She's sure sitting down more," Ricka responded.

"And sighing a lot to herself, like she's worn out."

"Ja, her life hasn't been a peach kuchen."

****

Harvest that fall was a much bigger affair than that of a year earlier. The Keller threshing rig had a full schedule, with twelve neighboring farmers joining the "Keller machine." The twelve would rotate, with eight providing teams of horses with bundle-hauling racks and four being "spikers" who would help load the racks out in the field. Since the fields were all considerably larger than just a year earlier, threshing would be a much longer process now.

For the women of each farm, the job had also grown into a formidable task, a feast of huge proportions. For the men, this was the prairie banquet they lived for since the middle of summer.

Ricka began preparing weeks before the threshing machine was to arrive. She and John began by digging potatoes from the garden and storing them in the granary. Then they butchered twelve chickens and hung them down the well, ready to fry in the big black cast-iron frying pan half filled with lard. After that, it was time to churn a gallon of cream into butter and hang it down the well in a tin to keep it cool. Next, Ricka got out some cheesecloth and hung up some curdled milk to turn into cottage cheese. Finally, the day before the machine arrived, she had to knead bread dough and kuchen dough and, when John had stoked up the kitchen stove with wood to heat the oven, bake a dozen loaves of fresh bread and another dozen custard and prune kuchen. Two neighbor women would each bring another dozen kuchen and several loaves of bread as well for the hungry men.

It had become tradition that noon meals would include at least three meats, most often fried chicken, sausages, and ham or beef roast. Ricka mashed a big kettle of potatoes, made a serving bowl of gravy, then went to work setting out tomatoes, corn, creamed peas, squash, pickles, pickled beets, pickled carrots, cucumber salad with onions and fresh cream, and, of course, mandatory bowls of steaming hot sauerkraut. This year the season was right for peppers maturing, so she added *haluptze*, peppers stuffed with spiced-up hamburger and rice. Finally, German chocolate cake, carrot cake, lemon and mincemeat pies, and kuchen would finish the festive feast.

They were fortunate that the weather held because there was no room to feed the entire crew in their little soddy, so they took two doors off the sheds and laid them across sawhorses in the yard, covered them with oilcloth, and surrounded them with wooden boxes and chairs borrowed from the neighbors.

At the threshing machine, the men unhitched their teams of horses and, climbing up into the grain wagons, led their teams, eight horses following each wagon, up to the farm to water and feed them.

When the horses were settled in, the men walked to the well and drank deep from the tin dipper, then rolled up their sleeves and washed off the thick layer of dust that plastered their faces and necks. Half the fun of coming in to dinner came with the jokes, the laughter, the good-natured shoving and jostling, even a quick wrestling match or two. When Ricka called them all to table, John, as host, led them in the table prayer, "*Komm Herr Jesu,* Come Lord Jesus, be our guest . . .," and they ate until all desire was gone and food was done.

Pushing away from the tables, the men stretched out for a quick nap in the yard while the women ate. Later, over laughter and news, they washed and dried the piles and piles of dishes.

These pioneers rose from bed long before sunrise to do their chores at home and then drove to the threshing rig to be there the moment the sun broke the broad eastern horizon. Not only were they hungry by noon, but, to keep their energy up, the women also brought lunch out to the fields at mid-morning and mid-afternoon. Those "light lunches" came in dishtowel-covered baskets filled with mounds of ham, chicken, and liverwurst sandwiches, pickles, kuchen, and cakes. A five-gallon cream can of piping hot coffee, several clay Red Wing jugs of cool well water, and another cream can of refreshing cool nectar, orange or strawberry, parched dry throats. Thirsts were big, cups were large, and the tin drink dipper made many a round during the welcome breaks.

This sort of meal was too much for one woman to handle, so three or four neighbor women all worked together, often bringing extra dishes and silverware along to supplement the meager cupboards of each house. When the women arrived at Ricka's, she chuckled, "I can't help but think of the saying the old Russian women had, '*Too many cooks spoil the borscht.*'" The women all laughed as she added, "But, *ei, yei, yei,* am I ever glad all you good cooks came to help."

For this band of sturdy prairie women, these were not only meals, nor just food, but a testament to their culinary skills. Threshing time became county-fair time, and no higher compliment could they receive than for the men to lay down their fork, wipe their hands on their pants, and pronounce a contented, "*Dass war sehr gut,* that was really good."

When the men drove back out to the field, they remembered that one of their crew, Immanuel Geist, had a huge phobia about snakes, and they hatched a plot to have some fun. Whoever found a black bull snake—it had to be a fairly large one, and not a rattler, so he wouldn't be bitten—would take it in to the machine and have Keller secretly throw it on Geist's rack when he pulled up to unload his bundles.

Sure enough, they found one, and everything went according to plan. Geist began pitching bundles into the threshing machine feeder and got down into the load when he suddenly saw the snake slithering between bundles near his feet. To him, the thing was instantly eight feet long and life threatening, and he came near throwing himself into the feeder chain to escape. He let out a scream that could be heard all the way out in the field and vaulted off the rack in one Olympic leap, landing on his feet and rolling in the dirt.

Keller had stationed himself on the steam engine, just in case, and immediately pulled the power lever to stop the belt and shut down the machine. All the men around the machine raced over to Geist, fearing a broken leg for their fun. When they saw his ashen face and heard him shrieking, "Snake, snake!" as he struggled to his feet, they doubled over in laughter. One of the other men had to finish unloading Geist's rack because he was an emotional wreck for the moment. The next two days, you could hear scattered shouts of "snake" all over the field, and Geist died a little inside every time he heard it.

During the days of threshing, there was much serious talk as well. The men felt a deep spiritual vacuum in their lives and now spent time talking about church. The closest church was in Krem, thirteen miles away, and they felt the neighborhood was ready to organize their own church. They decided that after threshing was finished, they would have the Krem pastor come over and talk about starting their own congregation.

Several weeks later, a delegation drove to Krem and talked to Reverend Adolph Zeiszler. He was more than happy to meet with them since he considered their area a mission field of his own congregation. "Yes, I know," he mentioned, "a baby from your area died not long ago, and all of you had to make the long trip over here for the funeral."

Together they set a date for the last Sunday of September, with all those interested being asked to meet at the Henry Renner home at 2:00. They would have a worship service first, and if the group so decided, they would then organize a new church.

When the day came, a crowd of some twenty families assembled at the Renner farm. Reverend Zeiszler drove in with his one-horse buggy, arriving amidst a great deal of scurrying and debating about how to conduct the service. A number of families brought extra chairs, but only thirty chairs could be packed into the little house. Finally, they decided to have the women in the house, with a number still having to stand along the walls, while the men would stand around the open door and windows, listening as best they could. The children were excused to play down around the barn, out of earshot so they wouldn't disturb the worship service.

Mrs. Renner dug into her steamer trunk and took out a precious ivory-colored crocheted sofa runner, which her grandmother had given her as an heirloom before she left the old country. This she now draped across the black cast-iron kitchen stove, which she had polished to a shine, and that would be the day's altar-pulpit-lectern-baptismal font.

The pastor placed his books on it, as well as a two-foot high walnut cross that Father Christian had crafted in Krem and sent along as a gift to the budding new church.

All the busy chatter immediately died when the pastor, standing beside the stove-altar, faced the group and proclaimed the opening invocation, *"Im Namen des Vaters,* In the Name of the Father, and of the Son, and of the Holy Ghost. Amen." He spoke with a voice rich and full, hoping the men outside could also hear him. Barely had he raised his hand to trace a cross in the air and uttered those first majestic words before powerful emotions began to sweep over the little group. For some of them, this was the first opportunity for formal worship since they left the old country, and it brought back a huge cloud of both feelings and remembrances. As they again found themselves shoulder to shoulder with other believers, they suddenly felt lifted from the open prairie into the Spirit's presence, and this humble house transformed into a living cathedral of praise. Their hearts were suddenly back in glad weddings, confirmations, the mystery of deeply spiritual Christmases and Easters, back to the hope restored in funerals when cruel death threatened to crush the soul.

When the pastor led into the first hymn, they needed no books. They knew those familiar hymns from memory through repeated use in the old country, Sunday in and Sunday out. With practiced voices, they easily swung into four-part harmony that came near to growing the sod on the roof by an inch a hymn. The rich melodies and lofty biblical word struck an overpowering chord that had the force of summer thunder in these waiting, hungry hearts, and hot tears rolled up to sit in the corner of many an eye.

Reverend Zeiszler preached a mini-sermon, holding himself to just forty-five minutes, and conducted three baptisms of children whose parents were convinced that the far road to Krem was too long to travel for church. Several more rousing hymns, a prayer, and the pastor once more made the sign of the cross and pronounced the powerful benediction that God laid on Moses's tongue to bless the people of Israel some three thousand years earlier, *"Der Herr segne dich*, The Lord bless thee and keep thee. The Lord make his face to shine upon thee and be gracious unto thee. The Lord lift his countenance upon thee and give thee his peace. Amen."

The pastor bowed his head in silence, and not a breath stirred inside the house or out as each heart realized that with the presence of God in this worship, a new chapter was indeed being written in their lives and in this little spot of earth. The Bible reminded them that they were but "strangers and pilgrims on this earth," and "they desired a better country, a heavenly one," but for the rest of their days on this earth, however many or few that be, this would be their abode, and all these souls around them who shared the mother tongue were their people.

After a long moment of soul-satisfying silence, the pastor walked outside and gathered the men beside the house to talk about forming a congregation. The women could not vote, but they had given their men careful instructions at home. *"We need a church here,"* was the message delivered to their men, so there were no dissenting votes. After a few more moments of discussion, the men elected three of their number to serve as deacons. Then they selected *"Friedens Gemeinde,"* Peace Church, as their new name and asked Reverend Zeiszler to contact the closest synod office in Iowa about the possibility of sending them a permanent pastor. Reverend Zeiszler also agreed that in the meantime, he'd come every second Sunday afternoon of the month to hold services and Christmas afternoon as well.

In short order, the soddy was cleared of extra chairs which were moved outside, planks laid across sawhorses to make tables, and bowls and bowls of soul food set out to satisfy the desire of every Germanic palate, young and old. They ate and visited and ate some more until the sun made serious overtures to the beckoning western horizon. One by one, the women slipped their Sunday-apron loops over their head and climbed up on the wagon seats beside their husbands, pointing home for daily chores that brooked no Sabbath rest.

One of the families invited Reverend Zeiszler to spend the night, and many a heart felt much lighter again as harnesses jingled their way home.

By the time John and Ricka finished chores, the orange harvest sun had pulled a blanket of blackness over the earth behind her, and reaching into her jeweled bag, she flung huge handfuls of glittering diamonds into the vast umbrella of the heavens. No vain empress of earth could match her majesty or inspire the awe she drew forth from those thankful pioneers.

The day had indeed been a time of rejoicing. When John came into the house, Ricka was finished feeding a tired, fussing little Phillip and gotten him to bed. She laid out cold sausage and bread with some cheese for lunch before bed, along with leftover church kuchen and soothing chamomile tea.

"Lord willing," John said, looking across the crude kitchen table with renewed admiration for this tremendous helpmate that God had given him, "by this time next year we'll have both a school and a church up and running."

"It feels so wonderful, like we're part of the world again," she replied with a glad sigh.

Along with all their neighbors, they would once more be part of a civilized community, as they understood the ordering of life among God-fearing people. With these twin corner posts of life now set, whatever else might happen, together they would somehow be able to handle it.

The next morning, John finished milking, and as he came around the corner of the house with his pails of warm milk, he came upon

Ricka retching with great heaving eruptions just outside the door of the soddy.

"What happened?" he shouted, quickly setting down the pails and running to hold her shoulders. "What's going on?"

"Well, I didn't want to tell you like this," she replied, "but Phillip's little sister seems to be disturbed with the breakfast she's getting."

Wiping her mouth with her apron, she looked up at him with tear-stained eyes, afraid that he might be upset with her.

"Oh, Ricka, my dear wonderful Ricka! How could I be upset with you over having a baby?" He took her in his arms and held her for long moments until her shoulders relaxed and he knew she felt comfortable with this sudden new turn in their lives. "But how do you know it's a sister?"

"Well, I suppose I don't, but wouldn't it be nice to have a little daughter?"

"I'd be so glad, so glad. You've just made me so happy."

They kissed in a long embrace that warmed their toes to the temperature of the steaming pails of milk.

The next morning Ricka asked John to harness the team so she could drive to Mina's and share the news with her.

Barely had she driven into Gottfried's yard when Mina came dashing out of the house, half dragging little Joseph who was pedaling as fast as his short legs could carry him, waving her arms and shouting, "Ricka, Ricka, guess what!"

"What?" an alarmed Ricka shouted back from atop the wagon seat.

"I'm going to have another baby!"

"Oh, Mina, I'm so happy for you."

As Ricka climbed off the wagon, Mina walked over and helped to unhitch the horses. Hitching the traces and reins to the hooks on top of the harnesses, she left the bridles on and tied the halter ropes to the wagon wheels. Then they both walked to the soddy, Ricka carrying little Phillip, who squealed and waved his arms, wanting to get down to play with his young cousin, Joseph. With Phillip just learning to walk, Joseph grabbed his hand and dragged him, and in a moment, they were gone, toddling and shouting, stumbling, falling, getting up and starting over, laughing until even the two mothers couldn't help but laugh as well to see such pure, excited joy bursting out of the little ones.

In the soddy, Mina poured a cup of coffee from the ever-ready blue, enamel pot on back of the stove, and they sat across from each other, both with so much to talk about that neither had time to listen as each poured out a torrent of words at the same time.

Suddenly, Mina stared so hard at Ricka that Ricka said, "What?"

"What indeed? Why didn't you tell me, you sneaky one?"

"Yes, I'm going to have one, too."

"Have you told John yet?"

"Yesterday morning. He caught me throwing up so I had to spill it."

"I hope he wasn't mad."

"He was glad, but I suppose he wants another boy."

"Oh, men. They're kinda dumb sometimes. Anyway, I hope we both have girls, don't you?"

"So do I."

Chapter 38

The Prairie's on Fire

After their blissful cups of coffee and piled-up conversation, Ricka moved her chair and got up to leave. The two mothers, still busy talking, stepped outside and called the boys. Their calls were still echoing back from the ravine when both were suddenly struck by the acrid odor of smoke.

Scanning the wide horizon, they looked toward the northwest hills and saw a huge plume of gray smoke billowing high into the air and bending in their direction. With a brisk wind from that direction, they instantly knew it meant trouble. The horses had smelled the smoke for some time and instinctively reacted with an inborn fear of fire. Schwartz snorted and snapped his nose up and down, rattling his bridle. Sophie whinnied and stomped her left foot, pawing the ground, trying to say, "Let's get moving." Both turned their heads toward Ricka, eyes glazed and nostrils flared, signaling, "There's trouble. Let's go."

Both women hurried to hook up the team of horses, and while Mina finished, Ricka ran to pick up her stubborn little boy who was way too busy having fun to listen to a worried mother's urgent call. Tossing Phillip into the bed of straw in the back of the wagon, she hurdled up onto the wagon seat, snapped the reins, and yelled, "Sophie, Schwartz, giddyup!"

The team needed no encouragement. In a flash, they were out of the yard, back on the trail home, and moving at full, synchronized gallop. Ricka gave them free rein and let them fly, wagon wheels sometimes on the ground, and as often off. Thankfully, the trail had only little bumps and rocks so the wagon sailed upright, if on seas that were rough. Little Phillip, on the bed of straw, bounced around like a rubber ball, arms and legs flying all directions, and loving every moment of it. But Ricka hardly heard his gleeful shouts. The great gray wall was rising higher and wider across the sky by the minute, and she knew, only too well, the fire was moving in their direction.

The strangely satisfying bittersweet smell of dry burning grass and sage was growing stronger with every hill she topped as the racing team sped home, into the mid-morning wind that was blowing with ever more determined force.

Suddenly, a pack of three tall gray jackrabbits went bounding in giant leaps like kangaroos across the trail in front of the team, and a little further on several coyotes raced across, ears back, tails flat out behind them, all moving away from the terrifying flames that were yet invisible but surely speeding their way. The creatures of the earth had no words for what was taking place, but all else was forgotten and none were enemies in this sudden flight for survival.

Sophie and Schwartz raced right into the yard, braking just in front of the earth-barn. Leaving Phillip on the wagon for the moment, Ricka, with heart pounding, was all thumbs as she jumped off the wagon and scrambled to unhitch the panting team, their flanks still heaving, their nostrils flared from their harried race the long mile home. Fumbling with the harness chains, she finally had them free of the doubletree hitch and clapped them on the rump to shoo them into the barn, harness and all.

Then she reached for Phillip, who by now had begun to sense the fear in mother and horse alike and was standing up and screaming at the top of his lungs. Stepping on a spoke of the wagon wheel, she was able to reach him and pull him out of the box. She hugged his wailing head tightly against her breast and raced for the house, all the while looking around to see where John might be.

Just before she reached the house, she saw John to the west of the buildings. He saw the smoke earlier and raced in from the field to hitch up the sulky breaking plow and turn several furrows of raw plowed earth around the buildings. Now he was on his third furrow, snapping the horses' reins to move at a faster pace. He quickly looked over from his perch on the front of his plow seat, as relieved to see her as she was to spot him, and waved her into the house.

She threw the soddy door open and dashed inside. She wanted to be brave, but with Phillip's crying and her own fear exploding, she burst into tears along with the little one. Their wails together brought *Schutz* charging into the house, barking to scare off any intruder that might be frightening his family. As soon as Ricka sat down at the table, *Schutz* stood up on his hind legs and quickly slathered the baby's face with his best comforting tongue, then looked into Ricka's eyes to see what could be so troubling.

Schutz, too, had smelled the smoke and seen the nervous animals all over the yard, but he had not yet experienced the terror of the verdant prairies being scorched, so he did not feel the full fear of his mistress. He only knew she was troubled, and he was there to help. As she stroked his head, she felt more calm herself, and when she softly spoke, "Ja, *Schutz,* it's all right," he felt better as well. Even Phillip ran his hands up and down *Schutz's* fur and stopped crying, his drippy nose running across a sudden smile. *Schutz* nuzzled against Ricka's legs and rested his head on her lap beside Phillip. Whatever was so terribly wrong, they could surely face it together and make it better!

John quickly plowed a fourth furrow around the buildings, hoping the six-foot band of raw earth would stop the flames from reaching his home. Then he kicked the pedal to lift the plow out of the ground and snapped the reins to trot the horses up to the house.

As soon as he opened the door, Ricka flew into his arms, crying, "Oh, Johnny, I'm so scared."

"Well, the fire is still quite a ways off, so maybe we can stop it before it gets this far."

With that, he quickly kissed her and pulled away, trotting out the door. At the granary, he grabbed several brown gunnysacks and ran to the barn. Moving rapidly, he unharnessed all four horses and hung the harnesses up on their pegs. Then, since Schwartz was their fastest horse, he took down the riding bridle and touched the bit against the horse's mouth to get him to open up and take it in. After the hard run he had just finished, Schwartz wasn't eager to have more work thrown his way. He laid his ears back and tossed his head, shaking his nose away from John's hand, as if to say, "Hey, I don't like this. Get somebody else."

"I know, old man, you don't want to fly again," John softly told him as he stroked his head and rubbed his ears, "but we have to get out there and fight this terrible fire. I hope you got enough guts left to run some more." Schwartz seemed to understand his master's tone. He put his head back down and let John open his mouth to take the bit.

Quickly, John finished slipping the bridle over his ears, then slipped the saddle blanket and saddle from their peg and swung them on the horse's back. Briskly, he tightened the girth, with Schwartz trying one last protest by pulling in a deep, deep breath and expanding his belly, trying to keep the girth just a little looser.

"Oh no you don't, old friend," John added, gently rubbing his flank, until he let the breath back out so the girth could be tightened to ride. Quickly, John tied the gunnysacks on the leather saddle strings behind the cantle and vaulted into the saddle. On the way out of the barn, he reached down to grab a four-tined hay fork standing beside the door, gently kicked his heels into Schwartz's sides, and they sped northwest toward the dangerous flames that were spitting black destruction across the valley and surrounding hills.

As they galloped toward the heavy smoke, more riders were converging as well, along with several wagons racing along in the distance. Drawing closer, John noticed several with water barrels and one with a plow in the box, along with shovels and fork handles sticking out of the boxes.

Three miles farther, and they met the lead fingers of fire. Fanned by the growing wind, the flames were shooting ten and twenty feet into the air and racing at running speed. Further to the right, the flames were gulping toward the Andreas Renner farm, and several wagons veered off to help protect the buildings there.

A buck and two does with half-grown fawns came out of the east, racing across in front of them toward the safety of the unburned western hills. They were in a gear higher than John had ever seen deer run.

John and some others veered around the left flank of the fire, driving into the area already burned, to park the wagons and tie their horses. Further north, they could see heavy plumes of gray smoke where several straw piles continued to burn. The Mostel and Christmann farms were still standing, somehow having survived intact, but with everything around them scorched.

Tying a nervous Schwartz to a wagon wheel, John patted his nose, "It's all right, Schwartz. You'll be safe here until I get back. Stay."

Schwartz somehow seemed to understand and stopped pawing the ground, only snapping his head as he watched his master go.

John quickly untied the gunnysacks from his saddle, soaked them in one of the water barrels, and throwing them over his shoulders, grabbed his fork and ran to join the men already battling the flames ahead of them. They formed teams of two and took sections forty feet apart. Striking at the flames with the flat of their forks and beating them backward into the burned area, they were able to stop the fire in that little space. Leaving one man to guard the area in case sparks should ignite it again, they raced further on and continued battling the moving blaze that seemed to have a mind of its own.

John was beating at the racing flames with his gunnysack when the man beside him suddenly yelled, "Hey, you're on fire!"

In that instant, with the angry fire attacking his left pant leg, John felt the sting of a dull horse-vaccination needle and slapped his gunnysack around his leg. As the fire was choked, smoke rose up his leg and with it rose the sour stench of burned flesh.

The flames ate the top of his sock and peeled the skin off his calf, ankle to knee.

When John pulled the sack off his leg, the neighbor knelt down to take a look and pronounced, "Uh-oh, that's not so good."

John twisted his leg to see, and before he could get a good look, the fire ran with new life just beyond them. "Ach, it's not so bad," he shouted and ran to beat the flames down once more, making the stunned neighbor rush to catch up.

As soon as they killed the fire in one small area, it broke out in another.

Dozens of men and boys on either side of them were each attacking their own area, but the wind was pushing the crackling fire faster than they could beat it down, and it was now scorching an area three miles wide, taking everything in its path.

At the Andreas Renner farm, toward the center of the blaze, everything was confusion. Othelia Mostel had raced in with her injured husband and two children all in the back of the bouncing wagon. Her husband severely sprained his knee and could not walk. Somehow, they hobbled him up into the wagon, and the terrified family raced ahead of the flames, leaving their farm to whatever would befall. Several other neighbors already at the Renners helped them off the wagon and into the packed soddy.

Outside, several men brought two-bottom sulky plows and were breaking the sod in a circle fifty yards away from the Renner buildings. On the south side they elongated the circle, out to a hundred yards up a slight incline, plowing four furrows to form that stretched-out circle. Then, moving twenty feet out beyond the first circle, they plowed a second, and finally twenty feet more they plowed a third circle. Working in teams, they struck wooden matches and lit a number of small fires between the inner circles, setting a controlled backfire against the wind.

When that circle had nearly burned itself out, they quickly lit the area between the outer circles and burned that area as well. Quickly beating out any little remaining spots of lingering fire, they now had a forty-foot-wide burned-out circle around the entire farm, an area they hoped would be big enough to turn the flames away from the farm and the haystacks close to the buildings.

The boys, meanwhile, were turning the crank at the well as fast as they could possibly power it, drawing up buckets of water to fill the stock tank and the barrels others had brought. Several wagons were busy running the barrels to the house, where buckets of water were thrown on the sod roof to water it down and then to the barns and finally to the haystacks to water them down, even if only making them slightly moist.

Inside, women and girls quickly made sandwiches, which the boys carried in dishtowels to the men on the lines, along with water jugs to slack the serious thirst.

By now the air was becoming heavy with smoke, and feathery pieces of black-and-white ashes were raining down all around.

Many a prayer was lifted to the heavens during all this time, but finally, Rosina Renner wiped her hands on her apron and announced loudly, "I think it's time to pray." With many a "yes, yes," all abruptly stopped what they were doing and bowed their heads as Rosina lifted her voice and implored, "God, our father, we know thou hast all power in heaven and on earth. If it be thy holy will, still the blowing wind again as thou didst in Bible days and cause the terrible fire to die. We humbly beg thee, give us all thy strength and save our men, our animals, the farms that we've worked so hard for. Amen."

Aprons were lifted to moist eyes as all realized again just how small and vulnerable they were in the great scheme of things and how these vast prairies could bless them and curse them, all in the space of a few hours' time. Glancing from face to face, Rosina saw the fear in the set of many lips, but now they also had the strong hope that their God who had seen them safe through the great waters of the deep would not abandon them on the seas of waving grass. Nothing more was said as all turned back to their tasks recharged.

As the backfired circles finished burning themselves out, the men saw dozens of loose cattle and horses moving across the prairies to stay ahead of the fire, some coming toward them and others running past. Suddenly, they realized why a higher hand had reached out and caused them to elongate the circle and stretch it out further. Four of the men mounted their horses and rode out to round up the terrified animals and get them into the protected Renner farm.

In half an hour, they gathered most of the strays from as far as half a mile away on either side of Renners. Rounding up the frightened animals was like herding fish—they bolted and ran blindly in every direction. Finally, with furious riding and wild shouting, they got the animals corralled on the lee side of the farm, away from the advancing fire.

The older boys circled the wagons and formed a temporary coral, with barbed wire strung between wagons, and rags tied on the wire so the frenzied animals could see it better. Here the milling strays would hopefully be safe. Just as they were about to finish tying the wire, a large fire-crazed brown steer let out an unearthly, high-pitched bellow and charged through the line, eyes wild and tail high, circling right back toward the fire. "He's gone crazy," yelled one of the men, "let him go."

In all that barely controlled panic, wild upheaval seemed to sweep man and beast alike. Calves bawled, cows lowed and sniffed for their little ones, steers bellowed and suddenly charged wagon wheels for no reason at all, horses whinnied and snorted, rearing on hind legs and pawing the air, scaring the defenseless cows even more. And the smoke was becoming ever stronger, the falling ashes thicker.

"Hey," one of the men shouted, "feels like the lower deck of Noah's ark in a three-day typhoon!"

"Pretty close!" shouted another voice out of the dust.

Inside the stuffed soddy, several infants felt the chaos all around and set up squalls challenging the trumpets of Jericho. Mothers tried to shush them, but no shushing did any good.

Suddenly, the dark rolling clouds shot a horrific bolt of lightning straight down into a rock atop a hill close by and with it, shattering thunder that froze every being that bore a brain. In one instant, all sound was swallowed up in a black hole of silence. All, that is, except the stunned infants that bounced in their mother's arms and howled even louder.

Outside, in that profound silence, the men noticed a most amazing thing. The fire was now approaching close enough so they could see the wind lifting the flames into the air. Suddenly, ahead of the flames, came a pair of terrified red foxes with a gray coyote not far behind them. Running at full sprint, they came toward the farm and then swerved sharply around it. When they drew even with the corralled animals, they slowed to a loping trot, crossed the burned-out circle, and wove in among the surprised herd of anxious cattle and horses. Several large, horned yearlings nodded their heads and showed a horn to the audacious intruders, then flicked ear and tail and dropped it. Under any other circumstance they would have gored these slinky cousins of Fido. Not today, when old instincts were paralyzed in the swirling smoke. Cow stared at fox; fox—paw in the air, wondering—stared at cow, neither one moving. Men looked at both and marveled.

"Ever see a thing like that before?" asked one of the stunned men.

"Never."

"I'd never believed it, if I didn't see it."

"Maybe the lion and the lamb *can* lie down together."

"And death can make friends out of old enemies."

This mysterious event would be talked about in the valley for many years. Some believed it. Some never did.

By now the flames were at the edge of the firebreak and started crackling around the farm. A number of the crew had wrapped gunnysacks around their fork tines and soaked them in water, ready to attack any flames that leaped across the firebreak. Now they took positions just inside the back-burned circle and waited. Flames and soot blew over them, smoke almost choking them with every breath.

"Ouch," cried one of the boys, "the fire stings like a hundred needles poking my face."

"Feels like my skin is on fire," another yelled back over the noise. Those with big red handkerchiefs tied them over nose and mouth; the rest raised their elbows and tried to breathe through their shirtsleeves. Eyes watered, and lungs coughed back the heavy smoke that got sucked in. The blistering heat grew more intense, searing nostrils. The crackling of the fire as it devoured the grasses grew to a fearful, unending drumroll. Sparks flew across the scorched circle and started small fires inside. They were quickly spotted and doused.

Nervous animals felt the biting heat and milled around the enclosure, crowding closer together to get as far from the flames as they could.

Apart from the great Missouri, this area had no rivers, no lakes, no wet marshlands, and no roads of any kind to stop the fire. The wagon trails leading to Krem and Kasmir would not slow the flames. The only hope now was the dark, overcast sky, which looked like the strong winds could possibly pull down some life-saving rain.

"*Treuer Gott*, Faithful God," prayed Rosina as she looked out through the window to the darkened west, "please open your heavens and send water to kill these awful flames."

Just then, with more lightning and shattering thunder, big drops of rain splattered in the dust. Two minutes more and driving rain pelted earth and living being alike.

Several more minutes of heavy downpour and the fire sizzled, sputtered, and died.

A great shout went up from the Renner farm. More shouts echoed back from all along the firewall, as bone-tired, sooty firefighters looked to the heavens and shouted, "Thank you, God! Thank you! Thank you!"

At the west edge of the fire line, John and those with him were now done and turned around for the long trudge back to their horses and wagons. Others along the fire line did the same, stopping here and there to pound out a smoldering pile of something still smoking. As they looked up, a dozen great black turkey vultures with naked red heads and wing spans the size of a man were already circling, looking for supper ready roasted, finding a snake here, a porcupine, a badger that didn't make it back to the hole. Farther on, a single file of still-soft cow pies laid down in a blowout by a frightened, fleeing cow.

Fire, thought John with a smile, *sure scared the poop out of that old girl.*

When circling vultures suddenly dropped down anywhere on this scorched picnic ground, they'd soon be engaged in a feast and the prairie cleaned of death.

All the farms in the path of the fire had survived. Some haystacks and a lot of straw piles were gone, but the neighbors would all chip in and provide help.

Back on his horse, John quickly stopped at the Renner farm, where people and animals were now beginning to disperse.

Spotting the Mostels, he quickly told Othelia that their farm was all right, to which more neighbors added, *"Danket dem Herrn immer wieder,* thank God again and again!"

Taking a drink and a sandwich, he turned Schwartz for home and an anxious Ricka. His leg stung something terrible by now, but in all the commotion, no one had noticed the raw wound under his shredded pant leg.

When he walked into the house, Ricka broke into tears and ran into his arms, but he was so sooty that she stopped short and couldn't help but laugh, "You look like that clown with the black face that we saw in New York!"

Seeing little Phillip's large, frightened eyes and his mouth starting to twitch, John turned and walked out to the stock-watering tank, where he stoically ignored his burn, took off his shirt, and doused himself with the most refreshing water he felt in many a month.

Back in the house, he pulled a chair up to the table and took Phillip in his arms.

"Oh, little one," he said softly, "you don't know how precious you are in my heart and how blessed we all are today!"

He buried his face in the little one's *strubled,* messed up, hair. Ricka saw a tear rolling down his cheek and scooted in to sit on his other leg, all three of them now hugging, with tears of thanksgiving flowing in glad streams.

In all the excitement, Ricka missed seeing the big hole in the back of her husband's pant leg, and when she got up, she suddenly caught sight of the raw, scorched skin now mottled in dried blood.

"Oh, Johnny, you're burned," she shouted and ran to get the can of lard that was standard medicine for emergencies like this. She quickly applied a thick layer of lard on the burned flesh, wrapped it with a dishtowel, and taped it in place. "I just hope it doesn't get infected."

"It'll be fine."

"We'll take another look at it before we go to bed."

Ricka threw a quick lunch together, and as they ate, all talked at the same time, trying to get out their frightened feelings from this day.

At Renner's, the wind finally finished blowing all the smoke away, but the smell of burnt grass still hung heavy in the air. The foxes and the coyote felt the lure of home and quietly wove their way out through the cattle, timidly setting out across the scorched ground to find their dens or maybe dig a new one. On a normal day, seeing them go, someone would have taken a gun off the hook, but today, all nature seemed at one, thankful to have survived the flames.

For these swift and stealthy creatures of the wild, returning to their sanctuaries held only naked promise at best. Their favorite foods were mostly wiped out, and their territorial cousins did not take kindly to aliens intruding on their turf, fire or not. For them, winter would be bleak and long. Some would have to battle for new territory to survive. Some would have to die. Sister Fire extracted a high price from all the earth, with no exemptions offered.

At the farm, the corralled cattle and horses were stunned, in animal shock, and milled around, not knowing what to do next. Slowly, they began to drift out toward the south, grazing on the unburned prairie but still feeling like the Renner farm was now their home. After grazing a while, a few at a time returned to the stock tank for a drink of water, and several neighborhood boys stayed on till night to keep cranking water for the thirsty, lost animals.

The next weeks were a continued flurry of activity as farmers in the burn area continued to ride around searching for animals that fled before the flames. Others joined in hauling hay and straw to those who had lost theirs. Andreas Renner put out the word that several unmarked cattle were still at his place, but no one ever claimed them, so Andreas had a small increase in his herd, along with an unclaimed sorrel horse that now claimed him.

The scared cows were nervous for weeks, and milk production in most of the farms dropped by pails. Renner's brother visited one evening at milking time and commented, "The old Russians used to say, '*A scared cow is afraid of a bush.*' You can sure see that around here."

"Ja," Renner replied, "I still have nightmares about that fire, too."

"He wakes me up screaming," said his wife. "Scares the plum pits outa me."

Renner, sitting under a cow, pulling teats, shot a stream of milk at a nearby cat, and all could laugh again.

Chapter 39

Lightning in the Flour Mill

John's leg took weeks to heal, but with Ricka's daily care, the oozing finally stopped and the wound scabbed over.

His leg got better just in time to haul their wheat to market. With gunnysacks and scoop shovels in hand, the brothers started the backbreaking task. John held the sacks while Gottfried shoveled a hundred pounds of wheat to fill each sack. After half an hour, they switched jobs.

They cut ten-inch pieces of string from a ball of binder twine and hung them over a nail, and as each sack was filled, they tied and set it in a row. When they had thirty sacks filled, they loaded them on the wagon, John hoisting them up and Gottfried stacking them in the wagon box.

For men under five and a half feet tall, handling these weights was indeed a day's work. They had to be rugged and in shape, but they were up to it.

The first ten sacks were easy. Then Gottfried blew out a big breath and said, "Hey, I think each of these sacks is getting heavier!"

"Yeah, I used a bigger shovel," laughed John.

When John's wagon was loaded, they parked it in the yard and drove to Gottfried's to load his. This year they started sacking up the wheat for hauling, so in case there was an accident of any kind or a wagon broke or rolled over, the wheat would not be spilled into the grass and lost.

Five o'clock the next morning, they were up, the wives cooked a big breakfast of sausage and eggs, and they drove to the high plateau north of Gottfried's place. Here, their two wagons met two more Keller and two Eisenbeis wagons, and they caravanned to the elevator at Expansion, where the wheat was loaded on steam barges and shipped down the Missouri.

They had all pulled the wheels off their wagons, greased the axles and checked the iron wheel rims and the hound assemblies as well as the entire leather harness for each horse, to make sure everything was up to heavy transport work. The horses were well fed, watered, checked over, and brushed down the evening before, to have them ready for the task. Each wagon was loaded to a ton and a half, and the four-horse teams would have a hard pull on the twelve miles up to Expansion.

When all six wagons arrived, John shouted, "Let's roll 'em out," and they began the trek to Expansion, the horses leaning serious into their collars, straining to keep the lumbering wagons moving on the grassy trails, and the men bantering back and forth in a relaxed convoy. They had filled their pockets with fresh sunflower seeds from the gardens, and spitting was easy as they slowly ground their way across the upward sloping prairies to their destination. Each of the six drivers sat high on the grain sacks with their legs dangling over the front of the box, and as they kept grinding northeast, talk became less, chewing sunflower seeds more numbingly routine as each man settled into his own thoughts. These men were not rookie one-sunflower-seed-at-a-time chewers. They were professionals, heirs who stood in a long tradition of seed chewers: toss a whole handful into your mouth at a time, store them in one cheek, then with your tongue move one seed to the other side, crack it with your teeth, spit out the husk, chew the seed and swallow it, move on to another, with no hands involved.

Dogs barked from nearby farms as they passed, a few horses whinnied, and neighbors waved them on.

As the horses strained into their collars crawling across the prairie, John reflected on the quiet life these prairies afforded. You needed neither clock nor fancy-colored calendars. *Here*, he quietly reflected, *you count by nature's steps.* His mind drummed the cadence of the seasons marching across the stage. *After the deep snows melt and the frozen ground thaws, comes the season of bright purple crocuses poking their heads up across the prairies, then the chattering mallards flying north, with a few mavericks settling in to homestead in the grass on top of the highest hills. They, and the litters of little coyote pups barking outside their dens on the high ground, all tell you it's time to drill the wheat and poke your potatoes, eyes up, into the freshly turned earth.*

He couldn't help but chuckle as the next season flashed by. *Then the wild onions come up in the pastures, and to the milk cows, they are sweet dessert. But, ei, yei, yei, how their bowels splatter in the barn, and the milk takes on an onion tang. Pffff . . ."* He blew out a breath at the thought.

When the sun stands over your head, she tells you to cut the grass for hay, and when the chokecherries turn and the fields take on gold, it's the season to thread the canvas in the binder and get the little kids ready for school.

Then the crows sound muster and collect, so the young ones can learn from the elders about the great heavenly highway they're going to fly after they've sneaked as much of your corn as they can pick. They, and the cows putting on an extra coat, tell you to get everything buttoned up for deep snow and bitter cold. And if you don't listen good, you'll wish you had.

These were the things that shaped life and that baked daily bread. *Oh Lord,* he breathed softly into the wind, *thank you for the precious three-score years that you have hopefully laid into our hands.*

When they rolled into Expansion and pulled up to the elevator, there were already several dozen other wagons ahead of them, so it meant several hours wait.

One of the Keller men decided he'd stay with the wagons, allowing the other five to head over to Doherty's Saloon to slack their thirst and catch up on the latest news around the world.

They relaxed around the table when talk turned to Louis Reuter. He was the operator at the flour mill in Krem until he was struck by lightning and killed. And it happened on a Sunday morning when he was on the way to church!

There was a long debate, which now continued, over whether it was perhaps just a freak accident or whether he had done some great secret evil and God nailed him for it in divine retribution.

"Everybody I've ever talked to," opined one speaker, "said he was a good man all around, as honest as they come."

"But you don't know what was in his heart, do you?" added another.

"Well, think about Job in the Bible and how his friends tried to blame him for secret sins when he had all kinds of bad troubles."

"You know, maybe it's like Sodom and Gomorrah. God sure fixed them for the bad stuff they did."

"Ja, but that doesn't mean God still works like that. Otherwise, we'd all be cooked."

"I think Reuter was just in the wrong place at the wrong time, and you can't blame him *or* God!"

So the conversation went, as it would long afterward as well. About that time, Keller came over from the elevator and told them they would be next in line to unload.

Each driver saved one sack of wheat to take to Krem and have some of it heated into "puffed wheat" cereal and some ground into flour for their winter's supply. For thirty-five cents a hundred pounds, it would be milled into flour, the same as the "American Eagle" brand, which the mill shipped out for sale around the country.

After having their wheat ground and some puffed, the Oster brothers decided to make a quick stop at Netzer's General Merchandise to have the manager order a Singer treadle sewing machine for each of the wives.

"Those are forty-five dollars apiece," the manager told them, looking over the top of his glasses as he held open his company catalog.

"That's twice the price that Sears and Montgomery Ward want for their machines," said Gottfried, scratching his head.

"Ja, but those are Burdick or Minnesota brands, not Singers," replied John.

Standing at the counter, the men were both struck by a sudden attack of extreme generosity and decided nothing was too much for a Christmas present for the little women at home. Besides, few of the neighboring women had one like it.

After returning home late that night, they spent the next day filling and loading thirty more sacks of wheat. The following day all would again meet and caravan to Expansion.

The next week they would repeat the grueling process twice more, and one final time the week after that.

Five trips and they held good hard cash for getting supplies. Before each trip home, both John and Gottfried stopped at the sawmill and picked up a load of lumber for building additional sheds at home. On the last trip, the women came along again to do some shopping and to spend several days with Grandpa Christ and Grandma Karolina, as well as time with Sister Katherine and her family Baisch.

As soon as they had unloaded, John and Gottfried, with the wives and sons, drove over to the lumber mill to see Peter Miller and pay off the last installment on their loan.

"Glad to see you, boys," exclaimed Miller. "I figured you'd be in one a' these days."

He chuckled as he repeated an old saying that seemed to fit the moment: "*Schulden sind keine Hasen, die laufen nicht fort, gel?* Debts are not rabbits, they don't hop away, right?"

"Ja, had a good crop," replied John, laughing at Miller's picturesque business mind, "and we're glad to be out of debt."

Every face in the office broke into a big smile when he handed over the bills and Miller finished counting them.

"Right on the money," said Miller, digging the promissory note out of a box in the corner, signing it with a smile, and handing it to the men.

"Thanks for helping us out of a big pinch," John replied.

"Sure appreciate it," Gottfried added as they started for the door.

Walking to the wagons where the women were waiting, Gottfried let out a deep breath and whispered loudly, "Last time I felt this good was when we got off the ship in New York."

Reaching Krem, they arrived to bear hugs and laughter at the parents' house. Karolina tossed an apron to each of the daughters-in-law, and in a short time, they were ready with a large supper of recently butchered chicken, new potatoes, cucumber salad, and—of course—custard kuchen that filled them all up to the brim. There was so much to talk about and two little grandsons to tickle, that before they knew it, dark had settled in and sleep beckoned mightily.

The next day, the women cleared the dishes early so they could get to both Netzer's and Richter's General Merchandise stores to stock up on winter supplies and get some warmer winter coats, mittens, and overshoes for the little boys. Of course, they also wanted to look at the new items on every shelf and all the hooks on the wall.

"Just look at the pretty prints on those percales," said Ricka, softly running her fingers over the heavenly bolts of cloth.

"And I love all these beautiful colors," Mina added.

"If we just had a sewing machine, wouldn't it be fun to sew up lots of things?" But they didn't, so why waste time thinking about what couldn't be?

John had Grandpa Christian resole his boots, which were scorched cardboard-thin fighting the prairie fire. While Christian removed the old nails and cut the new leather, it gave them good time to talk about how life was going in this new land of promise. Soon, the boots were back on the metal forming last and resoled, good as new.

John also asked Father to make a pair of soft leather moccasins for both Ricka and little Phillip to wear on the dirt floor of the soddy at home. With winter coming, they needed to keep their feet warm. "Especially," John added with a little shudder, "when she jumps into bed with those cold feet of hers."

"Ja," Christ replied, "I know."

Returning home, the days sped by with butchering, canning meat and garden produce, hauling hay, and building a new granary to store more wheat and flax, along with more oats and barley.

Getting up before daylight and working into total dark at night, John was able to break up more stubborn prairie sod for added plowland to raise crops, and before the ground froze too hard, he went full throttle to pound in more fence posts and string four strands of barbed wire fencing so he could increase his cattle herd next summer.

Ricka began to worry, and as he ate his supper, she quietly said, "Johnny, maybe you should slow down a little. You look like you're getting tired."

"I can't slow down now. Have to get this stuff done!"

And from the fire in his eyes when he looked at her across the flickering kerosene lamp on the table, she knew that was the end of that conversation.

After the freeze, the brothers set to work building new sheds for both the hogs and the chickens, finishing just two days before the first snowfall and the beginning of some bitter cold. The winter sun got up late and went to bed early according to people-time, but with all the work, the days were still long and exhausting. Through it all, life was good, and when the neighborhood gathered at Henry Renners for worship services on Sunday, they were indeed thankful for the good life that God was setting before them with each passing day.

Christmas brought Ricka and Mina each the delight of a new Singer treadle sewing machine, while the two women splurged to give their men each a black ankle-length Russian buffalo calf coat which they had found in the Sears catalog for the princely sum of twenty-five dollars and just couldn't resist. For four dollars more, they also added fleece-lined bear-fur mittens with full leather gauntlets. They topped it off with a black muskrat fur cap with a turndown neck flap and extra wide earflaps that tied with a braided string under the chin.

Those presents not only cleaned out the sisters' hoarded up savings, but they had to secretly rifle through their husband's little money box a number of times. Still, they had the comfort of knowing that during the long winter drives in the sled, their men would be a little safer against the hard-biting north winds.

"From a ways off," Ricka laughed, "the men look like something from the high mountains in Manchuria that we saw in pictures."

"All they need is those funny beards," Mina chuckled, "but they'll sure be warm."

The little boys received new caps, hard rubber horses and cows, a set of wooden blocks with English alphabet letters, and a big, shiny red apple that soon had teeth marks in it.

For the two sisters, the days after Christmas included long visits back and forth to learn how to operate the delightful sewing machines that occupied them for hours at a time.

Winter also brought long visits to relatives and neighbors. It was a time to share news, to play relaxing hours of cards—mostly whist—while the little ones were all stacked beside each other like little logs to sleep on the big bed, and of course to enjoy to the full the wonderfully rich, sugary delights at the table of each aspiring bakery chef who well-knew the tried and true German soul-food desserts that so satisfied the men.

"Best thing I ever had," said Brother-in-Law, Jacob Dschaak, one night at the end of one of their get-togethers.

"Well, maybe second best," replied John, looking at him straight-faced. Everyone roared, and no one challenged him. When they glanced over at Ricka, she was blushing a deep cherry red.

"Ach, you men," she muttered and walked away, swinging her hips.

Chapter 40

We'd Like Papers

The same year was also settling-in time. All the Osters and in-laws traveled to Stanton to begin the naturalization process toward becoming American citizens. By 1905, an emotional divide had melted into their lives. As they talked, they began to realize that the land of the czars was no longer "home."

They discovered how deeply they had become rooted to these prairies, and in their hearts, home had become America. German was still the mother tongue in home and church, but America was now spelled with a "c," no longer Amerika.

Trooping their entire body into the small county courthouse in Stanton, Father Christian informed the clerk, "We'd like papers to fill out to become American citizens."

Since only the head of the household had to file the application for the family, the clerk counted out the sheets and directed the men to start filling in the blanks. Unfortunately, all the men were educated to read and write in German and now could not understand the English form placed in front of them, nor could they write with English script. Even though daughter Katherina and her husband had lived in America for some ten years, they were ensconced in the German enclave of Krem and had learned only scant English. Now there was a lot of throat-clearing and embarrassed glancing from face-to-face until the clerk finally motioned to Christian and said, "*Komm hier, ich will dir helfen*, Come here, I'll help you." At the same time, he asked for help from another office, and soon, the two clerks were busy asking the questions and filling in forms.

Name, birthplace and date, port of entry, and previous citizenship were asked of all, and after half an hour all were sweaty and done. The clerk told them that in five years they would be notified to return to file their final papers and be sworn in as American citizens and then gently tried to remind the entire restless group to work on their use of English, to which all quickly replied, "Oh yes. For sure." They filed out of the courthouse, looking from one to the other, glad but very silent.

Before long, Mina had her girl, another Katherina. A short time later, Ricka had a boy, Gottfried Peter. For each birth, since the sisters now better knew what to expect, word was sent to the neighboring midwife, and she soon arrived to bring the little ones into the world.

While the birth of the new baby went fine, now Ricka found herself having a hard time keeping up with her firstborn. She had forgotten how total "total care" really was and how a baby sucked up nearly her whole life, while at the same time she still had to care for little Phillip, along with a husband, her garden, the house, and on top of all that, still somehow try to take care of herself so she wouldn't go under.

After John left for the field, she dressed Phillip, glad to turn him loose outside. He was yet neither fast nor dexterous, but he loved to get *Schutz* riled up enough to chase chickens in the yard, forgetting over and again that if they got too rambunctious in the chase, Mother would soon be shouting angrily from the house.

Today his little brain hatched a new challenge—run the big, heavy white geese around the yard. They were slow, they waddled a lot, and they didn't have sharp claws to scratch him. And to little ears, their irritated honking was a most delightful sound.

As he toddled toward the flock, the dog was instantly wary. *Schutz* had chased them alone before this and learned they had an attitude. Now he hung back, trotting several steps behind his overeager little master, ready for quick retreat if need be. Phillip charged happily toward the grazing geese, flapping his arms and squealing in delight. The lumbering geese saw him coming and, backing off a few yards, sounded a group retreat. But when Phillip kept coming at them, the closest goose suddenly stopped and wheeled around to face him. Instantly, she drew herself up to full height, her neck at maximum stretch, and took several quick steps toward him, ready to do battle eyeball to eyeball with this impious upstart. She spread her five-foot wings out wide like a thirsty, white-robed Dracula, flicked her orange tongue, and with bill full open, hissed at him so ferociously that he wet his pants right on the spot.

He turned on his heels and stumbled, wide-eyed, to the house, bursting in through the door and whining, "*Nass, Mutte, Nass,* wet, Mommy, wet."

"*Ach, Liebling,* oh my little pet, won't you ever learn?" was all she could get out before she laid him on the rug and changed his soaked pants.

When John got home from the field, he rode out to the mailbox to get the mail. When he got home, he sat down for a quick look through the *Staats-Anzeiger* newspaper and noticed an article they had picked up from a paper in Bessarabia, Russia. "Says here," he called out to Ricka, "that the Russians and Japanese are going at it. Big battle at a place way in the east called Mukden, not too far from Vladivostok on the Pacific. Says Russia shipped one hundred thousand soldiers east and laid rails on the ice of that big Lake Baikal."

"Oh," Ricka's eyes grew large, "that must have been scary for those men."

"Says twenty thousand Russian soldiers lost their lives, and fifty thousand were taken prisoner."

"Ei, that's horrible. And think of all the mothers!"

"Ja, and they say Tsar Nicholas is to blame for the whole defeat—they want his head."

"I'm just glad we're out of there!"

"Uh-oh."

"What?"

"On the bottom it says a couple of battalions of our German soldiers from Bessarabia were some of the first sent into the battle. You know my little brother, Frederick, got drafted."

"Ei, you think he was in it?"

"Dear God, I hope not."

John's mind was in a daze until Ricka sang out, "Remember, kids, Saturday night. Time to clean up."

John busied himself by hauling three pails of water from the well and putting them on the stove. Next, he took the four-foot circular tin bathtub down from its peg in the shed and set it on the scatter rug laid over the dirt floor in front of the stove, ready for bath time.

Ricka, meanwhile, got out a fresh bar of lye soap, which they made last fall when they were butchering hogs. Using lye powder and lard boiled down from the pig fat, they poured it into pans and let it harden. After it was cut into four-inch bars, they now had nice white bars of soap, stinky perhaps to more cultured noses, but effective dirt removers nevertheless. Now she started a fire in the cookstove to heat the water.

Little Phillip was yet too young to know the days of the week, but he knew the Saturday night bath routine, and he started stripping down, ready to enjoy his weekly soak.

The routine in their house, as in nearly all the prairie soddies of the area, was that Saturday night was cleanup time, getting ready for church and visiting neighbors on Sunday. Since every drop of water had to be hand-carried, one tub of water had to do for bathing the entire family. The normal order for baths was youngest to oldest. In other families with a number of children, the boys were sent outside, while all the girls took turns. Then the girls went out while the boys bathed. As time went by and houses had added rooms, it became much easier, of course, for the sexes simply to go into the next room.

Now, with one bound, Phillip leaped into the beckoning water.

"For goodness sake, little one, can't you ever learn to step into the tub, instead of jumping in?" snapped Mother. "Look how much water you splashed all over the floor!"

Phillip slid low into the bathtub, chastened but blowing bubbles until Mother couldn't help but laugh at his exuberance in the tub.

Then, while Phillip dried off and ran naked around the room, John scrubbed off a week's worth of grime and sweat before he, too, stepped out. By now the water had cooled down so he dipped a pail of water from the tub and threw it out the door. Then he added another pail of hot water from the stove for Ricka.

Ricka undid the bun in her waist-length hair and knelt in the tub. Even though the water was murky by now, it was soothingly warm, and she held the bar of Joro Shampoo which she and Mina had exchanged as Christmas presents, knowing they would not get such luxuriant personal articles from their men. When she finished kneading her hair and massaging her scalp, John poured half a dozen dippers of clean, warm water over her to rinse off her hair, and she sat with her legs curled up in the tub, enjoying the luxury of the comforting water, grungy though it be.

While she was drying off, John dipped out two pails of water, and then lifting the tub by its handles, he carried it to the door, gave it a backswing, and heaved the water as far as he could into the hardpacked yard. In an instant, the chickens raced in, pecking at every little droplet of water they could find and scooping up the little bugs caught in the unexpected deluge.

When they lit the kerosene lamp and gathered around the kitchen table, John got out his confirmation Bible and began to read their Saturday chapter for evening prayers. He just read several verses in Romans 2 and started to pray for Brother Freddy in Russia when there was a quick knock at the door and Gottfried walked in.

"Keller stopped at my house and said he was in Krem today. Katherina saw him and told him to tell us to come to Krem tomorrow."

"That's kinda quick."

"Ja, she said she got a letter from Natasha in Russia and that we should come."

John felt a lump in his throat, but he only said, "Doesn't sound good. Wonder what happened?"

"We better find out."

Both families rose early, finished chores, and loaded everyone into John's wagon for the trip. He held Sophie and Schwartz to a steady trotting pace to get to Katherina and Adam's house in time for Sunday dinner.

Grandpa Christ and Grandma Karolina were also invited and enjoyed a wonderful reunion dinner and hugs from the grandchildren.

When the final pieces of cake were finished, Katherina wiped her hands on her apron and coughed several times. Her breaths suddenly became short and her lower lip quivered ever so slightly, her hands trembling as she reached into her apron pocket.

With her eyes fixed steady on Karolina, she announced, "We just got a letter from Brother Frederick's wife, Natasha, in Russia."

Everyone held their breath, afraid of what the letter might bring, but even more afraid of Grandpa's reaction at the mention of son Frederick.

"We have no son named Frederick!" Grandpa snapped, with venom in his voice. "When he married a Russian, he fell dead to this family. I told you that!"

So softly they could hardly hear her, Katherina slowly replied, "I, I think you better listen to the letter."

All eyes turned to Christ as the edges of his lips curled down and his great mottled gray beard jutted out into the room. His cheek muscles rippled with anger.

Suddenly, Grandma Karolina jerked her head up from under her flowered *deechle*, bandana. Her eyes flashed lightning, and with cold steel in her voice, she looked at him with furrowed brow and shot out, "Old man, close your mouth and listen!"

The family sat totally stunned, all staring down into a whirling black hole of silence. None dared lift their eyes to check Grandpa's reaction. They did not see the sharpened leather-punching awls that his eyes shot in violent disgust at Grandma as he turned his chair and spat on the floor. But he remained sitting, and silent. Katherina slowly, haltingly started to read.

Chapter 41

Letter #2 from Russia

Liebe Katherina und Familie in Amerika,
My heart is heavy as I write to tell you that my dear Frederick
was killed in early May, fighting the Japanese. The army letter said
it happened in a place called Mukden, in the far east of our land.

They said his battalion of South Ukrainian Riflemen numbered
700 bayonets, and they fought bravely against the enemy, but many
were called to give their life for the tsar. They singled my man out
for bravery, but in the end he was one of the many killed.

People here are very angry. Many are saying bad things about
the tsar, and a few young hot heads have left for St. Petersburg to
join in protests against the tsar.

I don't know what the children and I will do now, and how we
will live. I wish I were with you right now, but I know Papa Oster
will never let that happen. Pray for us.

Eure, Natasha.

While she was reading, John's mind flashed back to the horror of
Private Wiedeman being kicked to death by Russian officers on the
forced march of his own army days, and now his mind went reeling, *I*
wonder, were the German conscripts put in the front lines at Mukden,
to take the first Japanese steel and give their blood for the unholy
tsar? The rest of Natasha's letter was lost to him.

As Katherina whispered the closing words of the letter,
handkerchiefs crept out on every side of the table and tears rolled
down the hole that sprang open in every anguished heart.

"*Ach, Lieber Gott, mein kind, mein kind,* Dear God, my child, my
child," sobbed Karolina as Ricka reached over and hugged her tight,
pulling Grandma's wet cheek against her own.

Grandpa Christ shoved his chair back and walked out. He spoke
not a word, though he felt like beating Karolina for her blatant
insolence in humiliating him in front of the children. But the slump

of his shoulders as he stepped through the door spoke of pain in his heart as well.

Despite his earlier bluster, the stark reality of this news now hit him.

They killed my son, was all he could think as his eyes clouded over with unexpected tears. *They killed my youngest son.*

John got up and walked out to where his father was leaning with his arm up against the side of the house, his face to the wall. John put his arm around Father's shoulder, squeezing the quivering arm. Neither said anything, but a deep bond grew stronger in that hurtful silence as both felt the comfort of a broken heart beating next to theirs.

In the house, the rest continued to feel Natasha's pain as well.

"We have to do something for Natasha," said Gottfried, drying his eyes. As eldest son of the family, he felt a sudden load on his shoulders and added, "She *is* our sister-in-law, and her little boys are our nephews."

Then, reaching in his pocket, he pulled out a dollar bill and said, "I will give a dollar a month for a year to help her."

Mina picked up on it, and turning to Katherina, she said, "Would you buy some flour and sugar and coffee and things like that here in Krem with our money and send them to her each month?"

"That sounds good. Yes, I'll do that, and I'll write her back right away. We'll give the same."

"Yes, we will too," added Ricka, "and we'll tell the other three sisters out west what happened and ask them to help too."

"I won't ask Father," Karolina chimed in, "but I'll find a dollar each month, somewhere, and I'll ask Anna and Jacob too."

"Eight dollars a month should help with food and maybe some clothes, to keep them going," Gottfried responded.

As soon as the dishes were done, the women gave their aprons back to Katherina and helped load the wagon to go home. Farewells were bid with blowing noses.

The road home was shrouded in a heavy blanket of grieving silence. The merry meadowlarks and red-winged blackbirds had laid down their happy choruses and left for warmer climes. Several small V-formations of geese called from high above them, but they, too, were in a hurry, heading south before bad weather iced their wings.

Only the rustling symphony of the tall, ripe buffalo grasses waving together in the blowing north wind and the jingling harnesses spoke to the melancholy silence in their souls.

The flaming summer sun was riding its celestial chariot far in the southern sky by now, and its powerful rays were turned to dull arrows that seemed to land with a hollow thud, bringing hardly more than turgid warmth.

The brilliant black-eyed Susans and prairie coneflowers scattered in the grass had long committed their eye-catching yellow petals back to the earth and now stood silent brown, waving them good-bye into winter.

The year '05 was indeed a year of triumph and of tragedy, of bane and of blessing. So much had happened, and each of the sad party was in their own vortex of thoughts on this lonesome trail home.

Breaking into their silent soliloquies, Gottfried piped up, "Remember how the old folks put it, '*Es gibt kein Fleisch ohne Knochen*, you can't have meat without bones.'"

"*Ja*, so true," John replied. "The good and the bad come all jumbled together and get mixed into one big bowl in life, ja . . . ja."

The two brothers were, such a short time ago, carefree young bachelors, galloping the Russian steppes, not adverse to the charms of comely young Russian beauties, and here they were family men on whose strong shoulders rode a new civilization out on the wild American frontier.

The Boeshans sisters, as well, so recently nonchalant in learning wifely skills at their mother's hand in faraway Klostitz, now found themselves life partners in raising a generation who would tame these rolling hills and reshape them into a verdant breadbasket of the world.

Where they and their friends had lived in homey, little old-country villages, only a door away from ever-present help and friendship, now they, like all their neighbors, lived in solitary soddies, that threatened to undo them with bitter loneliness while howling things in the dark brought fear to the soul.

So many thoughts raced through each silent mind as harnesses softly jingled to the steady beat of the hooves and the quiet wagon rolled on.

They were crossing soil that lay unchanged since the last ice age refigured the virgin prairie. The buffalo by the million here grazed where his tongue led him, and the red man walked free. No more. In one brief generation, all this was forever changed. A whole new day was dawning, new sounds vibrating the placid buffalo grass, a new world aborning. Their hearts felt strangely sad and deeply hopeful, all puzzled together.

"I wonder," Gottfried idly replied, shifting the reins to one hand and stroking his beard, "I just wonder what it's gonna be like around here a few years from now."

"Wonder if we aren't driving into a whole different world," John added.

All this talk left Mina's cheek twitching. "Everything is so different now than when we got here, and I'm not sure I like it," she insisted, her fingers drumming on her long dress. "What else can they possibly change!"

Suddenly, after another long silence, Ricka looked around at the beauty surrounding them and piped up from the back of the wagon, "You know something? I think this place is beginning to grow on me."

Acknowledgments

Where does one begin to express gratitude that stretches beyond anything that words can deliver, to people that stretch around the globe, across time that stretches over so much history?

I am hugely indebted to:
- Delores, lifetime helpmate, organizer, for her patience when she was more single than married during my surges of writing.
- faithful friends, teachers, authors, mentors, at every age of my life, some degreed and some "wisdomed," who sculpted my whole being.
- Father Joseph Height, pioneer priest of the German colonies in South Russia's Black Sea area, who chronicled those times and provided a glimpse into daily life in that era.
- the cadre of writers who mined the voluminous archives and told the czarist Romanov stories, some flattering, some scandalous, that have made this royal family both loved and hated.
- the Mercer County (ND) and the Freeborn County (MN) Historical Museum staffs (especially Linda Evenson), who provided invaluable information of so many kinds about people and days gone by.
- Catherine Ost, Paul Goodnature, and Susan Carlson, editors, shoulders, voices of correction and encouragement, who helped to shape thoughts into readability.
- Gilbert Ost, rememberer and storyteller of the first order, who will sit back and say, "Ah, I remember."
- the host of precious tantas, grandmothers, across two continents, whose hands I held as they shared a treasure-trove of memories. They suffered much, and their holy tears and blessed laughter are seared into my heart and woven into the fabric of these pages so the world will know the story.
- that Holy Source beyond all knowing, for gifts beyond telling, the Author whose story goes on . . .

Summary

Heinrich and Anna Marie Oster are invited by the czar to move to Russia. Their excitement runs high when a son of their family is selected to serve in the czar's elite bodyguard, the Imperial Hussars, and life is good.

Life next to the royals is full of thrills and color, but before long, the corruption and greed in high places are exposed, and soon bitter persecution of the family makes their days difficult. Their children flee to America and accept the government's offer of free homestead acres on the great prairies of the heartland.

The free land, however, extracts a heavy price. As they wrestle their sod house out of the stubborn buffalo grasses, they discover that their new "palace on the prairies" is only three miles from the native sons of the warriors who scalped George Armstrong Custer. It leaves their days uneasy, their nights uncertain.

At every turn, nature confronts them with immense battles, from killing blizzards and sweeping fires to plagues of grasshoppers. From years of death-dealing drought where nothing grows but tumbleweeds and biting flies to international conflicts that drastically change their lives. Through it all they come together in faith and turn their little spot of earth into the breadbasket of the world.

Author's Blurb

Milt Ost is a retired minister, and now lives with his wife, Delores, in Minnesota.

23518760R00160

Made in the USA
San Bernardino, CA
23 August 2015